ALSO BY CHELSEA ICHASO

They're Watching You
Dead Girls Can't Tell Secrets
Little Creeping Things
The Summer She Went Missing

WE
WERE
WARNED

CHELSEA ICHASO

sourcebooks
fire

Copyright © 2025 by Chelsea Ichaso
Cover and internal design © 2025 by Sourcebooks
Cover design by Casey Moses
Cover images © Nic Skerten/Arcangel, Rekha Garton/Arcangel
Internal design by Laura Boren/Sourcebooks
Internal images © Yongcharoen_kittiyaporn/Shutterstock

Published by Sourcebooks Fire, an imprint of Sourcebooks
P.O. Box 4410, Naperville, Illinois 60567-4410
(630) 961-3900
sourcebooks.com

Cataloging-in-Publication Data is on file with the Library of Congress.

Printed and bound in the United States of America.
PAH 10 9 8 7 6 5 4 3 2 1

For Julie and Laura

PROLOGUE

THE FIGURE KNELT OVER THE BODY AT THE EDGE OF the ruins. Nearby, a streetlamp crackled before succumbing to the night. Gray clouds tumbled closer. As the ocean waves crashed, the wind whipped against the figure's black hood and rattled the chain-link fence.

The figure glanced back to peer beyond the mist. A rock wall lined the front of what was left of Fairport Village, separating the clifftop property from the beach below. Among the other rocks, a long granite one stood out, smooth and flat as a tabletop, specks of mica gleaming beneath the moonlight. It formed a plank over the sandy beach below: the Founder's Slab. Back in the 1800s, a horrible plague struck the first settlers, and it's been said that in their desperation, the sick carved their prayers into that sacred rock.

Only those prayers went unanswered, as if the land had other ideas. The figure could almost hear its call, a wicked drumbeat, demanding more blood. The figure turned back to the body.

This girl—this *child*—sprawled lifeless on the gravel was far from the first to die on this land.

This child wouldn't be the last.

And so, tucking the note within the girl's sweatshirt pocket, the figure scanned the ruins once more, then vanished into the night.

October 4

Dear Diary,

I saw her again today. In the girls' bathroom. I had just washed my hands when I heard a noise. A swish. I spun around as the tail of her long black shawl fluttered across the back wall. Just a flicker before disappearing into the bathroom stall.

The stall door rattled, and my heart stopped. For a moment, I watched that door with my feet frozen in place, hands dripping water on the floor. I didn't dare take a breath. I wanted to sprint for the exit and never look back, but some reckless part of me had to face it. Had to find out for sure. Legs quivering, I forced two quick strides and flung open the door.

She was gone, of course. Vanished, like the ghost she is.

But I know what I saw.

She's following me.

1

THE MOMENT THE CORRODED FENCE COMES INTO VIEW, the sky betrays us, clouds shifting to cover the crescent moon. I click on my flashlight, even though Fairport Village isn't something you need to see to know it's creepy.

You can feel it.

Not just the smooth sand from the beach below transforming into rubble and grass up on this cliff. It's something in the air. Something darker than a pitch-black night that seeps into your skin whenever you get this close to the ruins. Something that makes the little hairs on your arms stand up, that whispers with a tiny buzzing voice, *Go back.*

I'm tempted to obey the voice. When Henry De Rossi's wide brown eyes meet mine, I can tell he feels the same way.

But I'm going in if it's the last thing I do. And let's be honest, if the legend is true, it very well could be.

Everyone else has already made it inside, which means we're missing valuable footage. "Go on, or I'll murder you myself," I say, because I've never been good at encouraging words, and I need this paycheck.

Henry adjusts his glasses. His dark-brown hair flutters in the breeze as he raises his video camera to his eye and clicks it on. Then he waves me along, and we approach the rusted chain-link fence, broken hinges reinforced with steel chains wrapped around the posts. The weathered *No Trespassing* sign has been there since before I was born. I hike his equipment bag up higher on my shoulder and ignore the words, along with the enormous crooked *Condemned* sign, its letters flashing white in the silvery moonlight. I pry the two flaps of chain link open. Henry takes a deep breath, staring down the gap while I try to avoid cutting myself on this broken, rusted metal.

Finally, he exhales, the sound lost beneath the whistling wind and the crashing waves, and ducks through. His sweatshirt snags on a sharp steel end, but I jostle it loose, and he slips free.

He turns the camera off and lowers it, meeting my gaze through the chain link. I pass the equipment bag through to him. "Well, good luck to you, sir," I say, saluting him. "I just remembered there's a thing I've got to do." I spin around on my heels.

"Oh, come on, Eden!" Henry bites out. "Thought you weren't afraid of some stupid curse."

"I'm not," I say like a defiant toddler. "It's the tetanus that worries me." I gesture to the fence. "And, you know, the prospect of falling through a rotted floorboard."

He rolls his eyes in the filmy moonlight and tugs the fence open. "You want to get paid or not?"

Letting out a huff, I duck through the opening. "Two hundred bucks seems like a lot until you crack open your skull." I grab his equipment bag and heft it over my shoulder. Henry and I aren't exactly friends, but we had a film production elective together last year. He heads the audiovisual team at school, and now he's in the advanced film class. As part of his application to some fancy film school, he's chosen to make a short documentary on the Fairport Village legend. Capturing the senior overnighter will be a huge part of it. I opted not to stick with the film classes, but apparently Henry liked my short feature titled *Fairport High Teachers Who Are Secretly Aliens* enough to offer me a paid assistant job tonight.

Either that, or everyone else was too scared of the curse to take the job.

Voices trickle out of a nearby bungalow, and Henry doesn't miss a beat, his camera rolling, its light illuminating the broken cobblestone path.

"Which bungalow is that?" I ask, struggling to keep up with his long strides, the equipment bag slapping at my side.

"Shouldn't I be asking *you*?" he says without slowing.

"Oh, right." I dig into my pocket, pulling out the little map Henry told me to study in preparation for our documentary. In its heyday, the six cottages of this bustling clifftop resort were painted various shades of pastel—delicate pinks, greens, and blues—so they lay like seashells under a glimmering sun. The Blackmores gave each one a charming name, like Sunnyside Cottage and the Village Jewel. Unfortunately after the resort closed down, the effects of salt water and wind took their toll. The new paint began to oxidize and peel. The walls rotted and buckled. A storm tore apart roofs and the once-pristine Fairport Village sign. Looters, either ignorant of the curse or unfazed by it, shattered windows and removed anything of value from every residence.

In the daylight, you can still make out the faded hues from the beach. But here in the dark, they all look identical, except for the varying degrees of devastation. I squint down at the map, still scurrying along after Henry. "It's the Darling Daisy," I say, reading off my own scribbles as I add, "known to the Fairport youth as Aunt Gertrude due to the facade's uncanny resemblance to an old lady's face."

I glance up, and a chill snakes through me. There's no electricity in the place. Of course, there hasn't been in twenty-five years. So when light gleams through the cracked window eyes and spills through the open mouth of a door, it's like seeing the dead raised.

My heart hammers as we tiptoe closer. I peek through to find what seems like half the senior class holding up their lit phones and chanting, "Do it!"

Henry and I exchange a wary look and make our way through what was once a living room to what was once a bathroom. The dank, rotten scent of the place is spiked with beer, thanks to the Fairport High seniors, who have already spilled several cans over the moldy carpet. Henry pans over the room, landing on the group of chanters.

It soon becomes clear that they're daring Jameson O'Sullivan—a linebacker for our football team and all-around loudmouth—to look into a cracked and cloudy vanity mirror and chant, "Old Mrs. Blackmore," three times. Which isn't actually a Fairport Village superstition. But after all the beer they've ingested, who could blame them for mixing up the local mythology with the legend of Bloody Mary?

Jameson yanks a beanie over his buzzed ginger-colored head and curls his fists. Jumping around like a heavyweight fighter before a match, he nods, at which the crowd goes wild.

Henry keeps the camera rolling as Jameson lifts a hand, stilling his audience in an instant. "Old Mrs. Blackmore," Jameson whispers. A shrill gust of wind trails his voice, and the girl in front of me squeals. Jameson turns to dart her a look before repeating the words. "Old Mrs. Blackmore," he says, drawing it out with a ghoulish flair.

I nudge Henry. "Since when did this become a Jameson O'Sullivan documentary?"

Henry swats an elbow at me, camera still aimed at Jameson, who has the entire crowd hanging on to his every word like he's some sort of prophet. "Old Mrs...." Jameson's head snaps to the side. "Did you guys see—"

"Oh, come on!" shouts Diego Rodriguez, who shouldn't even be here because he's only a junior.

Jameson laughs and adds in a barely audible purr, "Blackmore."

Then he points a meaty index finger toward the window. Before we can look, he clutches at his throat, throwing his enormous body to the floor with a thud.

The room bursts into laughter.

Henry attempts to tug me along, but I stand my ground. "Hold on," I say. "I really think we should stick around for the part where he falls through the floor." To behold such a sight would be worth more than two hundred bucks. After the way Jameson, Diego, and the rest of that group have treated me over the years, I hope he gets stuck below the floor and has to live out the rest of his life down there.

Henry takes the camera on a tour of the place as I wait for my dream to materialize, only to watch a very pleased-with-himself Jameson pick himself up off the ground. He dusts off his pants and turns to meet my gaze. "Hey there, Stafford. Surprised to see you here."

"Why's that?" I ask, trying to look bored.

"Just a spooky place is all," he says. "And you come from a family of cowards."

My fists curl at my sides as I charge over the cracked bathroom tiles straight for him.

I only make it a few steps before a hand grips my bicep. "Whoa, whoa," says a deep voice.

I wrench my arm away, spinning to stare down my new target. Except I have to stare up, because my target is Caleb Durham, an irritatingly gorgeous boy with a soccer player's physique.

He's also someone I despise with my whole being. Caleb is just as bad as Jameson—probably worse, because as kids, he made me believe that he and I were best friends. And the second my dad bailed, Caleb joined Jameson and the rest of those jerks in making my life a living hell. Every year it got worse, from stealing my lunch in grade school to spreading a rumor that I copied Jameson's math test in eighth grade. Like the guy can even *add*, much less solve linear equations.

"I don't think you want to do whatever you were planning," Caleb says, voice as cool as his expression. His charcoal-gray hoodie is pulled up over his dust-brown hair, casting his face in shadow. I make out only a vague outline of his perfect nose and strong jaw, but those hazel eyes glimmer through.

"Are you threatening me?" I ask, glaring at him.

"No," he says, lifting a hand and taking a step backward. "I was trying to help."

He's pretending to be nice, so I won't see it coming when he and Diego trip me or barricade me inside one of these godforsaken cottages. All the girls in school swoon over Caleb, but I'm done falling for his act. His charm makes him all the more diabolical. Like a handsome, hazel-eyed anti-Christ.

"Instead of *helping* me, you should go do the stupid chant so the old lady can feast on your soul."

"Eden," he starts, but Victoria Whitlock, junior class president and last year's sophomore homecoming princess, steps in between us, holding a can of beer.

"Let her go," Victoria says, turning to give me a once-over. Her long shiny dark hair falls in smooth waves despite the humidity, and she grins at me with perfectly painted red lips. "Eden versus Jameson is a fight I want to see."

"Isn't it past your bedtime?" I snap at her. Like Diego, Victoria is only a junior. But it's typical for the two of them to show up at senior things. The clique members barely function as individuals. And from the way Victoria's fingers are trailing over Caleb's arm, there's obviously something going on there too.

For a slice of a moment, her eyes narrow like I've hit a nerve. But she takes a swig of her beer and lowers it with a smirk. "Like I'd miss the last chance to do this."

"Do *what*, exactly? Get wasted or murdered? Because I think we could probably arrange bo—"

"Eden!" Henry interrupts from the far side of the room, camera poised. "Do you even want this job?" He crosses the room, still filming as my classmates proceed to drink and chant into the murky glass.

"Hey!" Kayla Díaz shouts at him, covering her face. "You can't film me, De Rossi! My mom will flip if she finds out about all the laws I broke tonight."

Henry ignores her, stopping at my side. "We're heading out," he tells me.

"Aw," Victoria says. "You two are so cute together. The job is… what exactly? Pretending to be your girlfriend?"

Henry turns the camera on her. "Victoria Whitlock, Fairport High junior," he says in his deep reporter's voice. "What brings you to these cursed grounds tonight? Does this mean the seniors failed to keep their secret under wraps?"

Not one to miss a camera opp, Victoria shoves her beer into

Caleb's hand and runs her polished fingertips through her hair. "Oh no, your secret is very safe. Trust me, I don't want parents or cops showing up any more than you do. I just have my ways of finding out stuff. And with this being the last chance to repeat that horrible night ten years ago, I had to be here. I mean, come this time next year, this entire place will be a brand-new resort."

Ten years ago, the Fairport High senior class held the first overnighter here in the ruins. That was when the first alleged victim of the curse was found. Farah Palmer. She was three days short of her eighteenth birthday when they found her in one of these cottages with her skull smashed in. "Aren't you nervous though?" Henry asks. "After what happened to Farah? After what happened to Esther Lamb?"

Esther was the second and most recent victim. Only two years ago, at just sixteen, she was found murdered, just like Farah—only more injuries had been inflicted upon Esther's body, which lay crumpled and bruised just outside the Village fence. Like she'd been killed and then tossed back over.

"Hell yeah, I'm nervous," Victoria says with a laugh. "Isn't that the point? Two kids died after stepping foot inside the Village ruins. Any of us could be next."

A thread of guilt spins in my gut. I know this documentary is important to Henry, but it's starting to feel very wrong. People laughing and making jokes about all this when Esther was a friend and classmate. When her younger sister, Naomi, who's been through hell and back, is a fellow senior.

"So then, you do believe in the curse?" Henry asks, bringing me back to the task at hand.

Victoria shrugs. "I might become a believer by the end of the night."

"Or you might become dead," I mumble under my breath.

I hear a chuckle come from beneath Caleb's hood, but when I glance over, he's back to eyeing me icily.

Henry lowers the camera. "Great. Thank you, Victoria. I'll cut the beer out of the beginning—you know, *if* I use this footage." He snaps his fingers. "Eden, the form."

"The what?" I ask, still savoring Victoria's open-mouthed expression at possibly being cut from the documentary.

"The consent form. You got everyone to sign one, right?"

Oh. "Uh, still working on it," I say, digging out the forms from Henry's bag.

"Well, hurry up. We haven't seen any of the key locations yet."

"Right."

By *key*, Henry means the places people died. He made me study up on those too, not that I needed much studying. Every kid in this town grew up whispering about the murders at sleepovers. Eavesdropping at beach barbecues when our parents' conversations inevitably turned that way after one too many drinks. We even covered the murders as part of our local history unit in fifth grade.

The first location was the Blackmores' personal residence, the mansion set at the edge of the cliff. That's where they found seventeen-year-old Nicolas Blackmore twenty-five years ago. The story goes that Hazel Blackmore, the boy's mother as well as the founder and owner of Fairport Village, slit his throat that cold December night. Mrs. Blackmore had been slowly losing her mind, they say. The town saw it. Fairport Village guests saw it too. Even the woman's husband had called the police on occasion before that fateful night, when he'd failed to calm her out of a fit.

I finish collecting signatures from the kids in the cottage, a couple of whom decline permission. I can't say that I blame them. Sure, Henry says the most you can get for trespassing around here is a small fine. That he can even change the names and do that freaky face-altering technology if participants request it. But taking part is a risk, especially with college on the horizon for many of us. And the school year starts in three days, so we're just in time for some hefty suspensions.

I shove the forms into Henry's bag and squeeze past two girls huddled beneath a blanket on the decrepit porch steps.

"Did you see that?" one of them squeaks, pointing at the rock wall on the beach side of the resort. The blanket shrouds the girl's head, so I can't tell who she is.

"I think so," the other one whispers. "You want to just go?"

"Mm-hmm," the first answers. They stand, blanket still draped over them as they hurry down the porch and back toward the busted fence.

I shine my flashlight at the place the first girl pointed. I only see rocks and the palm trees dancing in the breeze.

"Coming?" Henry asks, which makes me jump. "I think I want

the thirty-five for this," he says, and it takes me a second to realize he's asking for his other camera. I locate it inside his bag and we swap. He doesn't say another word before striding ahead, camera filming. I follow, wondering if I should tell him about the girls who left—and what they said—before someone tries to pin their disappearance on the curse.

Overgrown weeds and shrubbery consume the cobblestone path, forcing us to step over broken cement, gravel, and some mystery terrain that squelches and bubbles underfoot. I aim my flashlight ahead until it lands on something at the edge of the property that makes my insides drop, like the final roller-coaster plunge.

The Blackmore mansion, the family's residence. Formidable, even in its decrepitude, it looms over us like a ravenous creature. From the minimal research I did for this gig, I know the house was constructed back in the 1920s. When the Blackmores purchased the property, they focused on building the cottages, neglecting the paint and new windows their own home desperately needed. The porch pillars were tilted and patches of shingles were missing from the roof, but the Blackmores never got around to renovations before the murder.

Now, there's hardly a roof to speak of, and the pillars look like they could simply topple over and plummet into the ocean with one strong gust of wind. The mansion is visible from down on the beach, but this is the first time I've seen it up close. In the thick darkness, it takes every ounce of my willpower to not drop Henry's bag and turn around.

"This mansion is where the legend began," Henry narrates, his voice slicing through the stillness. "When the police showed up, they found Nicolas dead, his sister hiding, his father weeping, and his mother covered in blood. They dragged Hazel Blackmore away in handcuffs. Several Fairport Village guests had awoken and made their way to the mansion, where they witnessed the woman screaming and thrashing like an animal. By the time her case was set for trial, the Village had shut down, and her husband, Silas Blackmore, and their daughter had moved away to avoid publicity."

Moonlight pierces the clouds, illuminating the dilapidated manor sitting on its sandstone throne. "The town of Fairport and the media had questions," Henry continues. "For example, why did she do it? What happened to the murder weapon? Mrs. Blackmore never answered any questions and never proclaimed her innocence or guilt. The first time she ever spoke publicly about the case ended up being the last. When she was moved to the county prison preceding trial, handcuffed and clothed in prison garb, she proclaimed to the gathered reporters at the top of her lungs, 'From this moment on, anyone who sets foot inside Fairport Village will die!'"

The words, though familiar, hit me like an icy wind. "That night," Henry says, voice quieting, "after settling into her new cell in the county prison, Mrs. Blackmore slit her own throat with a stolen razor. The case never went to trial."

Even from outside the building, I can picture the blood spattering the foyer where that boy found. I try to imagine his last minutes. Had he seen it coming? Had he known he was about to die at his own mother's hand?

When I agreed to help Henry, I knew I'd have to go inside that house. But now I'm not sure I can do it.

"Hey, Henry," I say, still inventing my excuse, "what if we—"

"This way," he says, heading toward a gravel path instead of the house.

A whoosh of relief floods me as I hurry after him over the path that snakes between two cottages. We reach a courtyard with a monstrous fountain at its center—a headless stone mermaid surrounded by murky sludge. Nearby is a crooked picnic table with an inverted bench on one side, its legs sticking straight up like impaling posts.

I'm about to ask where we're headed when the bushes off to my right rustle. I turn, Henry's bulky bag knocking my arm and startling me half to death.

My gaze darts over to the bushes, its leaves swaying with the coastal breeze. Of course it was nothing. Just some stupid legend.

That's when I catch a flutter, quick as feathers.

I watch as a figure rises up behind the shrubbery. Like a shadow, it swells and pulses, stretching tall. Shivering silver-black in the glow of my flashlight.

Her.

2

MY HEART LEAPS INTO MY THROAT, STIFLING MY scream. I take a step backward, but my foot lands on some kind of old water spigot, throwing me off balance.

Finally, the scream struggling deep in my chest bursts free, and I topple over. With a smack, I land on the damp ground, Henry's bag breaking my fall. I spider-crawl backward, palms scraping over the gravel and debris, and scan my surroundings for the figure. That flash of black fabric whips into my periphery again. A dark hood.

I try to get to my feet, the bag heavy and my side aching. The figure is past the shrubs now, gliding straight through the courtyard toward me. My heart pounds in my ears, loud enough to rise above the sound of the waves.

"Eden?" Behind me, Henry is making his way back through the courtyard. "What the hell?"

He reaches me. The camera bobbles at his side as he extends an arm to help me.

"Henry, watch out!" I scream just as the figure lunges at us, a hand grasping at his jacket.

Henry darts a glance behind him. "Get the hell off me," he snaps.

The figure takes a lumbering step backward. Thick fingers emerge from the cloak sleeves to tug the hood back.

Jameson freaking O'Sullivan. Rage boils deep in my gut.

He doubles over, hands on his knees as he lets out an obnoxious belly laugh. "Oh my god. Your face, Stafford."

"Are you okay?" Henry asks, at which my cheeks heat through.

"Of course I am," I mutter, wiping the muck off my jeans. "I knew it was a hoax. I screamed because I almost knocked my teeth out tripping on this sprinkler thing."

Diego steps out from behind the nearest bungalow, laughing as hard as Jameson. "That was hilarious."

Victoria is at his side, holding up her phone. "Henry, if you need me to send this to you for the documentary," she says through a giggle, "I got the whole thing."

If I weren't dizzy from the fall, I'd rip that phone out of her hand and chuck it off the cliff. Not just because of the video. Because of all of it. From all four of them. The years of giggles, the torment, the snide remarks. Rubbing their money in my face. Manipulating my friends into turning on me.

And all because their parents hated my father, Greg Stafford. All because he cheated them in the cleaning company that he helped to found, nearly bankrupting them.

I can't even blame their parents, really. I hate my father too.

After my father's friends caught him siphoning money from Surfside Cleaning, they fired him. Instead of dealing with his mistakes, good ol' Greg chickened out completely and left Fairport. Even though my mother and I were still here. All he left behind was a lousy goodbye email to Mom, explaining how he was sorry but couldn't face jail time. He needed a clean start.

I've already been punished for the sins of my father. He left my mother and me to deal with all of his financial problems. That's why I've ventured into the Village of the Damned tonight to scrounge up a couple hundred bucks. My volleyball team has an out-of-town tournament, and I can't exactly ask my mother to cover the travel expenses. Not when she's already working two jobs just to put food on the table. My father's former friends and business partners cut my family out of the business entirely and then slapped us with a lawsuit which my mother never forgave them for.

That's why there's a feud, this grudge between their families and mine. And I'm caught right in the middle of it.

Victoria is still beaming. "Seriously, Henry. Look at this."

But Henry isn't paying attention. His eyes are on his bag, which lies in a puddle between the weeds and the gravel. "My equipment."

"Oh, I'm sure it's fine," I say, this job and my money drifting away like a boat at sea. If anything, I'm going to owe *him* money for whatever expensive equipment is broken in there. "I didn't fall that hard."

"No, you definitely did," Jameson says, wiping tears from his eyes.

"You want to see how hard she fell?" Victoria asks. "Or should we just wait until I post it tomorrow?"

The one silver lining. We're forbidden from posting anything about the overnighter on social media until tomorrow. That way, no authority figures discover we're here and try to end this. Maybe I can steal Victoria's phone before the night is up and delete the video.

"I just sent the video to, like, half your class right now," Victoria says. "I mean, why make them wait?"

On the other hand, there's always jumping through a rotten floorboard in this place and living out my life underground.

"You did not, V," Caleb calls out, nearing us on the pathway. "You sent it to Diego and me." He turns to me now, hood falling back to reveal tousled brown hair. "You can't even tell it's you in the video."

I flinch. How dare he speak to me twice in one night? "What are you talking about?"

"I just watched it," he says. "The image is too dark. It could be anyone."

"Oh good," I say, "because Victoria will totally leave off the caption that says, *Eden Stafford looks like an idiot.*"

"That's a good one," Victoria coos, pretending to type. "Thanks."

Caleb rolls his gorgeous eyes and steps closer, causing me to flinch yet again. "I'll get her to delete it." His voice is low and quiet, meant for only me. "Okay?"

He's doing it again. That thing where he tries to lure me in with his soothing voice and that concerned expression. Anyone who sees Caleb and this act would take his side. They don't know what happened the last time I fell for it.

I flash him a sugary-sweet smile. "You really expect me to believe you weren't in on this?"

He lets out a long sigh, his gaze roaming to his shoes. "I wasn't."

I glance down at Henry, now crouched in the rubble, going through the contents of the bag. "Everything intact?" I ask, shutting one eye as I cringe.

"Seems to be." Gingerly, he places a spare lens back in its case and zips the entire bag shut. He stands, slinging the bag up onto his shoulder rather than passing it back to me.

"I'm fired, aren't I?" I brace myself.

"What?" He squints at me, his foot jouncing in impatience. "We've got work to do. If these morons are done harassing you"—he darts a look at the four of them—"then we'll be going."

Delight swells in me. "Work to do. Absolutely."

He starts to move but stops abruptly. "Sorry, I got distracted with my bag. You *are* okay, aren't you?"

Shame courses up my neck. I'm supposed to be helping him, but so far, I've only gotten in the way. Made him abandon the documentary to come defend my honor like some Knight of the Round Table. I stand taller, shoulders back. "Completely unharmed and ready to make movie magic." Extending a hand, I nod toward the equipment.

Cautiously, he transfers the bag to my shoulder, then proceeds through the courtyard with the camera raised. I start after him, unable to resist a look back at the fiendish foursome to see their reaction to someone actually defending me. Three of them are huddled together, laughing and messing around with that stupid cloak costume.

But the fourth stands apart. Caleb's hood is up now, but his focus hasn't shifted from earlier. It's fastened on me.

Nearly tripping on a crack in the cement, I face forward and chase after Henry.

When he ventures onto the path that leads left, my heart sinks. "We are now approaching the infamous Village Jewel," Henry says, his voice deepening again as we head toward the faded purple cottage the town refers to as Motel Hell. The name isn't just for the old *Hello* sign that crookedly dangles from the front, missing the *O*.

It's because of what happened there.

"Ten years after Nicolas Blackmore's murder," Henry continues, "the senior class of Fairport High decided to put Mrs. Blackmore's infamous words to the test by holding an overnighter on the forbidden grounds. It didn't end well. At least, not for Farah Palmer."

I tuck my map away and watch Henry pass through the open hole where the door should be, narrating as he goes. Then I follow, trying not to break an ankle as my feet creak over the rotted steps.

Inside, Henry's light flits around the dark space like a firefly. I tiptoe precariously over the splintered threshold, inhaling the scent of mildew. Then I press on past a matted couch through the living room. I note the closed shutters and yank one open. Dust rains down. It coats my clothes, my mouth, my throat. I cough and tug the next one open, letting the moonlight pour through the cracked windows.

"Thanks," Henry says, kneeling in the corner of the room.

"No problem. Shouldn't we focus on the kitchen?" Once the words are out, I want to take them back. I have no desire to go in there.

The kitchen is where Farah Palmer died ten years ago. Where she was murdered, her head smashed open on the corner of the granite countertop. Her body left in a pool of blood that spread over the tiles and stained the grout.

"In a sec," Henry replies, buying me one more precious moment.

All of the seniors who attended the overnighter were interviewed. Everyone swore Farah was loved by all. That there was no one in the group capable of committing this atrocity.

But a few students mentioned that she'd gotten jittery shortly before her body was discovered. That she'd claimed to have seen someone in a black cloak wandering through the Village ruins.

Authorities never managed to find Farah's killer, only theorizing that the girl must've had an unfortunate encounter with a squatter. Then they left the story of her murder to the Fairport townsfolk, to spin it like silk into the legend we have today. The first victim of Old Mrs. Blackmore's curse. Proof that one step onto the Village grounds could be your last. Ever since that day, people around here say that if you cross into the ruins and see a woman in a black cloak, it's your time to die.

This legend is the basis of Henry's documentary. That's why it strikes me as odd when he sets the camera down on the floor and begins scanning the place with a pocket flashlight. He seemingly combs every nook and cranny of the living room, from the spiderweb-strewn corners to the peeling walls.

"What are we looking for exactly?" I zigzag my own light over the room.

"Evidence," he says.

"Oh, like of who murdered her?"

He shrugs and picks up his camera again. "Let's do the kitchen."

His tone is so cavalier. Just the thought of getting closer to the crime scene makes my stomach churn. I try not to let my gaze drift to the tiles as he adds, "We'll need the light for this."

Kneeling, I rifle through his bag, removing the parts of the LED kit and piecing them together. Between the dark and my quivering fingers, it's no easy task.

Once it's all together, I set it down and watch its glow spread over the floor, over the dark-brown stains that cover the tile and grout, everywhere but a large body-shaped space.

Henry's camera clicks on. "We are now standing inside the kitchen of the Village Jewel, where Farah Palmer's body was discovered ten years ago. You can clearly see the bloodstains from the **massive head** wound she suffered. Though two students were taken in for questioning in the weeks following the crime, no one was ever charged for the murder." He pans over the rest of the kitchen and over the entirety of the living room again. "But was it part of the curse? Was it truly Mrs. Blackmore's words on her final day in the land of the living come to fulfillment? And was the woman Farah claimed to have seen in the dark cloak Mrs. Blackmore herself, come back from the dead?" The camera pulls back around, lens aimed at the massive stain. "That's what we're here to find out."

He shuts the camera off and glances around the room. "Pack up. I'm going to get some shots of the bluff, maybe another interview."

He takes off through the open doorway, and I immediately start to fold the light. There's no way I'm hanging out inside this murder cottage all alone.

Finished, I hurry outside. The area is vacant. Clouds cover the moon again, forcing me to use my flashlight. I locate the path we came on, shoving aside the branches of large birds of paradise until I'm back in the courtyard. I listen for the sounds of drunken laughter from earlier, but there's only the waves crashing on the beach and the howling wind. Where is everyone?

I press on, weaving through the beach-view cottages. Once free, I scan the rock wall for Henry. He said he was getting shots of the bluff, so I pace down the long stretch of boulders. The fog thickens near the end where the Blackmores' mansion is perched atop the ocean. The cold seeps through my sweatshirt, and I can barely see a thing through the haze. "Henry?" I call out.

No answer. He must've finished the shots and started an interview. Or maybe he ducked inside the next cottage without me.

Except that doesn't make sense. The final murder didn't happen inside a cottage.

I bounce in place for warmth, searching through the fog for a new route. "Henry!" I call out again.

When no one answers, I let out a growl and hike the bag up

higher on my shoulder. He couldn't actually be inside the mansion, could he? A little gust of panic kicks up. Because of course he is. That's where the legend started after all. That's where Nicolas Blackmore was murdered.

I continue along the rock wall, gritting my teeth. I haven't heard a peep from the other seniors in ages. I'm alone with the salty mist, the waves, and the night sky. Out here by the cliff, it might as well be the edge of the world.

I shine my light ahead and through the fog, where the vague outline of a girl stops me dead in my tracks.

Naomi Lamb—Esther's younger sister—stands, peering out over the cliff, pale blond hair billowing in the moonlight. Her back is turned to me, but I'd know that hair anywhere.

What is *she* doing here?

"Hey Henry?" I call out, my eyes glued to Naomi. She doesn't so much as turn her head at the sound of my voice. I rub my hands over my arms, which prickle with goose bumps.

"Henry?" I try again, my voice drowned beneath the sound of the waves. I head back in the direction of the Blackmores' mansion, using the rock wall to guide me.

I wave at Kayla Díaz and Amy Park, sitting beneath a blanket on a rusted metal bench. "Have you two seen Henry?"

Kayla rolls her eyes. "I hope he went home," she says, words slurring. "That bastard is going to get me in trouble with his stupid film." She slumps lower, and my gaze slides to Amy, who's holding a bottle of something, the neck peeking out from the blanket.

I wait for her to offer me a sip, just to warm me up a little. But she tucks it deeper beneath the fabric, like I'm some sort of narc. "Well, thanks anyway."

I continue my trek along the rock wall. Through the mist, something stands out among the geological formations. A plank-like slab that juts out from the rock wall, extending over the sand down on the beach, more than a hundred feet below: the Founder's Slab. Where people say Mrs. Blackmore used to sit and watch the sea.

The slab was here long before Hazel Blackmore's day. After settling this prime location overlooking the water, the founding citizens of Fairport came down with a nasty case of the plague. The sickness took its time, sending victims into fever-mad spells before claiming their lives. The few surviving founders fled, moving farther from the beach, where we still have our town center to this day. The story goes that this oval rock was used as a last-ditch effort to save the suffering plague victims. Like giving them a good soak in the midday sun would somehow burn away the sickness.

Spoiler alert: it didn't.

I run my fingers over the edge of cold stone, watching the flecks of granite glimmer gold beneath the moon. There are still scratches where it's said the founders attempted to carve their prayers into the stone.

Why anyone decided to rebuild on this patch of land after such tragedy remains a mystery. It seems clear that death and madness live here in the soil.

On my right, I see a thin gravel path that appears to lead to the mansion. I take it, shining my flashlight over the ground.

When footsteps crunch behind me, I startle.

In the glow of my light, Henry's face is pale, eyes wide behind his lenses. His hands are empty.

"Henry, where's your camera?"

He only stares at me, brow crinkled like he doesn't understand the question.

"Henry, your camera."

This time, he blinks, as though coming out of a daze. "I—I think I dropped it."

"Dropped it? Geez, Henry. You said it took you three summers to earn that thing. Where is it?"

His eyes, wild and unfocused, scan the ground before him. The path. The ocean. "I, uh, I had it with me in Sunnyside Cottage. But then"—he glances over his shoulder to peer into the black night—"*she* was there."

"Who was there? And why did you go into Sunnyside Cottage?" I take out my map, unfolding it and fumbling my phone as I search. "It's not a murder site."

"I think she knows what's buried there."

3

A CHILL DANCES UP MY SPINE, AND I GLANCE UP FROM the map. "What?" The thin paper crumples in my grip. "Who are you talking about, Henry?"

"Mrs. Blackmore. I…" He checks our surroundings again, then lowers his voice. "I *saw* her."

I inhale a long breath, letting my head tip back. "Damnit, Henry. You really had me. I swear, between you and Caleb's little band of jackasses, I'm ready to drop-kick someone into the ocean. Can we just finish the documentary, please?"

Only Henry doesn't laugh. Doesn't move an inch on the pathway.

"Is this—" Suddenly, I realize *exactly* what this is. "You've got someone else filming us." Cracking a smile, I shine my light into the nearby shrubs. "This is live-action curse content, right? Sorry. If you'd given me a heads-up, I would've played along."

He merely yanks on a tuft of hair, distraught. "She knows, Eden. She knows about everything."

A prickle of fear slithers along the nape of my neck. "Henry, seriously. It's Jameson messing with you. He got one of those witch cloaks from Party City, that's all."

He doesn't nod.

I don't get it. He didn't fall for Jameson's stunt earlier. But something scared him this time. Scared him so bad that he abandoned his precious camera. I've got to get him back on track. "I saw Naomi Lamb," I offer.

At this, a glimmer of recognition lights his brown eyes. "What?"

"I saw her. At the edge of the cliff."

"Naomi is *here*? That's—" He looks over my shoulder to where the cliff juts out over the water. "We have to interview her."

"What? Oh, I don't think that's a good idea." Naturally, I would do too good a job getting him back on track.

"Eden, this is a documentary on the Fairport Village curse. Naomi's sister was a victim. No one's ever gotten the full story of why Esther Lamb was even in the ruins that night in the first place. Naomi could be the most important interview of all."

He's right. There was no senior overnighter when Esther was murdered. There were no witnesses. All we know is that there'd been a note left with Esther's body, all the words cut from magazines and newspapers like in those serial killer movies. It said, *I warned you never to set foot in here again.* As if Old Mrs. Blackmore thought we all needed a reminder.

"So, we're going back to Sunnyside for your camera?" I ask.

Henry licks his lips, eyes darting to the sea. "I guess we have to."

I sigh. "Look, I've already gotten the hell scared out of me tonight. What's one more time? I'll get the camera. You check if Naomi is even here anymore. It's so quiet, I'm starting to think everyone went home."

"Okay," Henry says, nodding adamantly. "Yeah, it should be on the floor in the front room. You have your map, right?"

"Yeah. But text me if Naomi isn't at the bluff. I'd rather not spend another hour tracking you down."

"Sorry. Will do." He tugs the zipper on his hoodie higher and trots off toward the bluff, looking more like himself.

I examine my map again, shoulder sore from the weight of the bag. I head straight for the center of the ruins in the direction of Sunnyside. But I barely make it ten yards when my light illuminates a dark object off the side of the path.

I inch closer, finding Henry's camera, lying there in a patch of weeds.

I pick it up, relieved that it's seemingly undamaged. The weeds must've cushioned its fall. When I power it on, all I see is black. The lens cap is on. That means Henry's lens should still be okay. At least the thing works.

Spinning around, I tuck it beneath my arm and hurry the way Henry went.

It isn't long before I spot him through the mist. He's up against the rock wall, facing Naomi Lamb's thin figure. Like earlier, her white-blond hair floats like a cloud in the night sky. The same hair her sister Esther had, though where Naomi's is messy and free,

Esther's was always perfectly coiffed. I still remember the elaborate braids and twisted buns from the school halls back when I was a sophomore and Esther was a junior. And then when her picture was plastered over every newspaper.

As I near them, Henry's voice, strangely brusque, punctures the sound of crashing waves. "Just a few questions. That's all I need."

Naomi shakes her head. "I told you. I don't want to be on camera."

"Come on, Naomi. This could be the interview that brings everything together."

Head down, she attempts to brush past Henry. But he reaches out, grabbing her wrist. "Just wait a second."

"Hey!" I shout, breaking into a run now. The bag knocks against my arm, its strap digging into my sore shoulder. "Let go of her, Henry!"

He stiffens, releasing Naomi's wrist. Then he takes a step back from the rocks. "Sorry," he says, lifting both hands. "Sorry. I just— I'm really sorry."

Naomi tucks her elbows into her body, head still bowed low. Without a word, she skirts past Henry, taking to the path through the cottages.

"What was that?" I ask Henry, letting the bag slide down my arm to give my shoulder a rest. I lower it onto the ground, setting the camera on top.

He grabs at his dark hair, clenched teeth gleaming white. "I don't know. I think—it's this place, Eden."

"I would've talked to her, you know. If you hadn't done whatever the hell *that* was."

"I really needed that interview. That girl…" Henry darts a glance back to where Naomi's figure has already vanished inside the ruins. "She *knows* things."

"Maybe we can still get it. Did she at least tell you why she came?" It was a terrible idea. She knew all these jerks would be poking fun at the murders.

He nods. "She said she wanted to feel normal."

I guess that makes sense. Life changed so drastically for that girl two years ago. She stopped being Naomi Lamb to take on her new identity as "the dead girl's sister." She used to play tennis, but I think she quit. Dropped out of every school activity. Maybe she decided that tonight would be the night. If all the seniors were going to act like idiots by braving the ruins, she would join them. Finally be part of something.

And then always-harmless Henry comes along and acts like a big bad bully with his documentary.

Henry's posture sinks, shoulders drooping and knees buckling like he's about to slump down onto the gravel.

But then he marches straight past me, close enough to rustle my hair as he snatches up the camera and slips by.

"Hey! Where are you going?" He'd better not be headed anywhere near Naomi Lamb.

Henry doesn't respond, only storms off into the night. I let out a growl and gather up his bag. By the time I look up again, I've lost sight of him. "Henry!" I shout. "You promised not to do this again!"

Tears sting at my eyes. I'm cold and alone with all of this equipment again. I should've stayed home, watching movies with my best friend, May. Ever the rule follower, she refused to come along, even after I begged her and then gave her the silent treatment. As usual, her instincts were spot-on. I knew tonight would be long, but I didn't think Henry, the definition of *calm and collected*, would be so volatile. I've never seen him act this way—grabbing a girl's arm, storming off, spouting nonsense about ghosts. The way this is going, I doubt he'll even pay me.

I'm tempted to head back out the ruins through that breach in the chain-link fence and forget this night ever happened.

But I need that money. So instead, I gather my resolve and scurry past Sunnyside Cottage, the one with the buckling porch swing. Into the thick of the ruins.

Batting away the untrimmed foliage along the path, I continue until I reach the large cement courtyard. "Henry?" I call out, still unnerved by the silence.

I press on past that freakish mermaid fountain and take to the path, listening for voices. Naomi must've joined the others, wherever they are. Maybe Henry's there too.

Over by the nearest cottage, a light pierces the fog. I turn toward it, unable to make out the wielder of the light. The glowing circle bounces over the porch before disappearing inside.

"Henry!" I yell again, picking up speed as I near the cottage known in Fairport as the Leaning Tower of Torture. It's an apt name, considering the place is so tilted it's practically parallel to the ground.

Ascending the steps, I note that the door to the place is wide open. I inch my way closer, that light I followed no longer visible. "Henry?" I whisper into the void.

"In here," a voice whispers back.

I sigh in relief. "You know, you really shouldn't ditch your crew like that," I say, crossing the threshold and shining my light into the space. A scratching noise comes from the back of the room. Like Henry is dragging something over the boards. I didn't find a specific event tied to this cottage in my research, so I'm not sure why he's in here. "Are you getting shots of all the cottages now?"

Henry doesn't answer, only continues to make that scratching sound.

"What are you doing back there?" Irritated by his silence and the utter lack of lighting, I make my way toward the sound, struggling to navigate through the moldy furniture and debris. "Henry?"

A low giggle. One that Henry definitely didn't make.

Terror lances up my spine. I halt, too paralyzed to turn around. I didn't follow Henry inside this cottage.

So who did I follow?

More laughter, soft as a woman's. Or a child's. I need to breathe, but I'm afraid to make a noise. When the scratching starts again, my heart lurches.

I take a slow, deep breath. *Turn around and run.*

That's when the front door slams shut behind me.

My heart skyrockets into my throat, and I lose my grip on the flashlight. It clunks to the floor and rolls toward the back room. Then it vanishes in the darkness.

I crane my neck to glance at the closed front door, but it's too dark to see anything. Only a sliver of moonlight seeps through a crack in the shuttered windows. Anyone could've slammed that door. They could be standing behind me now.

Shuddering, I venture a step toward the place my flashlight disappeared.

From somewhere in the bedroom, a footstep creaks over the ancient wood. "I warned you," the voice grates.

The same words from the note found on Esther Lamb's body.

I turn and sprint toward the front door, yanking on the knob. It sticks—locked or jammed, I don't know—but the footfalls behind me inch closer. Heart hammering, I throw all of my strength into one hard tug.

Mercifully, the door opens. I burst through, only to come face-to-face with a new figure.

I scream with everything in me. Hitting and clawing, I try to force my way past this person.

"Hey, hey!" The voice is low, not the childish giggle of whoever—or *whatever*—was back in that cottage. Strong arms envelop me, trapping me. "Shh, it's okay."

I struggle until the arms release me. My breaths are fast and shallow as I look the assailant in the eye. "Caleb?"

"Are you all right?"

"Of course," I spit, still wheezing and shaking. "You think you and your girlfriend can scare me twice in one night?"

Hood back, the wind ruffles his hair as he frowns. "I'm lost here."

I bite the inside of my cheek so hard I taste blood. *Liar.* But I can't let on that he's getting to me. "Fine." I try to bull past him, and it's like ramming into a boulder. It takes everything in me not to wince. "I'm in the middle of a job here," I snap.

"Oh yeah. Where *is* Henry?" Caleb shines his light in a circle around us.

"I don't know, but I've got to find him." I hear his footsteps behind me and turn on him. "Alone."

He pauses on the top step, scowling. "You shouldn't be alone in this place."

"What are you doing?" I glare up at him, forgetting that glaring requires looking at his face. And let's be honest, that scowl isn't hurting anything. "Why are you talking to me?"

He shrugs, running a hand through his disheveled hair. "You looked lost. And now I can see that you're also without a flashlight. Near some pretty treacherous cliffs, I might add."

"I've got a whole bag full of lights," I say, jostling Henry's equipment. "Plus, I'd rather fall off the cliff than stay with you." I spin around again, not sure where I'm headed.

That's when the smell of cigarette smoke punches through the brine. "Is someone there?"

A giggle drifts through the stillness. I squint into the fog until

Victoria and Diego emerge. Jameson trails them on the path, a faint red spark the only sign of his cigarette.

The back of my neck prickles. *Who the hell was inside that cottage?* I take two steps away from the porch, but Caleb stays behind, eyeing the place.

"What's going on?" Victoria asks, brushing past me.

"Eden heard something in here." Caleb pitches a thumb in the direction of the cottage.

"Scared?" Jameson laughs. "Like father, like daughter," he says, taking another puff of the cigarette.

"Have any of you seen Henry?" I ask, ignoring him.

"Aw, did your only friend ditch you?" Victoria asks, hooking her free arm through Caleb's.

"Look, mess with me all you want, but can you guys leave Henry alone? He has nothing to do with your stupid grudge."

"We didn't do anything to Henry!" Jameson barks.

"Right." I give myself a mental kick to the shins. "Forgive me for attempting to have a conversation with a pack of monkeys."

"*Barrel* of monkeys," Victoria corrects, ruby-red lips smirking in the moonlight.

"Of course. Thank you."

"We should check out this cottage," Victoria says brightly, ascending the steps. "I know *I'm* not afraid."

Diego follows like a puppy, and Jameson, not wanting to be outdone, flicks his cigarette to the ground. "That's a fantastic idea." The spark flickers in the weeds, one puff of wind away from igniting the whole place. Jameson stomps it out before following Victoria. "Coming, Stafford?" He glances back at me, sneering.

"Don't worry about them," Caleb whispers into my ear. I can't help the slight shiver that courses through me. "You don't have to do this. We can go look for Henry." His eyes find mine, penetrating my skull and likely my soul. Some part of me wants to believe he's being genuine.

Obviously, I don't. Instead, I lift my head and follow the *barrel* up the steps to the creepy cottage.

Inside, the silence is thick and consuming. At first, I think they're already hiding from me. But Caleb steps through the door, his light illuminating their still figures.

"So," Jameson hisses, "what did you see?"

"I-I didn't *see* anything," I stammer.

Victoria huffs. "Of course she didn't. This is why we—"

"Whoa!" Diego shouts suddenly, stumbling backward. "What the hell was that?" He points dead ahead, at the shadows in the far corner of the living area.

I'm tempted to roll my eyes, but my gaze lingers on that dark splotch a moment longer, as it slowly fades back into the darkness, like it never was.

And then, as it *moves*.

Fluid like a flap of wings. Faceless and lithe. So unlike Jameson's hulking body draped in a costume cloak. Slowly, the figure unravels itself from the shadows and slinks into the collected glow of the lights.

My heart skitters. I inch backward, straight into Caleb's chest. Flinching, I shuffle away from him. My sight shoots ahead again. To the shifting shadow.

The shadow that's headed straight toward us.

"Let's get the hell out of here," Jameson says, sounding terrified for once as he turns on his heels and barrels through the door. We race after him down the steps and into the fog.

When we reach the path, I stop, my gaze drawn back to the figure that now spills from the doorway.

"Come on," Caleb says, motioning me along.

I don't move. Partly because I can't stand to fall for another one of their pranks. Partly because my eyes are still glued to the hooded figure. A dark blur swathed in mist.

"Eden!" Caleb calls again, tugging at my elbow.

"I know you put someone up to this," I say, still watching the figure's cloak span and ripple in the wind.

"No, we didn't."

He tugs on me again, and I'm so torn over what to do, it feels like my insides are being shredded apart.

Finally, I give in to his pull. Together, we rush after the others in the direction of the water.

When I glance back at the shadowy figure, it's gone.

Caleb's hand is still on my arm, but my skin, my nerves—everything is numb with terror. I barely feel it when his hand slides down, gripping my wrist as he leads me along the broken cobble-stone path.

"What the hell was that" I ask, out of breath as we reach the rock wall. I pull my hood up to shield my face from the deadly wind.

"I have no idea," Caleb says. "It was just like… Well, it looked like—"

"No, it didn't," I interrupt. Because it couldn't have been a ghost. They're not real. "Where are the others?" I ask to change the subject.

"I don't know." Caleb surveys the long stretch of land at the front of the property. "Maybe they're looking for Henry."

He reaches out to take the bag from my shoulder, but I shrink back. "Nice try, but thanks to you and your friends, I'm nowhere near finding Henry."

I stride ahead, making it only three steps when a shrill scream pierces the night.

Dread pumps from my chest to my scalp. Somehow, deep in my core, I know this isn't a prank. That scream was as real as the gravel underfoot and the blood pulsing through my veins. Caleb sprints ahead, and I struggle to catch up.

The screams continue, half-drowned by the wind. They aren't coming from the first bungalow; they're coming from farther ahead.

From outside the Blackmores' mansion.

My adrenaline blurs the pain in my chest as my feet slap the cobblestone. We pass a ramshackle garden shed off the path, its metal door swinging back and forth with an eerie creak. When we reach the large mass of students, a buzzing ring blares in my ears, splitting my brain.

A loud sob throttles the night. It's from somewhere in the midst of the gathering at the cliff's edge. Everyone is standing there. Too silent. Too still.

I attempt to push my way through them to see what's the matter, but Caleb frees himself from the cluster of seniors and pulls me aside. "Don't."

Just one word that stops my rapidly beating heart, causing it to plummet straight into the rough sand.

I shake him off, determined to look. I shove my way through the group of wide-eyed onlookers staring open-mouthed at the water. A shaking Amy Park buries her head in Diego's chest at the cliff's crest. The Blackmores' residence towers beside us, overlooking the waves that lap at the sharp rocks below.

Everything is black but the foamy sea, rising at intervals to devour the rocks. The moonlight casts a reflection, and a dark shape emerges. Something sprawled out over the rocks, bent into uncanny angles. The waves spray and trample the shape, which bobbles in an inanimate way. My stomach turns.

"I saw him," Amy says, her words broken by whimpers. "He was just standing there on the roof, so I called to him. I went to reach for my phone to call someone for help. But when I looked up again… he was gone." She sobs again, and I dry heave.

At the edge of the cliff, a video camera lies among the tufts of grass.

Down on the rocks, Henry De Rossi's lifeless body gets pummeled by another surge of dark water.

October 11

Dear Diary,

I have a confession to make. Last summer, I went onto the Fairport Village grounds.

It wasn't a dare or anything like that. More like a compulsion. Ever since I started looking into the murders and the curse, it was something I _needed_ to do. Like an itch, it was going to drive me insane if I couldn't scratch it.

It was late at night, and I swear no one saw me. Afterward, I never told a soul.

And yet, somehow, _she_ found out. She knows, and just like she promised, she can't let me live.

I am now looking into a way to break the curse. If I fail, I'm not sure how much time I'll have left.

4

WALKING ONTO CAMPUS THE FIRST DAY OF SENIOR year feels like walking into an exotic reptile shop. The hissing sounds come at me from all sides. My schoolmates make no efforts to hide their stares, and a couple of underclassmen point at me. Apparently, word got around concerning who was at the scene when Henry's body was discovered. My best and only real friend, May Kimura, loops an arm through mine and says, "Ignore them."

Every senior present at the overnighter was questioned by the cops, and as Henry's partner for the evening, I was the most important witness of all. I kept expecting the officers to ask about the hooded figure, but they never did. Maybe, like me, the others stayed silent about what we saw that night. Because it would've sounded insane.

When I was finally allowed to go home, Mom took it easy on me, mainly due to my state of shock. It wasn't like I was close to Henry; still, he stood up for me Friday night. For a few terror-filled hours, it felt like he actually cared what happened to me. Like he might actually become a friend. And then, before I ever had a chance to see, he was gone.

Last night, every Fairport High student received an email from Principal Jiménez, instructing them to head straight to the gymnasium at the start of the school day for an assembly addressing Friday night's tragic event. I considered staying home—hell, I even hoped the email had been a notification of my suspension. But apparently the administration thought a student's death was punishment enough and turned a blind eye. In the end, I owe it to Henry to be at this assembly.

When the bell rings, May and I push through the horde to find a seat way at the back of the seniors' section of the bleachers. Some girls behind us are sniffling, and I catch a few kids wiping at their eyes as the rest of the student body settles in. Henry might not have been a "big man on campus," but he was well-liked by students and teachers. He was the guy responsible for running all things audiovisual, which explains why the enormous screen below shows nothing but an error message and why Principal Jiménez's voice is inaudible in the microphone.

Mr. Sanderson, the head of the AV club, swoops in. He adjusts a few cables and tests the mic, pausing to blow his nose into a tissue before getting it to work.

"Welcome, students," Principal Jiménez says in a frequency that causes everyone to cover their ears. Mr. Sanderson rushes to turn a knob, and then the principal begins again, somberly. "It is under extremely sad and tragic circumstances that we begin our year in this room together. As I'm sure you're all aware by now, our own incoming senior and AV club president Henry De Rossi passed away on Friday night."

The crowd breaks into a sea of murmurs as Principal Jiménez nods. "He was beloved by so many of you, and the staff and administration want you to know that Fairport High is a safe place. We will have counselors on standby if you need to talk, even if you didn't know Henry personally but might be silently struggling the way Henry must have been. Suicide is a topic that—"

"Suicide?" I blurt, and everyone below me in the bleachers turns their heads. May slings me a sharp look, and I mumble an apology and shrink down in my seat as close to invisible as humanly possible.

The principal, who apparently heard my outburst, is staring up in my direction. "I know some of you were present the night of this tragedy and were questioned about the events. The Fairport Police Department has determined that there is no need for further questioning." He clears his throat. "I know that the word *suicide* can be a hard pill to swallow. No one is grappling with this as much as Henry's family, so all I ask is that you give them space as they mourn the loss of this bright and talented individual. I'm now going to invite up Mrs. Franklin."

As the guidance counselor approaches the microphone, I turn to May. "This is bull," I whisper.

May shushes me but concedes with a look that says she promises to hear me out when this is all over. We listen to Mrs. Franklin rattle off some statistics and basically repeat everything that the principal already said. Then, we're excused to go to first period, like this is any other school day.

The second we clear the gym, I race to the lockers, dragging May along by the arm. "Nothing about Henry that night was suicidal," I hiss. "He went in there to film a documentary."

"But do you really think he was murdered?" May asks skeptically.

"Well, no," I admit, remembering Amy Park, who claimed to have seen Henry up on the roof all alone. If someone had actually pushed Henry, wouldn't she have seen them? "But maybe it was an accident? Henry was pretty shaken up before he…he said he saw someone."

"Who?" May asks, eyes widening.

"He, um…" I shut an eye. Does admitting that Henry claimed to have seen Mrs. Blackmore's ghost count as speaking ill of the dead? Though if I'm honest, even *I* saw something that night. Something that had Caleb and the others running like their lives depended on it. "He said that Mrs. Blackmore was there in the ruins."

May lifts a brow.

"I know, it—you'd get it if you'd been there Friday," I say, instantly regretting it.

She looks down at the linoleum floor. "You said you understood."

"I know. I'm sorry." This was a topic of contention between us last week. A topic I promised to be over. "Just forget it. You were obviously right to skip it." I offer a smile and bump her shoulder with mine, and the two of us head to first period.

But even as I smile, my mind is fastened on that figure draped in black. The one I saw with my own two eyes that night. Henry claimed that she *knew what was buried there.* What the hell did he mean?

———

Lunch rolls around, and I wait for May by the lockers so we can finally head off campus the way we've dreamt since freshman year. Only she doesn't show up right away. I foolishly forgot to get a copy of her schedule, so I'm left standing around like a loser when Caleb enters this stretch of hallway.

His eyes meet mine, and his steps pivot in my direction. My heart does this weird palpitation thing. I consider breaking eye contact and pretending to look busy, but his stare has me frozen in a trancelike state. Is he coming to talk to me about Friday night? I tuck a strand of messy hair behind my ear and force myself to focus on my shoes. When I glance up again, Caleb is no longer walking toward me.

He's headed to Victoria, who's leaning against a locker a few yards down, wearing a white minidress and heels like she's headed to Sunday brunch. She looks much recovered after Friday night's ordeal, her hair curled and her face freshly made up.

I barely have a chance to feel the sting before Victoria turns to catch me standing alone, staring like an idiot. My face ignites. *Damn you, May, for leaving me all alone here.*

But Victoria isn't giving me the smirk of victory. Not even

a glare. More like a look of confidence, two strangers sharing a secret unfit for words. There's a foreign expression on her always-composed face. Worry? Fear? She turns toward the exit doors, long dark hair rippling down her back as she ambles at Caleb's side, leaving me to wonder.

I pull out my phone to send off a text to May. Where are you??

After obtaining my stale burrito from the cafeteria, I finally spot her walking out of the science wing.

"Nice of you to finally show up," I say when she reaches me. "What happened to our lifelong dream of eating at Benny's Burgers instead of this prison?"

"Like Benny's food is any better," May says, stuffing some sort of flyer into her binder. "I'm sorry. Mr. Lombardi wanted to talk to me about heading up robotics club this year."

"Oh, May, no. I mean, god bless those robotics kids, but you cannot be their leader. If they revolt, you could wake up one day with artificial eyes and a hand that fires lasers."

"Eden, I don't think you have any idea what goes on in robotics club. I'm going to grab a bag of chips or something before the bell rings."

"Worst first-day-of-senior-year school lunch I've ever had."

"Make it up to you tomorrow," she says, shoving her binder into her locker and leaving me alone yet again.

I pull out my phone to kill some time playing Roblox when someone taps me on the shoulder. I spin to find Diego standing there, hair disheveled and dark circles rimming his eyes. "Geez, Diego, you look—are you okay?"

Not that I should care. He certainly wouldn't care if I weren't okay. But he looks like he hasn't slept in days.

He shakes his head and glances over to where Naomi Lamb is sitting on a cement planter, eating lunch by herself, then to where a boy is drinking from the water fountain. "I need to talk to you in private."

I smile and nod. "Didn't you also need to talk to me in private that day you and your crew locked me in the janitor's closet?"

"This is different," he says, still eyeing everyone who gets within ten yards of us.

"Look, it's not that I'm suspicious because I haven't heard Jameson's loud mouth all lunch period." I twist my lips. "Okay, it's exactly that. Where have you got him hiding?"

"I'm not trying to prank you, Stafford. I—look, only the ones who saw her that night will understand."

"Saw who?" I ask, trying to erase the lingering images even as I play stupid.

Diego's dark eyes sharpen. "The *thing* we saw in the Village. I know you saw it too! It's her! Mrs. Blackmore…or whatever she is now."

I have to stay calm, diplomatic. "Everyone was on edge that night. I barely remember what happened before…" I don't have to say what happened because it's the only thing anyone has been talking about today. "Besides, what does it matter?"

"It matters because she's following me," he grits out. His gaze darts to the lockers, then back down the long stretch of hallway.

I roll my eyes, trying to decide whether to respond or simply walk away, when he adds, "He knew. Henry was doomed, and he knew it." Diego's face goes white as a sheet. "And now I think I am too."

"What do you mean?"

"The curse. He was cursed, and now I am. Almost like he passed it on to me."

"Diego, I don't think curses work like the common cold. Unless, I mean—you didn't share a water or a beer with Henry, did you?"

I wait for him to crack a smile, but he merely stares off down the hall. "It had to have been the note. She must be looking for it."

"What note?" I ask.

"She was standing over my bed when I woke up in the middle of the night."

A chill rolls through me. "I really think you should take a sick day. You're sounding a little bit—"

"She's after me," he says, leaning in so close that I want to step back. "She knows what's buried there."

At those words—the exact words Henry used—I flinch as if slapped.

"You have to believe me," he continues. "If we don't do something—"

"We?"

"Those of us who were there, who saw her that night. We have to find out what she wants."

"I haven't exactly been included in your *we* in years, Rodriguez. Outside of your plans to use me for target practice."

"I wouldn't joke about this," he says, rubbing at a swollen red eye. "Please, Eden." The tears welling in his eyes look genuine. Like he actually might cry. "Will you meet us after school, at Fairport Brew?"

Fairport Brew, the coffee shop where Henry works. *Used to work.* The place where May and I used to annoy him by ordering under different names with ridiculous spellings every time we went in.

"I have volleyball after school." Relief sweeps over me; I have an excuse. We're getting ready for our first preseason tournament in a few weeks, which means Coach would never let me miss practice for some ghost club meeting.

"Okay, then, we'll go tomorrow morning instead." He nods as though it's been agreed. "Seven a.m. I'll tell the others."

Without another word, he scurries off down the hall, hood pulled up and shoulders hunched. I try to call him back, but he disappears into the crowd of students exiting the cafeteria.

5

TUESDAY MORNING, I WAKE UP EXTRA EARLY TO MEET
Diego and the others. Though I'm eager to hear what they have
to say about that night in the ruins, there's an anxious knot in my
stomach.

Of course, when I arrive at Fairport Brew, the only other
member of the ghost club there is Caleb. He's seated at a big table
in the far corner, and I pretend not to notice him as I approach the
counter.

The owner of this place, Miriam, is a thirtysomething woman
with purple frames. Her brown hair is pulled up into a bun. She gives
me a wave and proceeds to train a younger girl, who asks what I'd
like. Seeing this new girl behind the counter where Henry should be
hits me like a brick. Suddenly lightheaded, I consider abandoning
this meeting altogether.

But I think of Henry again and pull myself together. He's gone, and none of it makes sense. I order my latte under a fake name with a particularly challenging spelling; if the new girl can't hack it, she's not meant for this job.

When the doorbell chimes, Victoria enters the shop wearing three-inch platforms. They clack over the tile as she orders a sugar-free soy-milk latte with a dash of cinnamon.

I move toward the back of the shop to avoid her, only to remember the other devil there. The one lazily sipping coffee, chin resting on a hand and hair falling over one eye. Like he doesn't have a care in the entire world, even though his best friend is apparently fearing for his life.

"Sherlee with three *E*s," the girl at the counter calls out, saving me from having to make this impossible choice.

I grab the drink, then turn to find Caleb arching an eyebrow at me from his table.

"Got a problem?" I ask, dropping into the farthest seat away from him and mimicking his lackadaisical posture.

"I think you took the wrong drink."

"Most certainly did not." I take a defiant sip of my latte, scalding my entire mouth. I blink away the full-on eye watering to find him watching me with something like amusement. "It's important to protect one's anonymity," I say, removing the lid of this caffeinated lava trap. I blow on it, replace the lid, and then run out of reasons not to look Caleb in the face.

"Okay." He takes a sip of his own drink without flinching. The guy's mouth must be made of steel.

"Yeah, okay," I say to make it sound like I won the conversation and not like he simply lost interest in it.

There's a clacking behind me, and Victoria slides onto Caleb's bench, scooting until their arms brush. "Hey," she says to him sweetly before turning to curl her glossy red lips at me. "Why are *you* here?"

"Nice to see you too, Victoria. I was invited by your sleep-deprived friend."

"Speak of the devil," Caleb says, flicking his chin in the direction of the chiming door.

In walks Diego, who doesn't bother to stop at the counter to order anything before lumbering across the place to us. He looks worse than yesterday, eyes bloodshot and clothing wrinkled. "You came," he says to me with awe, squeezing in on the bench beside Victoria so that all three of them are facing me.

"Yes, I'm here. We're all here. Now tell me why you said the exact same words that Henry said to me before he died, so we can get to school before the tardy bell."

"In a minute," Diego says. "Jameson had to park down the street, but he's coming."

"Wonderful." If the caffeine doesn't jolt me to life, Jameson's thunderous voice will do the job. No one else says anything, so I start to fiddle with the zipper on my hoodie. The last time I sat at a table with this group was second grade, and I doubt they're still debating whether crayons or school glue tastes better.

A moment later, Diego motions toward the front of the shop. I don't have to look to know that Jameson's stopped at the counter to flirt with the barista-in-training. "I actually don't drink coffee," his voice booms across the shop. "Just a protein shake every morning to help my performance out on the field."

I suppress an eye roll, remembering Jameson's *healthy* smoking habit. "As fascinating as we all find Jameson's dietary habits and his...interesting conversational tactics," I say to the others, "can we please get this meeting started?"

"I'll go get him," Caleb offers, scooting off the bench and around the table.

When they return, Caleb sits in an empty chair beside me and gestures for Jameson to take the spot on the bench beside Victoria. She eyes Caleb, her gaze narrowing and zipping to me.

Jameson soon follows suit. "What's *she* doing here?"

"I asked her to come," Diego says.

"Keep your eyes on your wallets, guys," Jameson says with a laugh. "You never know what runs in the blood."

I start to get up, but Caleb lays a gentle hand on my wrist. Unnerved, I sink back down.

"Okay," Caleb says, folding his hands and leaning his elbows on the table. "Diego asked us all here for a reason. Let's hear him out."

Diego stares at the space between Caleb and me now. "I think we have to tell the cops what we saw that night."

"What we saw?" Jameson huffs. "We didn't see anything. Other than a dead body in the water."

"I don't mean the body," Diego says. "I mean the woman in black."

Jameson flinches, then glances around the place. "I thought we agreed we'd had too much to drink." *Agreed?* Why does it sound like he's convincing himself as much as the rest of us? Maybe someone as big and tough as Jameson can't have anyone thinking he's afraid of ghosts.

"Well, Eden didn't have anything to drink," Diego counters. "And she saw the woman too. Right, Eden?"

It's true that I had nothing to drink that night. Still, I'm not ready to admit anything to this group. "I'm not sure what I saw. I was under a lot of stress, with Henry being missing and all."

"Come on!" Diego says, throwing his hands up. He turns to the others. "You saw her, right? Caleb? Victoria?" They only avert their eyes in turn.

"She showed up again last night. Followed me home from soccer practice. My life is at stake here. You guys are supposed to be my friends." His voice cracks, and I'm tempted to get up and head for the door.

It's exactly what Diego deserves, coming to the realization that these people make the worst possible friends. Only it doesn't give me any sense of satisfaction at all. It just hurts.

"Why do you think your life is at stake?" Caleb asks, sounding concerned.

"Because of the note. Henry's note. The one that he passed on to me."

"Can we see this note?" Caleb asks.

Diego shakes his head furiously. "No! No, no, no. I can't give it to you. I don't have it, and even if I did, I wouldn't give it to you."

"But why, Diego?" Victoria asks, sounding irked even as she reaches out to lay a calming hand on his. It would almost be a sweet gesture if I didn't know her to be evil incarnate.

"Because that note is the *reason* I'm next. Don't you see? It's the way he passed the curse on to me. If I showed it to you, you'd all be doomed."

"I don't..." Caleb starts.

"If Henry had never found that note—if he'd never done any of it, we'd all be fine. We should've listened. This whole time, the curse was real. We *never* should've gone there."

"Okay, assuming all of this is true," I say, "this is really what you want to pitch to the cops? That you're being followed by a ghost because of the Fairport curse?"

"What else can I do?" he blurts, drawing the attention of the other patrons. "Henry was murdered because of that curse. It was no suicide—that's for sure. And now Mrs. Blackmore is after me."

"Okay," Caleb says, sitting up in his seat. "Vic, can you get him something to drink? And make it decaf, please?"

When Victoria slides off the bench, Caleb turns to Diego. "Did you get a photo of her? Something we can show the cops?" He looks to me. "Stalking is a crime, right? They should be able to do something if we show them proof."

I nod. "Yeah, but I think they have to threaten physical violence. I could be wrong though. A photo of her in your room might help."

"I don't have a photo," Diego says. "By the time my screams woke up my parents, the woman was gone." His lips press flat. "And last night, I didn't exactly pause to take a picture. All I wanted to do was get home."

I sigh through my teeth. "It's not enough."

"Not unless we all come forward with what we saw in the ruins," Caleb says, lifting a brow.

I study him, unsure what game he's playing.

Diego's expression shimmers with something like relief or gratitude.

Then Jameson pounds a fist on the table, nearly spilling my drink. "We didn't see a damn thing in the ruins," he snaps.

Caleb's hazel eyes meet mine, interrogating me the same way I did him a moment ago.

"I might have," I say just to rile Jameson up some more.

He grunts. "Like the word of a Stafford means anything around here."

Before I can throw my coffee in his face, Caleb says, "If the four of us go to the cops, they'll have to listen. Maybe they can take a closer look at Henry's death, for a start."

If there's one thing I stand behind, it's that Henry didn't commit suicide. Still, murder by ghost? That's too much to swallow. The curse isn't real, and Mrs. Blackmore isn't out there killing off kids.

But as I attempt to push the thought aside, a dark figure swoops into my mind. A flap of black fabric. Soundless footsteps that close the distance between us in a blink.

Victoria returns, placing a cup in front of Diego. "What did I miss?"

Jameson crosses his arms and slumps lower. "These idiots are claiming they saw Old Mrs. Blackmore in the ruins on Friday night."

"We're saying we saw *someone*," Caleb corrects. "Someone who chased us in the ruins."

"Well," Victoria says carefully, eyes on the table as she returns to her seat, "you're right about that."

Diego beams at her. "So will you come with me to the cops?"

She bites her lip for another beat, then leans to give him a side hug. "Of course."

I sip my coffee, wondering why Victoria has had this sudden change of heart. Is it because Caleb is on board now?

"I might not have any photos." Diego considers his words carefully. "But I do have something I can show the cops."

"That's a bit cryptic," I say.

"I'm trying to save your lives," Diego says, voice strained, eyes red and watery like he hasn't slept. And damnit, despite how many hours I've spent despising him over the past decade, I actually feel bad for him.

"We'll go to the police station after school then?" Caleb asks. "I'll drive."

Great, a truck full of them. "I have volleyball after school," I mumble, offering a regretful shrug.

"Then we'll go at lunch," Victoria says.

"You two can't leave campus at lunch." I flick an index finger from her to Diego.

Victoria's head flinches back. "What? You really never snuck off campus for lunch?" She smiles deviously. "That's so…cute."

"Okay then," Caleb says gruffly, erasing Victoria's smirk, "my truck at lunch."

As much as I want to avoid this trip, I also want to find out what happened to Henry. He set out to make a documentary on the Fairport curse, and it took his life. I don't believe in curses, but was it all really a coincidence?

Jameson continues to sulk on the bench, arms crossed, and my one consolation is the fact that he won't be joining us.

I grab my backpack, ready to blow this joint, when Caleb asks, "Need a ride, Eden?"

I freeze, my brain failing to make sense of his question, my tongue refusing to make words. His eyes are on me, and all I can think about is freshman year. The night I not only believed he'd abandoned this grudge against my family but that he actually wanted to be my friend again. Or even something more.

I think of the way that all turned out, tears soaking my pillow and a pain in my chest so bad I couldn't breathe. "I'm good."

6

"YOU'RE GOING TO TELL THE POLICE *WHAT*?" MAY ASKS, brown eyes wide as we pace the outer courtyard during nutrition. "With whom?"

I blow out a breath through my teeth. "I told you Henry's death wasn't suicide. Turns out, there are others who want to look into it. Others who happen to be…my mortal enemies."

"Oh my gosh," May says, a bit too excitedly considering my plight. "I should come. Let me come."

"You only want to come because you think Diego's hot." I've definitely caught her staring at the guy on multiple occasions.

"Do not," she says, reddening. "He's too young for me. And besides, any mortal enemy of yours is a mortal enemy of mine. I should come to be your bodyguard."

"I appreciate the sentiment, May. But you're not coming. I only told you in case I don't make it back. You can tell the police who kidnapped and murdered me."

"Are you sure you want to do this?" she asks.

"I've never been less sure of anything in my life. But Henry was my employer and almost friend, and I owe this to him. If Diego's claims about the threat on his life can get the cops to open an investigation into Henry's death, I have to back him up."

"So this means we wait yet another day for our Benny's Burgers excursion," May says wistfully.

"I know. It's the worst part of all of this, but imagine how good those chicken bites will taste after so much longing."

"Like high-quality cardboard, I'm guessing." She puts a hand on my shoulder. "You're a true hero, you know that? Getting into a vehicle with Caleb Durham after he stood you up? All in the name of doing what's right."

"Following my beliefs, yeah." I take a dramatic breath. "It will be a journey fraught with peril. At least Jameson isn't coming."

———

"Changed my mind about coming!" Jameson bounds through the parking lot toward us, skirting car bumpers and nearly bulldozing a pack of freshmen.

"I don't hear anything," I say, shutting my door in the back. "You can start driving. We don't want to be late to sixth period."

Caleb leans an elbow on the steering wheel and turns to roll his eyes at me. "The others aren't here yet."

"While we wait, maybe you could drive around the lot and make Jameson chase us until he tires."

He cracks the hint of a smile. "You know his testimony will help. His dad pulls a lot of weight in town." Like the rest of my father's ex-friends and ex–business partners, Jim O'Sullivan is well-liked by everyone because he has a lot of money.

"It's him or me."

Unfortunately, that sounded a lot more threatening in my head. Caleb's brows knit together. His phone dings just as Jameson lumbers up to the passenger's seat, pulling open the door.

"Where are Diego and V?" he asks.

Caleb holds up his phone. "Victoria just texted. She says Diego left fifth period early and never came back."

"What?" Jameson is still standing outside the truck with the door propped open. "Did you text him?"

"Yeah, a minute ago." Caleb unlatches his seat belt. "But he didn't respond. I'll check inside."

I open the back door and practically leap out of the car. There's no way in hell I'm going to sit in this truck alone with Jameson. "I'll help you look."

Jameson plops down in the passenger's seat and whips out a bag of chips. "I'll be here," he says, opening the bag with an unnerving pop.

I weave through the cars, following Caleb up the steps and inside the building. "Nothing yet?" I ask as he checks his phone again.

He shakes his head. "Victoria is headed to the office to ask if he went home sick."

"Without telling us?" After arranging that whole meeting this morning, then this plan—it doesn't make sense. "Maybe you should check the bathroom," I suggest. "I would, except…you know, reasons."

"Yeah, okay." He nods. "How about you check the boys' locker room?"

I turn to find him smirking at me, and my cheeks heat. "I'll check the cafeteria. Maybe he got hungry. It is lunchtime."

"Good idea. Meet back here." Caleb takes off down the hall, and I navigate the crowds to the cafeteria. I do a once-around, scanning the line and each table. No sign of Diego.

Out in the hall, I hurry to the front of the school to wait for Caleb. Knowing him, he found Diego in the bathroom, and the two of them got in the truck and left without me. That would be a relief, honestly.

I decide to wait another minute, just in case. As I pull out my phone to look busy, a crash sounds above the hallway din.

Every head in the hall turns toward the noise. "Was that a gun?" asks a terrified-looking freshman.

"No," another kid answers. "It sounded like something fell." Gradually, we stir, moving toward the gymnasium in herd formation. I try to push through, but there's a holdup ahead.

"It won't open," calls out a voice.

I get on my tiptoes and see a couple of boys attempting to tug open the gym doors.

"Locked," says another voice. "Someone get a coach or a janitor."

"I'll go try the back door," a girl says.

"What the hell do you think that was?" a kid next to me asks his friend.

"Maybe Big Jake tried to dunk, and the entire basket came down," one of the basketball players says, eliciting a hum of nervous laughter.

"All right, everyone," comes Coach Prescott's deep voice, "make room." He presses through with the key. But when he tries to yank open the double doors, they stick. "That's weird," he says, pulling harder. "Something's holding it shut from the other side."

Without thinking, I start toward the front of the school. A few kids are ahead of me, apparently having the same thought as they pass through the doors.

"Eden!" Caleb is standing on the school steps. "What's going on?"

"We're not sure," I say. "No Diego?"

"Nope. And he didn't go home. Victoria's freaking out. I told her to go check his house in case he left without telling anyone." He stretches his neck to peer beyond me. "Where's everyone going?"

"Come on," I say, following the ever-growing crowd of students around the perimeter of the school to the back entrance of the gymnasium.

We make it as far as the flower planter bordering the cement when someone screams. The sound freezes the blood in my veins.

Caleb's eyes, wild with fear, meet mine. In the gym doorway, the girl who first offered to check the back is gripping the doorjamb as if for dear life.

At first I think she's hurt, but the other students press past her to get inside the gym. I follow Caleb, my heart pounding so hard it could burst through my chest. On the ground lies a ladder—the source of the crashing sound.

There's a gasp, and I look to the girl who entered before us, whose neck is angled upward. The boy beside her is equally entranced by something overhead. I follow their gaze and drop to my knees, a scream caught in my throat.

Above the fallen ladder, Diego Rodriguez is hanging from the rafters by his neck.

Caleb lets out a muffled sob and rushes to the ladder. "Someone help me!"

I do, even though my legs are shaking as I get to my feet. Even though I'm not sure there's anything we can do for Diego now. We right the ladder, and Caleb climbs it. I try to hold it steady, focusing on the tread mark–streaked wood floor.

But my gaze sneaks upward, to where Diego's sneakers, the bottoms scuffed and worn, continue to sway back and forth.

7

I PICK THE PHONE UP OFF MY NIGHTSTAND AND STARE at the text again. Hey, it's Caleb. Can we meet?

It's Saturday afternoon. None of the teachers had the heart to give us weekend homework, so I'm tucked in bed, trying to avoid Mom's hovering presence. I get that she's worried about me; two of my schoolmates died this week, and I happened to see both of the bodies.

I've thought a lot about Caleb over the past couple of days. Not that I wanted to; it couldn't be helped. And now he's texting me like we're friends again. Like nothing happened freshman year.

When I deleted his number from my phone three years ago, it felt final. He'd hurt me so bad that I would've been happy never to have seen his stupid handsome face again. I never would've believed I could actually feel sorry for the guy. But after Tuesday, that face—twisted with panic, helplessness, then anguish—lives in my mind on a constant loop.

I haven't seen him or the others since that day. School was canceled on Wednesday, and though I attended Thursday and Friday, Diego's friends must've stayed home. Probably for the best, considering the school has been ablaze with gossip. Two "suicides" in one week.

Which is complete and utter bull. Diego didn't want to die. He was doing everything in his power to stay alive. To outrun death.

But he died anyway. And we still don't know why. Both boys mentioned something being buried in the ruins. Both boys mentioned a note.

Unfortunately, Diego withheld that note in order to "save" us, for some reason.

I'm still not willing to buy into the curse as an explanation, which means I have to find a rational one. Without that note, I'll have to look for another avenue.

I consider calling May and asking her to look into this with me. But as much as she loves me and would do anything for me, she simply wouldn't understand. She wasn't there for any of it.

I text Caleb back: Why?

He replies a minute later. What they're saying about Diego isn't true.

I blow out a breath, my own questions about Diego's death and how it connects to Henry's swirling around in my stomach to the point of nausea. Fairport Library in an hour. Don't bring your friends.

———

"I gave you one instruction," I snap at Caleb as Jameson and Victoria hop down from his truck.

He shrugs, lanky figure clothed in soccer warm-up pants and a black Fairport High T-shirt. "Sorry. They were already at my house when I got your text."

"We were planning Diego's vigil," Victoria says, even though no one was talking to her. "It's on Monday." Her eyes are red-rimmed and swollen, just like Caleb's, so I let it go.

"Whatever." I brush past them and head up the steps into the library. Passing the circulation desk and bookshelves, I slip into the computer room.

"Are you going to tell us why we're here?" Jameson asks, following too closely behind me.

"We're going to figure out why Diego died," I say. "Henry too."

"On a computer?" He gapes at me as I sit down in front of one.

"Pleased to hear that you know what one of these things is called, O'Sullivan," I say, typing in my library card number. "Now go sit down at one *way* over there"—I point to the end of the long computer table—"and start researching the Fairport murders."

"You really think they're all related?" Caleb asks. "Even though Diego died outside of the ruins?"

"In the ruins, out of the ruins. All I know is it seems pretty clear that someone is killing us off, one by one."

Victoria, uncharacteristically clothed in leggings and a sweatshirt, crosses her arms. "Diego said we're fine as long as the curse isn't passed on to us."

"You really want to sit around and wait to see if that's true?" I ask.

"No one's chasing *me*," she says.

"Okay then." I turn to face my computer. "Go. If you really don't want to know what happened to your friend, go home."

I start to type *Nicolas Blackmore* into the search engine when I hear the sigh, followed by footsteps. Victoria plops into the chair three computers down from mine and asks, "Why are we in the library? We all have computers. And phones with browsers."

I can't exactly admit that I feel more comfortable with them in a public place. Or that I would rather swim in a pool full of sharks than go to any one of their houses or have them in mine. "This way, we have access to that microfiche stuff, in case we need it."

"The first murder was twenty-five years ago," she says, "not two hundred."

"Could be an *ancient* curse," I counter.

She rolls her eyes. "What am I researching exactly?"

"You can search Farah Palmer's murder," I say. "We're looking for connections between the victims. Clues that can lead to whoever's doing this." I crane my neck to peer down the table. "Jameson, dig up whatever you can on Esther Lamb."

Jameson rolls his eyes, and Caleb takes the seat directly beside me. "Guess that leaves me with…"

"The curse," I say. "Mrs. Blackmore sightings, the lore, all of it."

He gnaws on his lower lip, facing me now. "It can't really be… you know. Can it?"

"No," I answer quickly. But my mind spirals back to that night in the ruins. To Diego's ill-fated words from the school hallway: *Henry was doomed, and he knew it. And now, I think I am too…almost like he passed it on to me.* "I don't know," I admit quietly. "But near the end, Henry and Diego believed it. So we have to consider it."

Nodding, Caleb turns to his screen and starts typing. I begin the tedious process of combing through articles on the Blackmores, dating back to the morning after the murder twenty-five years ago.

"I don't understand who put Stafford in charge," Jameson grumbles through his clacking.

"Ignore him," Caleb whispers.

An hour later, I've discovered nothing but facts I already knew about Mrs. Blackmore, Fairport Village, and her son's murder.

There's a rustle somewhere in the library, and I look up to see Jameson pushing out his chair and stretching his arms like a freshly awakened baby. "This is worse than school, and it's going nowhere," he says with a yawn. "I need a break."

"Me too," Victoria says. "Coffee run?"

"I'm pretty good here," Caleb says, digging for his keys. "You can take my truck."

She frowns. "We'll just go to the place across the street. You want anything?"

"I'm good, thanks." He glances pointedly at me until I blink. Surely, Victoria wasn't asking if *I* wanted coffee.

"Eden," Victoria says, tapping a foot over the carpet. "Your drink order?"

"Uh, I'm good too, thanks." Much like the rule that you shouldn't let anyone mix a drink for you at a party, you definitely shouldn't let a nemesis deliver your coffee.

"Fine," she says, flipping her hair behind a shoulder and following Jameson out the door.

"You can go with them," I say to Caleb, whose eyes are already back on his screen.

"Nah," he says. "I'm reading this story about a woman who went to the police and the local media claiming that Mrs. Blackmore stole her baby."

"Wow," I say. "That's…"

"And then the police discovered that the woman had never had a baby. She was either mentally ill or an attention fiend. So I'm quite entertained here. But thanks for your concern."

I scoff. "Like I'd waste energy being concerned about you. I wanted you to leave so I didn't have to be alone in a room with you."

Caleb rubs at his temple like I'm giving him a migraine. "We appreciate you helping us."

"I'm here because Henry was a good guy whose death should be investigated at the very least." But after a moment, this self-righteous statement rings false in my ears. "And I guess I'm here for myself. I was in the ruins that night too."

He turns his chair slightly to face me. "Why are you always pretending like you don't have a heart?"

"Does it matter? A *heart* isn't exactly a valued commodity among you and your crew."

Caleb's gaze averts back to his computer screen. "Diego was a good guy, you know. A good friend. I know he wasn't always the nicest to you—"

I let out a hollow laugh. "Oh, so it was just him then?" He's really going to play dumb about ninth grade?

"Eden, I'm sorry we're not close anymore, but I did—"

"Stop. Just stop. I'm here for Henry. Now, if you don't mind, I'm reading." This is a lie. I'm not actually reading because my eyes are blind with anger. My heart is thumping like I just finished a marathon. I swore to myself I'd never let him get to me again. He isn't worth it.

But before I can push back my chair, I make out a few words on the screen through my tears. It's an article from the *Fairport Fix*, an online journal of questionable journalistic value. The article is dated five years after Nicolas's murder and claims to contain insight into the Fairport Police Department's mysterious interview tape with the boy's younger sister, Adelina Blackmore.

FIVE YEARS LATER, MYSTERY TAPE LEAKED

It's been five years since seventeen-year-old Nicolas Blackmore was stabbed to death, four years and six months since his mother and alleged killer Hazel Blackmore slit her own throat in her prison cell. Though Mrs. Blackmore never saw trial, we now finally have pieces of the damning account that put the mother of two behind bars for the crime.

At the time of her brother's murder, Adelina Blackmore was an eight-year-old child. Her interview with the police has been sealed due to the girl's age and other reasons that remain classified; however, excerpts from this tape were recently leaked in a series of audio bites that were posted online.

During her heart-wrenching interview with police, Adelina can be heard sniffling and asking for her stuffed bunny.

The interviewer, lead investigator on the case, Detective Harry McGuire, then presses the child about her mother and the crime in a truly despicable display. Though the leaked audio has been removed from the internet, we were able to obtain the transcripts, which are provided below. Please note that parts of the interview are missing or damaged, so it is not presented in its entirety.

AUDIO RECORDING #1

Adelina Blackmore: "I want Hoppy. And I want my daddy."
Detective McGuire: "What about your mommy? You don't want to see her?"
AB: (Silence. Sniffling sounds) "No."
DM: "Why is that?"

(Silence)

DM: "You don't want to talk about it?"
AB: "I want my bunny. I want Hoppy."

AUDIO RECORDING #2:

DM: "Adelina, can you tell me about last night? What did you have for dinner?"

AB: "Nicolas made me peanut butter and jelly."

DM: "Why didn't your mommy make you dinner?"

AB: "She and Daddy went out."

DM: "So your mommy was out all night?"

AB: "Not the whole time. She came back later."

DM: "Was she back when you heard the screams?"

(Silence)

DM: "Adelina, can you please answer yes or no for the recording?"

AB: "Yes, she was home. She and Nicolas got into a big loud argument."

DM: "And what was the argument about?"

AB: "He was supposed to be running the Village, but he had people over. They were having a party."

DM: "So your mother became upset?"

AB: "She got real mad."

DM: "I see. Does this happen often? Your mother getting real mad at your brother?"

AB: (Silence) "Yes. She yells at him and says he's not responsible."

DM: "And that's what happened last night?"

AB: "Yeah. She screamed and screamed until his friends decided to leave."

DM: "And where were you when your mommy and brother were arguing?"

AB: "In my room, but...I was listening through the door."

DM: "Where was your daddy?"

AB: "I think he was checking on the guests, since Nicolas forgot. He wasn't in the house."

DM: "Can you tell me what you heard next, through the door?"

(Silence, static)

DM: "Adelina, can you please answer aloud for the tape?"

AB: "No!" (Sobbing) "I don't want to!"

AUDIO RECORDING #3

DM: "Adelina, now that you have Hoppy, do you think you can tell me what you heard last night?"

AB: "Arguing. Mommy and Nick. They were fighting. And then, there was screaming." (Crying sounds)

DM: "Who was screaming?"

AB: "Nick. Maybe Mommy too. And then..."

DM: "What happened then?"

AB: "I accidentally dropped Hoppy, and it made a noise. And
then Mommy started calling my name. I looked out the
door, and she had a knife. She was coming toward the
stairs, shouting my name, so I ran down the hall. I climbed
up into the attic and hid there." (Sniffling sounds) "I
wanted Daddy."

DM: "And did you hear anything else? Did you see anything?"

AB: "No. I hid there until someone dressed like you came
and found me."

I reach the end of the transcripts and realize that I've barely
taken a breath the entire time. I'm lightheaded, and my eyes are
bleary. "Oh my god," I breathe.

Caleb rolls his shoulders and leans in to check my screen. "What
did you find?"

Suddenly, it becomes extremely apparent that I'm alone in this
room with Caleb Durham. Only it isn't fear I'm feeling.

"See for yourself." I scoot my chair aside so he can skim the article.

"Wow," he says, sitting back in his chair. "That poor kid. How
do you get over something like that?"

"I don't know. But I think we need to find Adelina Blackmore
and speak to her. Maybe she can explain what we saw that night
and what's going on."

"Or maybe she can't," Jameson says, standing in the doorway.
He lets out an exaggerated sigh. "Can we please be done here? Our
friend is dead, and we can't explain it away with some wild story."

There's a shush from the librarian in the next room, so Jameson and Victoria press inside.

"Jameson's right," Victoria says. "Come on, Caleb. We have a vigil to plan."

"Don't you want to know how he died?" Caleb asks.

"Of course, but…" She looks down at her iced coffee.

"I knew Diego," he says gruffly. "*You* knew Diego. Both of you. He came to us, desperate for help. And we didn't"—his voice breaks, and my heart wrenches—"we didn't help him. We didn't save him."

"Caleb," Victoria says, looking like she wants to comfort him as her shoes stay stuck to the carpet.

"Hey! No food or drink in here." The librarian, a young woman with her hand on her hip, enters the room, looking like she'd be going ballistic if not for the whole quiet-in-the-library thing.

"We should go," Jameson says, taking a few steps toward the door before stopping. "And you're our ride."

Caleb casts an apologetic glance my way as he stands. "It is getting late. Can we drop you off?"

I turn to face my computer. "I've got more work to do here."

"Eden," he says, gripping the back of his chair.

"Come on, Caleb," Victoria calls, eliciting another shush from our librarian friend.

He runs a hand through the hair at his temples, and for the most bizarre reason, I find myself wanting him to hang back. I know he can't be trusted, and I despise him all the way to my core. I know he drove the others here, so it wouldn't make sense for him to stay. Still, when he turns to follow her, I get a familiar pang in my chest.

"Let me know what you find," he says as he walks away.

"Will do," I call out sweetly.

Will definitely *not* do. If I never speak to or text Caleb Durham again, it will be too soon.

8

ONCE THEY'RE GONE, I CHECK MY PHONE FOR THE TIME. Six p.m. This place must be closing soon. My phone has been on silent, so I failed to notice May's slew of texts.

> How are you doing?
>
> Want to come over and watch a movie?
>
> Are you ok?
>
> Why aren't you answering me?
>
> Should I call the cops?
>
> No but seriously, after everything this week, I'm worried

I quickly text her back. Sorry, my phone was on silent. I'll be at your house in an hour or so.

Turning back to my computer, I start to search for information on Adelina Blackmore. Maybe something can make sense of Diego's cryptic words.

It doesn't take long to learn that Adelina and her father moved away from Fairport shortly after Nicolas's murder. According to a true-crime online forum, she was eventually committed to a psychiatric facility. And after her release, she was sent to St. Andrew's Academy, a boarding school for troubled teens. She was moved to three more boarding schools before apparently aging out.

The best lead I can I find is the address of a group home in the Bay Area. There isn't much on the house itself, but I learn that it's a staffed residential care facility for adults with mental health or behavioral issues, with around-the-clock care, strict house rules, and monitoring.

I feel the bite of frustration, which soon gives way to sadness. That poor little girl. First overhearing her brother's murder, then that detective's line of questioning only hours after the traumatic event. It was enough to send anyone over the edge.

Or maybe Adelina never had a chance. There were plenty of comments in the true crime forum about how insanity runs in the Blackmores' blood.

I need to talk this over with someone, but Caleb's seat is empty. And I'm not quite ready to toss this load onto May's shoulders. Especially since, curse or no curse, someone is killing kids who know too much.

Next, I pull up Nicolas Blackmore's obituary. After a few minutes, I realize I'm not absorbing any of the text. My eyes skim the material, but my mind is on Caleb. On the way he seemed torn between staying with me and going with the others. It wasn't the first time.

Back when my father left—when he backstabbed all of his

partners and then took off—Caleb was the only one in the group to stay friends with me. The others acted like I'd caught a plague worse than the one that killed off the Fairport settlers. But Caleb still talked to me. He ignored the comments from his friends. He didn't treat me like trash, the way all of their parents did.

I think that was why, eventually, I started to develop a bit of a crush on him. In the midst of all the chaos, he seemed brave and noble. Steadfast.

In the end, he turned out to be as big a coward and a jerk as my dad. Too bad I didn't realize it before the homecoming dance in ninth grade. When he messaged me on Snapchat, asking if I wanted to go with him to the dance, I actually thought the worst was behind me. I believed his invitation meant that he was willing to show his friends and their parents—to show the whole school—that the grudge between our families was ridiculous. That he was squashing it, once and for all.

I was so excited. May helped me get dolled up, which essentially meant she brushed my hair and forced me to wear one of her dresses. That night, I waited for Caleb outside the gymnasium, my stomach buzzing with happy nerves. I finally saw him. He was handsome in his suit—unlike the rest of the awkward ninth grade boys. When he smiled at me, my insides melted.

And then, he proceeded to place a corsage on Victoria's wrist, right in front of me. The two of them walked into the dance, arm in arm, and I just stood there, feeling like my entire body had been beaten to a pulp. He'd done it—all of it—to humiliate me.

So yeah, he was right when he said we weren't *close* anymore. He managed to phrase it in a way that was not only accurate but diminished every real feeling I had for him. A way that made it sound like that night never happened.

My jaw aches from clenching it for who knows how long. The library is silent and still; at some point, the lights in the main room turned off without my notice. I'm hit with the sudden fear that the librarian locked up without realizing that I was still in here.

I go to log out when something in the article snags my attention, chilling me through. Dispersed throughout are several photographs of Nicolas, one with his sister, one with his dad. There are a few of him at the beach, holding a surfboard, riding waves, or making hang-ten signs. In one, Nicolas waves at the camera wearing nothing but board shorts, and I notice a tattoo of a shark fin on his inner wrist. It's still red and raw, freshly inked.

I email myself the article, then close the browser. As I log out and gather my things, my mind is reeling.

There's got to be a simple explanation. Maybe twenty-five years ago, it was a common tattoo in Fairport. It is a beach town after all.

Still, I can't help feeling unsettled. Because I've seen that tattoo before.

On my father, Greg Stafford.

I hurry out the door into the dark room. Moonlight spills in through the front windows, illuminating my path as I navigate through the tables and bookshelves toward the door. *Please don't be locked. Please don't be locked.*

Before I can try the door, something in the room rustles. I freeze. Then slowly, I turn around.

A light clicks on, blinding me. I blink until the librarian comes into view over by the circulation desk. "Sorry, I thought everyone had gone. Just closing up."

I mumble a thanks and continue through the door, head low. Outside, it's dusk, the remaining light rapidly fading. I walked here, which means I have to get to May's house on foot. If I hurry, I can be there in ten minutes.

I send off a quick text to Mom, letting her know that I won't be home for dinner, and proceed down the shop-lined sidewalk. Everything on this street closed an hour ago. Other than a few cars parked on the street, it's empty.

Part of me wants to ask Mom about the tattoo, just to make sure my memory isn't deceiving me. But questions about Dad tend to put her in a bad mood. Between the abruptness of his leaving and the shock at learning of his duplicitous nature, she never really got over it.

The streetlamps are lit. Overhead, the palm trees sway in the breeze, their shadows stretching across the road. I wrap my arms around myself. It was so warm earlier that I didn't think to bring a sweater. There's no one else in sight, so when I hear footsteps other than my own, my heartbeat skips and I speed up.

The footsteps quicken, mimicking mine. I leave the sidewalk, crossing the empty street to the other side to watch this person pass. But the steps crunch along the pavement, following me.

I make it to the opposite sidewalk and consider turning onto the next street, closer to residential territory. But that would be ridiculous. No one is after me. The librarian startled me earlier, and now I'm on edge, that's all. Besides, I'm almost at the main drag, which means more lights, cars, and people. I continue toward May's house, the footsteps echoing my own as they meet smooth cement.

Diego's words trickle back into my head. *It matters because she's following me.*

Unable to stave my curiosity any longer, I glance back, expecting to see the librarian on her way home. Maybe someone out for some early-evening exercise.

Instead, I see nothing. No one.

I stop walking and peer into the now-darkened street. The nearest lamp glows over the pavement, making shadows of everything around me. The buildings, the trees, the benches.

My heart is beating so thunderously I can hear it over the rustling palm fronds. I know someone was behind me. So where did they go?

Then I see it. Not on the sidewalk, but on the pavement. One of the palm tree shadows—it moves. Like the trunk split down the middle and half of it walked off.

My gaze shifts to the sidewalk in time to catch the figure clothed in black as it darts behind a parked truck.

I turn and run.

My sneakers whack the pavement so loudly I can't hear if the figure is pursuing me. I risk a peek back as the black hood rises from behind the cab of the truck.

Without slowing, I try to free my phone from my pocket to dial 911. Only it sticks. I glance down when a horn blares. Lights blind me, and I jerk backward, avoiding the fast-moving car by inches. My heart seizes in my chest, but I manage to dislodge the phone. I barrel ahead to the sidewalk, checking behind me again and whacking my left elbow on the corner of a postal box.

Sharp pain radiates up my entire arm, and the phone slips from my other hand. I hear it clank on the cement behind me.

I spin around to search for it in the shadows, barely registering the pain in my elbow anymore.

I feel the smooth, hard case, grasp it, and start to stand when the figure descends upon me.

9

THE CLOAKED FIGURE HAS ME BY BOTH SHOULDERS. I scream and thrash.

"Eden!" it screams, still holding me despite my attempts to claw its face off.

I suck in a breath, trying to fill my air-deprived lungs. Then I peel open my eyelids and squint into my assailant's face. The charcoal-gray hoodie falls back, revealing a tousled mess of brown hair. "Caleb?"

"Are you okay?" His hand is on my arm now, and he pulls me to my feet. "What happened?"

"Someone was following me," I pant, scanning our surroundings. "They were just…" But he's the only person on the street. I take a step back, shaking him off of me. After checking that the phone clutched in my grip is still intact, I return my attention to Caleb. "You weren't wearing that hoodie earlier."

He frowns and glances down at his attire. "It wasn't cold before."

I mentally swat myself, because it's true—I had the same thought about the temperature a few minutes ago. *Still*. Whoever followed me and then disappeared was wearing a dark hood. It can't be a coincidence. "What are you doing here? You left the library an hour ago."

He scratches at his jaw. "I wanted to see if you'd made any progress and"—he doesn't make eye contact—"make sure you were all right."

"But where's your truck?"

"At the Chicken House. We all drove over there together, and then I walked here." He gestures over his shoulder to the street that leads to the main drag.

"Do *they* know you came to check on me?"

He clears his throat. "Not exactly." He draws sweeping arcs over the sidewalk with the toe of his shoe. "I told them I needed some air and that I'd be walking on the beach."

I start to shiver. If he was trying to play a trick on me, he would've done it by now. There's no one else around, no witnesses. "Okay, well," I say, starting to walk, "you found me. I'm alive."

Barely.

"But you said someone was following you. Did you get a look?"

I rub at my arms, which are covered in goose bumps. "Looked like the same person from the ruins." If you can call what we saw that night a person.

Caleb unzips his hoodie and shrugs it off. "Here," he says, offering it to me.

I catch the scent of bonfire smoke, a dash of coconut sunscreen. *His* scent. "Ha. Right. I'm good, thanks." I bat it away and keep walking.

"Why are you always like this?" His massive strides catch up and overtake me in no time.

"Like you don't know," I snap, determined not to cry.

"Hey," he says, moving in front of me and stooping to meet my eyes. "What's wrong?" He glances down. "Oh. You're hurt. Let me see—"

I follow his gaze. Sure enough, my elbow is scraped from my run-in with the mailbox. In the scuffle, I managed to wipe blood on my cream-colored shirt. "Please, just let me pass."

"I should take you to the hospital," he says without budging.

"It's a scrape, not a compound fracture. I'll be fine." I better be. I've got practice on Monday morning, and arms are somewhat necessary in volleyball.

"Clearly you're upset." His finger moves up near my eye, like he's about to wipe that lone traitorous tear away. Then, thinking better of it, his hand lowers to his side.

"Am not," I lie, blinking. I can't let him see me like this. I can't let him... see how much power he has over me, years later.

"At least let me walk you home."

I press my lips flat and try to feel nothing. Not the stinging in my eyes, nor the throbbing in my elbow. Not the ache in my chest.

I don't understand his charade. It's sadistic, really. Why can't he just be a giant jerk like Jameson? Why does he have to keep pretending to care, only to force me back to that night? To force me to relive that moment when I actually did care for him, only to feel the twist of his blade. Because even now, as I look up into his hazel eyes, I let the same fantasies that played in my head as a naïve ninth grader revive themselves.

Knowing he still has that power over me hurts more than any pain in my elbow.

"I was headed to May's house," I say. "Over on Palm Drive."

"I'm walking you."

"Are not," I say, pushing past him on legs that haven't quite recovered from my fall. I cringe and shake out what must be a bruise on my left knee.

"Stop acting like a three-year-old, Eden. Someone was just following you." He catches me by the right wrist, and this time, I don't tug away. My skin blazes where he touches it. When he lets go, it's to drape his sweatshirt over my shoulders.

Instead of fighting it, I shiver, inhaling that saltwater and smoke scent. "You're getting your favorite sweatshirt all bloody," I say as our steps start up again, this time side by side. It's an admission, I realize only after the fact. I'd have to notice him—to be aware of him on a daily basis—to know that he's always wearing this sweatshirt.

"Maybe you should keep it. Beats that horrible puffy yellow jacket you wear when it's cold."

My mouth drops open. I look over to find him smirking.

"Kidding," he says with a laugh. "You've never looked bad in your life."

A flutter goes through me. "Not even in first grade, when my mom gave me that bowl cut?"

He laughs, a low sound that's somehow both thrilling and comforting. "Not even when that feral cat on the docks scratched your eye so bad it swelled shut."

"You would think an animal that begs for food all day would've been a little more grateful for my leftover ice cream."

"Didn't your dad make himself a matching eye patch to wear to the Founder's Day barbecue, so you wouldn't be the only one?"

The memory hits me like a gut punch. "Yeah, I was worried that I looked like a pirate, so he said we could be pirates together." My lips curve in a half smile. "Come to think of it, he also gave himself an egregiously bad haircut when he saw what my mom had done to mine."

Caleb nods. "That was epic. Your dad was pretty hilarious."

"If only being funny mattered half as much as being present." My voice catches, and Caleb nears me, making an awkward attempt to lay a comforting hand on my back.

"I'm sorry, Eden."

I can barely mutter a response through my swollen throat. This is why I don't like to talk about—even *think* about—my father. It brings on happiness and pain in equal doses, but in the end, the pain wins out.

Because in the end, none of that fatherly stuff he did matters. All that matters is that he bailed on me.

I actually defended him, back when everything went down. When Caleb's friends—*my* friends at the time—were still talking

to me. But I refused to believe that my father could've committed
such a crime. I told them that maybe their parents should learn how
to count their money better. Let's just say that didn't go over too well.
I was so ready and eager to prove to them that their accusations had
been unfounded, so positive that my dad and I would be vindicated.

Obviously, our vindication never came. My dad left me in the
middle of a war I never asked to fight.

We reach the downtown strip, and I glance at the lit sign of
the Chicken House. "Sure you don't want to head back before your
friends eat all of your chicken and steal your truck?"

He rolls his eyes. "They're not that bad."

"No, of course not. I mean, they wouldn't *seem* that way to someone who's equally demented."

"You know, I—"

"May's just up this way," I cut in, pointing to the dark end of the
street where the residential neighborhood begins. "I'm fine, really."

"That's good." He takes a large stride in the direction I indi-
cated. "Maybe nothing's broken after all."

I grumble under my breath and cross the street with him.

"So," he says, "did you find anything after we left?"

I think of the tattoo on Nicolas Blackmore's inner wrist, the
same tattoo I remember seeing on my own father. "I tried to find
Adelina Blackmore," I finally answer. "But she moved away, then got
bounced around various psychiatric facilities and boarding schools.
After ending up at some group home, she basically fell off the face
of the Earth."

"Not great news for her or for us."

"Nope. I think, as much as Diego wanted to keep that note from us, we have to find it. Whoever killed him and Henry came after me tonight."

"That's…" He shakes his head, features darkening. "I mean, I never thought Diego was making it up, but…still. The fact that someone's really out there, hunting us? Who the hell would do this?"

"That's what we've got to find out. That's why we need the note."

Something grates off in the bordering shrubs, and without missing a beat, Caleb steps in front of me. When we locate the culprit—a broken open house sign waving in the wind—he continues ambling on that side like he merely prefers it. "How do we find it?"

At first, I don't recall what we were talking about. Remembering the note, I shrug. "He was *your* best friend. Any idea where he'd hide it?"

"Maybe his locker. If we can get to it before his parents clean it out."

"Monday, then. You know his combination?"

"If I did, it wouldn't make a very effective hiding spot," he says as we reach May's porch. "But Victoria can get the combo from the office list."

"Of course she can." Part of the reason Little Miss Know It All *knows it all* is that she's always in the office, pretending to be doing stuff for student council.

I ring the doorbell, unsure how to explain this situation to May. "Thank you for walking me, but I'm good now." I make a shooing motion, to which he merely arches a brow and continues up the steps.

May answers the door, making no attempt whatsoever to hide her shock. She stands in the doorway with her mouth hanging open.

"There," I say to him, furling a hand. "I made it. Happy?"

"I am, actually."

My cheeks heat as he looks at May. "Eden's a little banged up. Can you please make sure she's okay?"

My teeth clench. "I told you I was—"

"Of course," May says, her cheeks rosy. "Thanks for helping her."

"It was nothing." His eyes are already on mine.

I know I should repeat the sentiment and express my gratitude, but my jaw stays locked. He starts down the stairs, and I remember the sweatshirt. "Hey!" I call out. "You forgot this."

"I'm not cold," he calls back.

I want to insist; instead, I tug the sweatshirt tighter around my chest as he heads down the driveway and onto the sidewalk. "Watch out for shadowy figures on your walk then, I guess."

"Will do." He reaches the street and adds, "Have a good night, girls."

When he's out of earshot, May turns to me, eyes wide. "Oh my gosh. You *like* him again."

"What?" I shuffle my weight from one foot to the other. "That's crazy, May. He's my mortal enemy."

"Mortal enemies don't walk each other home. Or give you their sweatshirts. At least, not last time I checked. You watched him walk away, and"—she makes a horrified expression—"I think you were *smiling*."

"Because I was contemplating his demise," I snap, pushing past her into the house. "Obviously."

"Right." With a barely audible laugh, she shuts the door behind us. "Obviously."

October 12,

Dear Diary,

I've been researching Nicolas Blackmore's murder, and I stumbled upon something disturbing today: there is no record of Hazel Blackmore being buried anywhere.

Is it because the state took care of the body when Silas and Adelina Blackmore left Fairport? Or is it because she never actually died?

All I know for sure is that if she is still alive, she has a lot to be angry about.

10

"YOU GOT IT?" I ASK VICTORIA, WHO'S STRUTTING UP
to me in the hall with her hands behind her back and a smug smile
that would be fun to knock sideways. Behind me, Caleb leans
against his locker.

"Of course I got it," she says, holding up a hot-pink sticky note.
"The combinations are stored in the database. All I had to do was
tell Miss Gibson that I needed the computer to look up class sched-
ules so I could call student council out of fifth period before the
lunchtime pep rally."

"You are a true evil genius. Well"—I tilt my head to the side—
"at least half of that's true. Now can we go check the locker?" I hold
out a hand for the note.

"Are you crazy?" She whips it out of my reach. "You don't think three
of us gathered around a dead boy's locker is going to look suspicious?"

"Fine, then you go." I glance around nervously.

She narrows her brown eyes at me. "Right. So I can find Henry's
note and be the next to die."

"Who's the coward now?" I resist the urge to grin.

"Whatever." She hands the combination over. "You do it."

"If I must," I say, feigning reluctance as I snatch up the sticky note and head over to locker fifty-seven. I only make it a couple of feet before Caleb catches up to me. "What are you doing?" I hiss. "You heard her. This is a one-man—er, -*woman*—job."

"Except she's wrong," Caleb says. "It's a two-man job. I'm your lookout."

"Fine with me, but…" I glance around nervously. "Where's the loud one?" He casts me a befuddled expression, and I add, "O'Sullivan. At what point does he waltz in and ruin everything?"

"Oh." Caleb nibbles on his lower lip. "We, uh, left him out of the loop on this one."

"Wow." I skirt past some boys huddled around a phone watching a video. "Definitely not geniuses, but you two might not be idiots. *Evil* not *idiots* has a nice ring, don't you think?"

He concedes an unamused smile as we reach Diego's locker, which stands out like a beacon among the rest. It's been turned into a shrine, now covered in photos and notes from the entire student body. I've got a minute at most before someone spots me digging through this thing. I start to turn the lock, and Caleb plants himself behind me, facing the crowd. When I twist the dial to land on the final number, my hand starts to shake.

Probably the whole covert-mission thing and definitely not my close proximity to Caleb.

I yank the door open. Out spills a Fairport High soccer hoodie and a massive textbook, which lands on my foot. I let out a yelp, causing Caleb to turn.

"Are you okay?" he asks as I hop on my remaining good foot.

"Yes, fine," I grumble, gesturing for him to pivot. "Just do your job."

"But I heard..." His gaze slides down to the ground, fastening on Diego's sweatshirt. He starts to kneel but remembers himself. "Okay, go," he says, spinning back around.

I dig through the remaining contents of the locker, which include a few spiral notebooks, textbooks, a gray half-full Hydro Flask, a snack-sized bag of potato chips, and a copy of *The Catcher in the Rye*. Immediately, I grab the paperback and shake it out over the floor. Nothing tumbles loose, so I move on to the notebooks, flipping through each of them in turn.

All around us, our classmates walk, talk, turn locks, and slam doors, allowing us to blend in with the commotion. "Anything?" Caleb asks, still playing lookout.

"Not yet." I stash another notebook back inside and remove a textbook.

The bell rings, sending even more students to their lockers. I glance back to see Caleb floundering as he attempts to shield me. Unfortunately, he can't cover every side. "Here," I say, passing *The Catcher in the Rye* over my shoulder. "Pretend to read this."

He takes it, and I continue riffling textbook pages. All that's left is a U.S. history textbook, which I reach for, defeat already setting in the pit of my stomach.

But when I remove it, I discover a crumpled collection of papers and scraps at the back of the locker.

Caleb clears his throat. "Teacher approaching." He inches close enough that our backs graze. "Eden, shut the door."

"Okay, but I'm almost—" I ignore him, shoulder-deep in the locker as I sift through the trash pile, and he nudges me with an elbow.

"Shut it now."

But I'm so close. I gather up the entire pile and stash it in the kangaroo pocket of my sweatshirt. As I shut the door, I feel Caleb pivot. I'm sure he's about to yank me away from the locker; instead, he wraps an arm around my waist. I start to sidestep away, but he whispers, "Play along," turning his face so that our foreheads touch.

My heart whacks against my rib cage. I do as he says but avert my eyes so that they rest on the locker.

"Hey! You two!" At the low voice, my body jolts.

But Caleb's fingers nestle into the crook of my hip, tugging me toward him as he casually lifts his head to glance back. "Sorry, Mr. Harrison. Eden was talking me through some stuff. Helping me write a message to Diego."

I turn to see the math teacher's face fall. "My deepest sympathies, Mr. Durham. But the tardy bell is about to ring."

"Diego was his best friend." Victoria marches up to us, a book tucked under her arm. I nearly jump again; I assumed she ditched us to get to class. "They haven't even held his funeral yet. Don't you have any compassion?"

This seems to do the trick. Mr. Harrison's shoulders slump, and his skin reddens. "I'll give you another minute," he says quietly before plodding down the hall in the direction of the teacher's lounge.

"What the hell was that?" I ask, turning on Caleb.

"Sorry." He cringes. "I panicked. He was coming, and you weren't listening. He was about to catch you in Diego's locker."

"So you thought canoodling when we're supposed to be in class would be the lesser crime?"

Victoria laughs. "*Canoodling*. In your dreams."

Caleb still looks distraught as he rubs his hand over the back of his neck. "I didn't want to have to explain to the principal or to Diego's parents why we were snooping through his things. It's bad enough that their son is dead. They shouldn't have to hear our wild theories as to how he died."

The fire inside me dwindles. "No, I guess not."

"Did you find the note?" he asks.

I dig my hands into my sweatshirt pocket, pulling the scraps of paper free. "Let's find out."

The three of us sort through everything, keeping an eye on the hallway. But it's only a bunch of old school event flyers, class handouts, and tardy slips.

"It's not here," Victoria finally says.

"Nope." Disappointment stabs my gut as I get to my feet, entering the locker combination again. "We should put his things back." I indicate the sweatshirt and book.

"Yeah." Caleb gathers the papers while Victoria picks the hoodie and book up off the ground.

"Anywhere else we can look?" I ask.

"Maybe his room," Victoria says. "Remember how he said he had *something* at home that he could show the cops? Maybe that was code for the note." She twists her lips. "Not sure how we're going to get in there though."

"What about after the funeral tomorrow?" Caleb asks. "Isn't the reception at his house?"

She side-eyes him. "You want to break into his room during his funeral reception?"

"Well, I don't *want* to. But we might not have a choice. What do you think, Eden?"

What do *I* think? I think I wasn't planning on attending Diego's funeral, considering we weren't friends. "You two should definitely give that plan a spin."

"I thought we were in this together," he says, sounding dejected.

"I'm not going to the funeral or the reception. His family hates me. Correction, *all* of your families hate me."

"That's why you should come," Victoria says brightly. "No one will ever miss *you* while you're hiding out in his room, digging through his things."

"I have volleyball practice," I say, utilizing my foolproof excuse yet again.

"Good news." Her obnoxious smile only grows. "All after-school activities are canceled due to the funeral."

11

"IT'S JUST SO SAD," MAY SAYS AS GENUINE TEARS SPILL down her face, smearing her mascara. She turns onto Diego's street, which is jam-packed with cars.

"It is." I nod. "Very sad." Though if we're honest, May's relationship with Diego was primarily in her head. Yes, we all grew up together. But the day she decided to be my friend was the day she crushed any real chance at talking to Diego and the rest of that group.

Eventually, May parks in the first open spot on the curb, two blocks away from the Rodriguez house.

"They do not need me," I grumble, getting out of the car and slamming the passenger door. When May meets me on the sidewalk, we amble behind the rest of the funeral-goers. "Look at how many people are here. Not even Victoria or that loudmouth Jameson's absences would be missed in this crowd."

"Maybe this is about more than the missing note," May offers.

"What do you mean?"

"Well…" She carefully avoids the next crack in the sidewalk, then sidesteps an insect. "Maybe they don't really need you, but they asked you to come because they've realized the error of their ways, and they're trying to befriend you again."

I laugh. "Oh, May. You sweet, innocent cherub. You're too good for this world."

"*I* think I'm right."

"I mean, crazier things have happened this week." I shove my hands into the pockets of my short black dress. "Thanks for coming with me."

"Of course," she says. "It's not like I'd send you into this den of wolves alone."

"I thought you said—"

"I didn't say their *parents* were going to have the same change of heart."

"Right." We make it to the porch as Diego's father, Arturo Rodriguez, greets the couple in front of us with a smile that doesn't reach his eyes. "Ann," he says with a nod. "Bill. Thanks for coming." They offer condolences and press inside the house, and Mr. Rodriguez's sad eyes drift to us, a glimmer of recognition in them.

"We're so sorry for your loss," May says before he can think too long about who we are. I haven't seen him since I was a kid, so there's a chance he won't recognize me. "Diego was such a wonderful soccer player and friend. Fairport High will never be the same without him."

Mr. Rodriguez's eyes fill with tears. "It's good to see Diego's school friends." He steps aside for us, and relief sweeps through me.

But it's short lived. Victoria's mother, Bianca Nielsen, is apparently overseeing the refreshments table in the foyer. Dressed like one of the *Real Housewives* in a glimmering long black gown, she's standing behind the table, counting snacks and adding lemon slices to the water pitcher. She has the same shiny dark hair and intimidating posture as her daughter. Her husband, Sam, ambles over to the table, and she immediately barks out an order, pointing down the hall. He strides past us, giving a small, embarrassed smile, and I offer up a *what can you do?* shrug. Unlike many of the adults here, I'm almost positive Sam doesn't know who I am. Bianca's divorce from Victoria's father came after my dad had already left town. I feel bad for the guy, who by the looks of things, may end up ex-husband number two any day.

Bianca's gaze lifts from the table, apparently in search of her husband.

"Go get snacks," I tell May, casually turning my back to Bianca.

She glances over at the table and nods with a look of understanding. When she has Mrs. Nielsen in conversation, I lower my head and search for Victoria.

On the way to the living room, I pass an easel holding a large photo collage of Diego at all ages. I get an acute pang seeing them, especially the ones where he's little. I remember many of the events, like kindergarten graduation and his sixth birthday party. Though it seems like whoever made this collage went to great pains to avoid my face.

The small house is so packed with bodies, it's difficult to breathe, much less move. The men are starting to remove jackets and drape them on the furniture. Through the sliding glass door ahead, I see people gathered on the patio. I navigate through the living room, nearly reaching the sliding door when an elbow jabs me in the chest.

The large middle-aged man turns to apologize, still attempting to get his arm out of his jacket in the small space. "Sorry, little lady," he says, and if his enormous stature weren't enough of a giveaway, his red hair, peppered with gray, seals the deal. It's Jameson's father, Jim O'Sullivan. The man who created the mold for Fairport High's current biggest jerk.

I keep my head low, letting my hair fall over an eye. "Oh, it's fine."

I duck outside, finding my three favorite people congregated on a wrought-iron bench beneath the shade of an orange tree. Jameson spots me first and scowls, finally giving me the welcome I expected.

"You actually showed up," Victoria calls out, sounding impressed.

Caleb stands and crosses the lawn to me. "Thanks for coming."

"No problem," I say, the toe of my nice black church flat tapping soundlessly against the grass. "So are we going to search for the elusive note, or what?"

"Yeah, but I've been wondering something. Diego said he was cursed because of that note, right? That the old woman started following him when Henry passed it on."

I give him a *proceed* look.

"But you said the woman followed you the other night. And you've never even seen the note."

I shrug. "Maybe Diego was wrong about who's being targeted and why. I still think that note will give us a clue."

"Let's hope so." He steps closer, lowering his voice. "Any more sightings of *you know who*?"

I shake my head. "I've been avoiding dark empty streets at night. Seems to help." Caleb fiddles with the top button on his dress shirt, undoing it, then buttoning it again. Almost like a nervous tick. "Wait a minute." I squint up at him. "You saw her too, didn't you? When?"

"Shh." He glances back at the bench, where Jameson and Victoria are too busy fighting over who was closer to Diego to notice us. "Last night when I left Victoria's place after we finished up the photo collage. I don't want to worry them."

"But you don't think you should warn them? Do they—did you not tell them about what *I* saw?"

His eyes lower to the grass.

"Why not?" Now the nervous foot tapping is more of an irritated clacking.

"I sort of..." He runs a hand over the back of his neck. "I thought maybe you'd..."

"That I'd what, Durham? Lied? Hallucinated?" I let out a hollow laugh. "That's great. I help you and your friends. I even show up here, where everyone hates me, and no one more than the kid whose life we're honoring. Meanwhile, you"—I throw up a hand—"don't give a damn about, or even *believe* what I say."

"Eden, wait. That night, you were on edge because of the fall. After I went home, I started thinking—"

"I'm out of here. If you want to snoop through Diego's room, go right ahead."

I spin around, already clomping over the grass when his voice, low and rough, reaches my ears. "I'm sorry."

I halt before the concrete patio edge, something about his voice ensnaring me, holding me in place.

He nears me, close enough that I catch his salty beach scent and feel his breath riffling my hair. "I did believe you that night. I promise." He moves around to face me. "But this is all so bizarre. By the time I finished my walk to the Chicken House, I'd talked myself out of believing it. I told myself there had to be a different explanation. That no one in Fairport would be targeting high school kids."

"It wouldn't be all that unusual for Fairport though," I say, my blood still simmering. "Don't forget Farah Palmer or Esther Lamb. They died, just like the legend foretold."

He gives a somber nod. "And we decided we didn't care. That we'd risk it anyway."

"Look," I say, knowing I'm only opening myself up to more disappointment, "I can understand not wanting to believe in a curse. Hell, I don't want to believe in it either. But two more kids are dead, and someone followed me Saturday night. It sounds like you saw that same someone yesterday."

"Thank you," he says, still looking down. "For understanding. We'll look for the note and let you know if we find anything."

"Okay." I step onto the patio just as Diego's mother wobbles through the back sliding door, wineglass in hand. The heel of her pump catches in the door track, and she stumbles, dropping the glass, which shatters. Mrs. Rodriguez nearly slams to the concrete before catching herself on the armrest of a chair.

Caleb rushes to steady her, but she swats him off and continues tottering across the lawn.

Over on the bench, Victoria nudges Jameson, and the pair hurry after her. Victoria places a soothing hand on the woman's back offers her a seat or a snack. All I manage to hear from Mrs. Rodriguez is slurred mumbling before she breaks down into sobs.

Standing helpless at the edge of the patio, Caleb stares after her.

"Everything okay?" I ask, wandering closer.

Caleb stirs, glancing at the broken glass.

"I should clean that," he says, gaze roving back to Mrs. Rodriguez. At the pain in his eyes, my heart twists.

"Must be hard to see her like that," I offer, even though I'm terrible at these types of talks. I consider fetching May, who sweats empathy from her pores and could talk a rabid wolf out of a henhouse. "She's been like a mother to you, right?"

Caleb shrugs. "I mean, it always *seemed* that way. I think I've had dinner at Diego's house as many times as I've eaten at my own house over the years. She was basically my second mom." He sighs. "Now she can't even look at me. Or my mom for that matter." That could explain why I haven't seen Caleb's mother here. Cecelia Durham is another of my father's former business partners—one I'd been preparing to dodge. "I know Mrs. R wishes it had been me instead of him."

"Don't say that." I reach a hand toward his arm before thinking better of it. "She's grieving. Give her time." His eyes remain latched onto where Victoria is attempting to coax Mrs. Rodriguez into a chair while Jameson offers her a cookie. "You know," I say, positive I'm going to regret this, "maybe I can stay and help after all." He gives me a confused look. "Those two have their hands full. And finding the note seems like a two-person job, at a minimum."

"Really?"

"Really. Two of us will cover the space faster." I flick my chin in the direction of the house. "But first, go in there and find a broom."

———

With Mrs. Rodriguez *occupied* outside and Mr. Rodriguez finally settled on the couch, surrounded by guests, it's fairly easy to slip past everyone and head upstairs.

The door to Diego's room is shut. Caleb pushes it open, and inside, we find the space seemingly untouched. As if no one has been through this door since Diego was last here. There's a wadded T-shirt on the floor, a notebook splayed open on the desk. It makes what we're doing feel like even more of a violation.

But I can't let the feeling stop us. Someone is killing teens who were in the ruins that Friday night. And the reason why could be hidden inside this room.

Caleb eases the door shut behind us, and his shoulders sink, like he's absorbing the weight of the world. For a second, I'm not sure he's cut out for this at all.

Then he blinks, straightening. "We've got to move. I'll start with the desk, and you can check the closet."

"Sure, but reverse that." Desk feels safer, somehow. I don't know Diego outside of his penchant for torturing me, and the last thing I want to do is uncover a secret collection of dummies or a bizarre shrine of authenticated soccer memorabilia that includes some famous player's left earlobe. "And you can take under the bed too, for that matter."

Caleb quirks a brow, then gets to work on the closet. I cross the room, starting with the notebook. Immediately, I can tell it's a school notebook and not some sort of diary. There's no loose note stashed inside. It's a dead end.

I lift the lamp, searching beneath the base and checking every knickknack. My phone buzzes in the pocket of my dress, startling me. Caleb casts a look of admonishment over his shoulder, and wincing, I silence my phone. The text is from May, asking if I'm okay. I text back that the search is on and I need a few more minutes.

Then I move on to the top drawer, and my heart sinks.

It's full of loose papers. And this time, I can't exactly fit everything in my clothing. I notice the two larger drawers to the side and, shutting one eye, tug them open in turn to find even more paper.

My head falls back, and I let out a groan. This could take an hour to search. Still, it's the most logical place to stash a note, so I begin the tedious process of combing through everything. It would've been nice for Diego to give us some hint as to what we're looking for. Size of the paper. Color. Anything.

I'm barely through one-third of the top drawer's contents when a *creak* tears through my focus. My gaze darts to Caleb, who freezes in the closet doorway. Slowly, he turns around to mouth, "What was that?"

I throw up a hand and mouth back, "What do we do?"

There shouldn't be anyone up here. The guest bathroom is on the ground level.

Maybe Mrs. Rodriguez decided to take a nap. I listen, willing the sound of the footsteps to fade away as they carry their owner to the far end of this floor.

Instead, the sound only grows. The footsteps are headed toward us.

My heart jolts. *Move.* I shove all the papers back into the drawer and ease it shut. Making a *get back* motion at Caleb, I attempt to glide across the carpeted floor as he presses farther into the closet.

Once inside, I roll the door shut and hold my breath.

The sounds outside the closet are muffled. I can't hear the footsteps anymore. I venture to take a breath, inhaling the scent of dirty shoes and mothballs. Then Diego's door creaks, the sound hitting me like a blast. I flinch, my shoulder whacking into Caleb's chest. His extremely firm chest.

Trying to steady or quiet me, he places a hand on my back. He leans closer, his chin brushing my head. "Shh," he whispers, his breath hot against my ear, sending tingles down my neck and arms.

I'm pretty sure I'm sweating. The footfalls continue around the room, followed by a rustling. *Please go away, please go away.* For a second, the steps sound distant, and it seems like whoever's out there is obeying my thoughts.

But the steps grow louder again, thudding right outside the closet door. I shut my eyes tightly, as if it will render me invisible. The door opens, and light radiates through my closed lids.

I peek to find Victoria looking very pleased with herself. But her eyes drift to where Caleb's hand is still on my back, and her lips curl in disgust. "What are you two weirdos doing in there?"

"Hiding from you, obviously." I shove past her, practically gulping in the fresh air.

"We thought you were Diego's parents," Caleb whispers, tone apologetic.

"Why are you all red, Eden?" Victoria asks coyly.

"Believe it or not," I say, already back at the desk, "it was warm in that closet."

"I'm sure that's it," she says with a laugh. But when I glance back, her expression is unreadable. She studies Caleb for a moment before rolling her eyes. "Good thing I'm not Diego's parents, because your attempt a being covert was pathetic. Did you at least find the note?"

We shake our heads, and she gives a knowing look. "Guess you two make a lousy team. I came to tell you guys to hurry up. People are starting to leave, and my mom wants our help with cleanup. *Caleb's and my* help, not yours," she clarifies, as if there were ever any confusion.

"Then let's hurry up." I yank the drawer open, picking up where I left off.

"Where haven't you checked?" she asks.

"Under the bed," Caleb says.

Victoria mutters something but gets to work.

A minute later, I hear the closet door shut. "If you're done over there," I say, "help me with these drawers."

But Caleb doesn't acknowledge me. I turn around to find him unzipping a gym bag on top of the bed. I take a step toward him, and when I view what's inside, my chest tightens. It isn't workout gear.

It's Henry's camera.

12

"WHY WOULD DIEGO HAVE HENRY'S CAMERA?" CALEB asks, standing awkwardly over by my desk with his hands in his pockets.

Back at the Rodriguezes' house, we agreed to watch Henry's documentary footage together. While the others finished cleaning up, May dropped me off at my house. I changed out of my dress into jean shorts and a T-shirt, and now, the four of us are finally getting settled in my room. Despite my conviction to keep the three of them out of my house, bringing them here seemed like the lesser evil. Plus, Mom is working late tonight and will never know they were here.

It doesn't mean I like the idea of Jameson O'Sullivan sitting on my bed or Victoria Whitlock laying eyes on the décor I haven't bothered to switch up since the last time she was in here, years ago. Not to mention Caleb Durham even setting foot in my room.

The thought sets my nerves on edge.

"No idea," I answer, settling on the side of the bed opposite

Jameson. "I figured the police had it." Suddenly, I remember exchanging cameras with Henry in the ruins. "Wait, Henry had two cameras. The police must've recovered the one left in his bag. Diego must've taken the thirty-five-millimeter to see what was on it." I recall the camera lying in the grass near the cliff's edge. "It was at the scene of the crime."

"Except there was no crime," Victoria says, taking the desk chair. "At least, according to the cops."

"There's a connection between Henry and Diego," I say. "That much is clear. The fact that Diego has Henry's camera can't be a coincidence." That's why, despite how little I want to see Henry's face or hear his voice after what happened, I know we have to do this.

The USB is already plugged into my laptop, so I set it up at the foot of the bed as Victoria moves her chair and Caleb crosses the room to get a better view. Then I pull up the file and press Play.

The first clip shows me mouthing off to Henry at the fence surrounding Fairport Village. "It's unedited, obviously," I explain with a shrug. I try to fast-forward through this bit, but Jameson pounds a fist on the bed, rocking the laptop.

"You said we would watch it all the way through! So we don't miss anything."

Sighing, I lift my hands. "Fine. Have at it. At some point, he filmed me attempting to befriend a seagull, so that should be a good time."

"Indeed," Victoria says, settling into her seat. "Where's the popcorn?"

I ignore her, and the four of us continue to suffer through segment after segment, reliving the entire night.

"When's this going to get interesting?" Victoria finally whines. "Like when do we get to the interview with Naomi Lamb? I still can't believe she actually showed up."

"We, uh, didn't get an interview with Naomi," I admit.

"Why the hell not?" she asks.

"Speaking of hell," Caleb says, "isn't that Motel Hell? What is Henry doing?"

"Oh," I say as the camera pans over every square inch of the living area. "I remember thinking it was weird. I assumed he was getting some scenic shots to sprinkle in later."

"Wait a minute," Victoria says, sitting up straighter. "Shh." She bats a hand at us and leans an ear toward the screen. "Rewind that."

"Why?" I drag the laptop toward me.

"Because I think he was narrating that entire time but, like, really quietly."

I go back to when Henry first enters the dark room and crank the volume up. "So far, no sign of where it could be," he whispers as the camera combs the rotted floors. "And if it were here, it would be almost impossible to find it at night." He kneels down, and the camera shakes as he attempts to film himself grabbing at a loose board. Then he sets the camera down entirely, giving us a close-up of his hands frantically yanking and pawing at the board. "I'll have to get back here in the daylight," he says. "It's the only way."

"What the...?" Caleb says.

"Eden, what is he doing?" Victoria stares at me expectantly.

"I have no idea. He sent me in the kitchen to set up the lights." I hear the defensiveness in my voice. "Don't you think I'd tell you if I knew? My life is on the line too." I remember Henry's ominous words about Mrs. Blackmore. "Look, that night, he was rambling and nothing made sense. He said that the old lady knew what was buried there." I throw up my hands when they narrow their eyes at me. "Weird, I know. It seems clear he was looking for something that night. Only I swear I have no idea what it was."

"Maybe it's money," Jameson says brightly. "Maybe Mrs. Blackmore came back from the dead to find the fortune her family buried in the Village."

"That's…" The least idiotic thing he's ever said, honestly. Apart from the coming back from the dead part. "Maybe Henry will tell us somewhere in the footage. I wasn't with him half the night, so anything could have happened." I start the video again, watching the trek from Motel Hell to the Leaning Tower of Torture.

"That's odd," I say, prompting Victoria to get up and hit Pause.

"What's odd?" she asks. "Spit it out."

I resist the urge to remind her that she's in *my* room. "When we finished up in Motel Hell, Henry told me he was going to get shots of the bluff."

"That's definitely not the bluff," Jameson says.

"Thanks," I say, my tone droll. "I'm just wondering if he changed his mind at the last minute, or—"

"If he lied," Victoria cuts in, starting up the footage.

We watch as Henry searches the place the same way he did in the previous location. Except this time, without me in the next room, he narrates at a normal volume. "I wish I'd been given more information," he says. "Unfortunately, all we have is this note, which a customer left on the counter at Fairport Brew." I can just make out a crinkling sound before Henry focuses the camera on a wrinkled scrap of paper.

"Whoa," Jameson says as the camera zooms in on the writing.

My breath catches. It's *the* note. It has to be. The one Henry spoke about in the video. The one Diego claimed was passed on to him. It contains one line that sends the hairs on the back of my neck on end.

The truth is buried in the Village ruins.

"The truth?" Caleb says, rubbing at his temple.

"Guess it's not money then," Jameson says dejectedly.

"Maybe it's about the murders," I say, just as Henry snatches up the note again on the video. He continues examining the decayed cottage interior.

As the camera focuses on the peeling wallpaper, something wavers outside the broken window. "What the—" Henry yelps. The shadow grows, hovering there in the window for another beat. Then it darts out of frame.

For a moment, the camera sways back and forth to the rhythm of Henry's labored breaths. "I saw something," he says. "I'm going outside."

Even though I know he's gone, my muscles clench up. I want to shout at the screen for him to leave whatever he saw alone. Instead, I sit and watch from his view as he descends the porch steps, swinging the camera wildly in every direction. "Damnit," he growls. "I should've been faster." He gives the foliage surrounding the cabin another look before letting out an audible sigh and turning the camera back to the porch.

That's when the figure swoops into the frame, exiting as quickly as it entered.

Henry starts to run after it, camera bobbing, footfalls crunching over the rough terrain. At first, I don't see anything. But when he spins around, the figure is already on him. He screams, backing away.

A second later, he recovers, his lens finding the still figure beneath the moonlight. It's the same silhouette we all saw that night. The one that followed me after the library. Long black hooded cloak. Henry zooms in on the hood, cinched tightly to create a faceless void. But a tangled strand of wiry hair escapes the fabric.

"Oh my god," Victoria breathes as the figure seemingly disappears into the thick fog before our eyes.

"She knows," Henry whispers. "She knows, and that's why she has to stop me. Before I find the truth about Nicolas's murder. But I will find it. I have to. It's the whole point of this documentary. That note was the reason I chose to make my senior project about the curse. It's why—" The frame starts to dive; Henry must've tripped on something. The image shakes and then lifts as Henry takes to the trail, weaving through the foliage. "It's why I planted this overnighter idea in the senior class's heads in the first place."

He searches for the figure again, the camera sweeping in jagged and nauseating motions as he tries to cover every angle.

Then everything goes black.

13

"THAT'S IT," I SAY WHEN THE TAPE STOPS. "AFTER THAT, Henry lost the camera. Eventually, I found it. But he must not have gotten another chance to film before…" The words hang heavy in the air, everyone quiet.

"So Diego watched the video footage and saw this note," Caleb says. "And that's how he thinks the curse was passed on to him."

"And now it's been passed on to us," Victoria says dismally.

No wonder Henry was so *off* that night. And I did nothing to help him. "H-he told me he saw the woman," I say, "but I didn't believe him."

"Hey." Caleb nears the bed to rest a hand on my shoulder. "This wasn't your fault. I didn't believe Diego at first, remember? All we can do is act on what we know now."

"Which is what exactly?" Victoria snaps, her eyes glued to Caleb's hand on my shoulder.

I ease myself out from under his fingers, feigning the need to pace the room. "We know that some sort of 'truth' is buried in the ruins. Henry said it was about Nicolas Blackmore's murder. What if there's more to the story than the town knows? What if there's concrete evidence that could disprove everything? Something hiding under all that rot. And whoever was there that night—whoever's beneath that black hood—knows about it too." With a shiver, I think about the unearthly movements of that figure. "And they're willing to kill to keep it buried."

"So," Jameson says, "who would drop that note in front of Henry?"

"Someone who wants us to know the truth about the curse?" Victoria suggests. "Maybe it is real after all. And the proof is somewhere in the Village ruins."

"Or it's someone who wants to expose the truth about Nicolas Blackmore's murder," Caleb says. "And maybe even wants to vindicate Mrs. Blackmore."

"Well, Mrs. Blackmore is dead," Victoria says. "She killed herself in that prison. So unless this really is her ghost back to clear her name, it's got to be someone else."

"The daughter," Caleb says, looking at me.

I furrow my brow. "Adelina Blackmore, who moved away from Fairport after the murder and was last seen in a group home with strict policies about residents' comings and goings?"

"Maybe she lied to the staff about where she was going," Jameson offers. "Or earned an overnight pass."

"That's…" Maybe the second smartest thing this guy has said

in his life. "I mean, it's upstate, so it would be a drive. But I guess you're right. She could be involved."

"What about the father?" Caleb asks. "Do we know where he is now?"

I open my browser and type *Silas Blackmore* into the search engine. I scroll the hits until I reach a headline that reads, *Husband of Child Killer Dead at the Age of Sixty-Two.* "Dead," I say. "Definitely not our guy."

"So then, it has to be the sister," Jameson says. "After all these years, she wanted to expose the truth about her brother's murder and prove her mother's innocence."

Caleb starts to nod but stops. "How would this woman know that Henry's a filmmaker? Or that he'd not only take the note seriously but would investigate it? I'm starting to think it has to be someone he knew."

"I mean, Adelina could've asked around, right?" I glance about the room for reassurance. "It wouldn't have taken much effort to locate the town documentarian."

Over on the desk chair, Victoria fiddles with a long strand of hair, lips twisted in thought. It's odd that she doesn't have an opinion here, since she has an opinion on everything.

"Victoria?" I ask. "Anything you'd like to share with the class?"

"No," she says too quickly. Her thin frame sinks lower into the chair, wrecking her always perfect posture. I exchange a look with Caleb, who seems torn between pressing her and leaving her be. Before he can decide, Victoria says softly, "I uh, found something. In my attic, a few months back. I never really gave it a second thought until now." She swallows, and her eyes roam the swirling pattern on my rug. "I was looking through an old box of photos for the family tree assignment in history, and I found this photo of my mom and Nicolas Blackmore. They looked...*close*. So I asked my mom about it, and she admitted that they used to date." She licks her lips, almost like she's nervous. "She said they were dating when he died."

"Whoa," Jameson says. "I thought your mom used to date my dad."

"Yeah, so did I—I mean, she dated him too. Apparently, when they broke up, my mom started dating Nicolas."

"Guess your mom really got around," Jameson says, to which Victoria leaps up from her chair.

"Okay, okay." I lift a calming hand. I don't really care if they kill each other, but I am responsible if they break something. I gesture for Victoria to sit back down. "So, what are you saying exactly?"

"When I asked my mom about her past with Nicolas, she sort of *changed*. She tried to brush it off, but I know my mom. She was still so sad about Nicolas's death, even after all these years. I don't think she ever really got over it."

"You think maybe she's the one who wanted Henry to make the documentary?" Caleb asks.

"I told her about him once, after that video he made about the class election." She runs her fingers through her hair. "I was complaining, to be honest. Henry included shots of all the other candidates. Some at the podium, others in school activities. But he only showed me putting on lipstick at my locker. I thought he was trying to make me look bad, so no one would vote for me."

Henry's photo of Victoria sounds like an accurate depiction to me. Still, I say, "So your mom knew he was Fairport High's resident filmmaker."

Victoria nods. "She won't want to talk about it though."

"She has to," I say. "If she's the one behind that note, she stirred something up. Something that caused that person—that thing—to come after us at the ruins and kill two more people. There could be more deaths—including her *own daughter's* death—if she doesn't tell us what she knows." Even though it's the last thing I want to do, I say, "Either you talk to her, or we'll all be paying a visit to Bianca Nielsen."

———

That's how we all end up in Bianca Nielsen's living room two hours later. Victoria thought it would be more effective to gang up on her mother after work. Fortunately, Mr. Nielsen is away on a business trip, since it would be awkward for us to ask questions about his wife's old dead boyfriend in front of him.

Jameson wastes no time taking the comfy leather recliner, and the rest of us gather on the couch, Caleb in between Victoria and me. Bianca, posture as perfect as her daughter's, settles into a stiff mauve wingback chair.

Bianca looks the same as she did a decade ago. Back when she and her ex, Travis Whitlock, were friends with my parents and she didn't look at me as if I were a rat scuttling through her living room. Her hair is still long, dyed brown to hide her roots, and her gray eyes rimmed by only the faintest of crow's feet. After working all day, she's changed into athleisure wear: black leggings and a blue drapey shirt with a wide-open, plunging back. From her place on the chair, the woman eyes me coldly. "What is *she* doing here?" she asks the others, still focused on me.

"Eden was there that night in the ruins," Victoria says. "When we saw Mrs....when it all happened. She's part of this."

I wait for the frown, or the snide "unfortunately" follow-up commentary from Victoria, but nothing comes.

"Well," Bianca says, crossing her arms, "you should never trust a Stafford."

I sense Caleb shift closer to me on the couch, and when I open my mouth to spit out some half-concocted retort, he lays a hand gently on my elbow. I take a deep breath and jounce my foot to keep from storming right out the front door.

As much as I want to start questioning Bianca so we can get this over with, I have a feeling that would get us nowhere. Instead, I glance pointedly at Victoria.

"Right," she says, nodding. "Mom, you know how I was asking you about that photograph of Nicolas Blackmore a while back?"

The woman's face darkens. "I told you, I don't like to talk about him."

Across the room, Jameson's footrest raises. "Sorry," he mutters, lowering it back down again.

Victoria glowers at him before turning back to Bianca. "Mom, have you ever suspected his killer was anyone other than Mrs. Blackmore?"

At this, the woman's eyes widen. "What do you mean?"

Victoria, apparently unable to accuse her mother of setting the past weeks' events into motion, looks to Caleb.

"It, um," he starts, rubbing at the back of his neck, "seems like someone is trying to tell a different side of the story. About what happened to Nicolas Blackmore that night. And to be honest, we're running out of people who might care enough about Nicolas to stir things up."

"I don't understand." She rubs a finger over the armrest, cleaning something.

"Mom, I told them," Victoria says, face downcast. "They know that you two were together and that you"—she swallows—"loved him."

Bianca's jaw tenses. "You shouldn't have done that."

"It's not like we're going to tell Sam," Victoria says, referring to her stepfather. "Is that what you're afraid of? That he's going to care about your high school boyfriend? This is about the kids—Diego, *our friend*—who died. We're just looking for answers."

"We already have answers," Bianca snaps.

"Can you at least tell us how you and Nicolas got together?" Jameson asks.

At this, the glimmer of a smile shines over Bianca's face. "I worked for the Blackmores," she says. "It was my first after-school job. Mrs. Blackmore hired me to clean rooms. That's where the idea for Surfside Cleaning came from, my experience that first year of working there. Eventually, Mr. Blackmore moved me over to the restaurant. That was always his area of expertise, handling the food and the staff. I started off as a host and, after a while, got promoted to server. That's where I first met Nicolas. I mean, I knew who he was. He was this handsome surfer boy at school—impossible to miss. But he didn't run in our circle, so we never talked until my job at his parents' restaurant."

"He worked there too, right?" Caleb asks. "We read that he was supposed to be overseeing the place the night he died."

Bianca nods. "He bussed tables, washed dishes, cleaned cottages. Whatever odd jobs his parents gave him. The summer after junior year, I invited him to a bonfire with the rest of my friends—your parents. And everyone hit it off. He became one of us. The guys hung out, surfing mostly." She wrinkles her nose. "Greg and Nicolas were the closest of all. Getting those kitschy tattoos. Well"—she shrugs—"they were close until the surf tournament. They always got so competitive when it came to sports."

"What do you mean?" I ask.

"Greg didn't want Nicolas to compete against him in the county surf tournament. He said it was because the waves were going to be too big for Nick, who wasn't nearly as experienced as Greg. But Nick said it was because Greg knew he was the only surfer who could beat him. Nick refused to drop out."

"What happened?" Caleb asks.

"Nothing happened," Bianca says simply. "Nicolas died the weekend before the tournament."

My stomach drops. There was a fight between my dad and Nicolas. Right before Nicolas was murdered.

"You said you were friends with Nicolas, but when did you dump my dad's ass for him?" Jameson lets out an obnoxious laugh.

Bianca looks unamused. "I didn't dump Jim. We were always on and off in high school. Never together more than a couple of months at a time. I guess I was tired of everything being so up and down. Nicolas seemed solid, steady. I thought he might be… I only wish I could've—" She shrugs, but I catch the tear welling in her eye before she blinks it away. "Like I told my daughter, I don't talk about it."

"You wish you could've *what*?" I ask, instantly regretting it.

Like a vulture, Bianca's neck stretches, her head whipping to peer at me. "I wish I could've saved him from the rot in his life."

The words sting; she's referring to more than Nicolas. Again, I feel a pull to get up and walk out the door. Instead, I scoot back until my spine sinks into the couch cushion. "The rot being what?"

"That woman. His mother. Deep down, I always sensed she was dangerous. I *knew* it. I see her wretched face every time I think about Nicolas. That's why I can't look at photos of him. It's why I can't talk about him."

"Because you think you could've saved him," Jameson says, looking pensive for once as he releases the handle on the recliner.

Bianca only sighs. "She wasn't just insane. She was evil. When she died in prison, I was glad. It didn't fix anything. It didn't bring Nicolas back. But I was glad she was dead."

"Then you never suspected anyone else of killing Nicolas?" I ask.

Like Jim O'Sullivan, for example. I make a mental note to bring this up with Caleb later in private. Are we really supposed to believe that Jim watched this other guy steal his girl and was simply fine with it?

Bianca shakes her head. "If you'd seen Hazel Blackmore, you'd know."

"Well," I say, shutting an eye, "that's the thing. We maybe did see her?"

Bianca looks to her daughter. "What is she babbling about?"

"In the ruins, at the overnighter," Victoria explains. "We saw someone before Henry died. And then…Diego said a woman was following him."

"But that's—" She frowns. "Don't be ridiculous, Victoria. The woman's been dead for years."

The room quiets, and shame creeps in. But then Caleb looks Bianca directly in the eye and says, "Someone is killing kids who were there that night, and we think it has to do with covering up the past. A past that Henry was starting to dig up. Are you sure there isn't something you're not telling us?"

"What would I be hiding?" She arches a brow.

"A note," I say, "left for Henry De Rossi at Fairport Brew. It said that the truth was buried in the Village ruins."

"The truth?" She doesn't move a muscle or even flit her eyes to mine. Only sits there, peaceful and still. Her calmness stirs a rage within me.

"About Nicolas's murder," I snap. "Someone in town knows something. They wanted Henry to go to the Village and find out the truth, and it got him killed. So did you leave Henry that note or not?"

"Of course not," she says, still without looking at me. "There's no mystery to uncover. Nicolas was killed by his mother. Look," she says to Victoria now, her posture suddenly easing, voice warming. "I know Diego was your friend, and what happened to him was unfathomable. But you have to face the facts. Diego wasn't murdered."

"And Henry?" I ask. "He just happened to commit suicide too? Right in the middle of making his documentary?"

"You know, you remind me so much of your father," Bianca says, and my first reaction is pride. It's a bittersweet, nostalgic feeling. Millions of memories of my dad and me come flooding in: Me wearing his San Francisco Giants baseball cap, even though I couldn't see past the bill. Him taking me down to the beach and trying to teach me how to surf, pulling me up on the board with him when the waves got too big. How in many ways, I wanted to be just like him—funny yet warm. I was only seven, so things like drive and ambition were far less impressive.

And then I realize that for the first time during this meeting, Bianca Nielsen is looking me dead in the eye.

At her seething glare, I remember that Bianca Nielsen loathes my dad, and the comparison wasn't a compliment. I remember that my dad walked away from me and the last thing I should want to be told is that I'm like the man in any way.

"Oh yeah?" I say, fists curling at my sides. "Why's that?"

"Neither of you can face the hardships of life."

It stings. I'm tempted to grab a precious trinket off the end table and shatter her window with it. "Isn't that what we're doing now? Trying to find who's killing kids and stop them?"

"No," she says, some mixture of pity and disinterest on her face. "You're avoiding reality, letting yourself fall into a story."

"But what about the note?" Caleb asks.

"Sounds like a hoax to me. It sounds like the exact type of thing you'd find in a town like this, where the people become so bored with their dull lives that they choose to live through legends and rumors." She stands up and moves in the direction of the stairs. "Now, I've had a long day, so if you'll excuse me."

Without another word, Bianca Nielsen exits the room.

14

THE REST OF THE WEEK, I KEEP MY HEAD DOWN, STICK-
ing with May so that I'm not easy pickings for a hooded stalker. I'm
also avoiding the others like you would a horde of plague-stricken
zombies—the kind that run.

This works well for me, to the point that I almost start to believe
that we all overreacted and that Bianca Nielsen was right about
everything. I've known from the time I could walk that this town
loves its lore. Is that all this was? Is someone out there messing with
us? I want to believe it.

I allow myself to shove aside the creeping doubts, the ones that
remind me that if the hooded figure and the note were truly part
of some hoax, that means Henry and Diego really committed suicide. I start to ignore how little sense it makes, so I can believe that
everything will be fine.

That is, until Friday afternoon, when I find Caleb Durham
standing in front of my locker.

I consider pretending like I was headed somewhere else entirely and walking right past him. But I've made a lot of progress in standing up to this band of bullies in the last couple of weeks. I hate the idea of taking two steps back. Inhaling a deep breath, I carry my stack of books like I could use it to knock his teeth out if I wanted to, and stride right up to him. "Excuse me," I say sweetly. "That's my locker."

"Yeah, I know it is, Eden."

"Well then." I flick my head toward the hallway. "Get lost, pretty please."

"I need to talk to you," he says without moving.

"These are getting heavy."

He blows out a puff of air and steps to the side. "I saw *her* again," he whispers before I can even finish twisting my locker combination.

"What?" I turn to check if he's serious, and my books start to slip from my hands, spilling onto the floor. "Damnit," I say, crouching to retrieve them.

Caleb kneels beside me, reaching for my history textbook, which lies sprawled open. Various notes and handouts have come loose, and he collects and stows them inside the book.

When he stands, I wait for him to place it on the top of my pile. Instead, he takes the rest of my books from me. "Sorry," he says, as if he's the one who dropped all my books. "I shouldn't have scared you like that. Go ahead."

Cheeks heating, I finally get my locker open. "You didn't scare me," I protest as he carefully waits for me to remove my backpack from it. Once I've collected what I need for the weekend, he pushes the stack of books inside.

"Thanks," I mumble, scanning the hallway for May. "So where did you see her?"

Caleb is eyeing the passersby too. "Can we talk outside?"

Reluctantly, I follow him through the crowd and out the door. When we reach the trees that line the parking lot, he stops in the shade. "Last night, I tried to get back inside the ruins."

"You what?" I nearly yell.

"Shh." He glances past me to where a couple of underclassmen waiting for their rides are watching us with concern.

"Sorry, but why the hell would you do that?"

"I don't know," he admits. "I thought I was helping. My plan was to check the cottages Henry never got to in that video. But it was all chained up, tape everywhere. Before I found a way inside"—he shrugs, looking down at his sneaker—"it—*she*—was there. Inside the Village, right up against the fence. Close enough that she could've touched me through the chain links."

"Did you see her face?"

"No, I…" He kicks at a patch of grass, then rubs his temple. "I didn't get a good look. She had that hood pulled up, and I—I panicked, okay?"

"Yeah, okay," I say before he can either break the skin on his temple or kick me instead of the grass. "Anyone would've panicked."

"I know, but I just…I should've gotten a look before I took off."

"If you'd stuck around, you'd be just as dead as—" I wince

internally. "Sorry, you know what I mean. It was good that you left. I still don't understand how you could be that idiotic in the first place. Someone is targeting people who snoop around the ruins."

"But we still don't have any idea who it is. Bianca denied knowing anything about a cover-up of Nicolas's murder."

"Well," I say, not actually wanting to suggest it, "we still have Adelina." If she was really granted leave or snuck out, then she could've left that note for Henry. Unintentionally, she could've sent him straight into the hands of the true killer.

"Did you read where this group home is located?"

"It's a couple of hours north, the Bay Area."

"Do you think they'll let us talk to her?" he asks.

"Wait—what do you mean, *us*?"

"If we leave in the morning," he says. "We could go up there, speak to Adelina, and be back here before dinner."

"Do you think they'll just—let us speak to her? Maybe we should call and find out."

Caleb shakes his head. "If we do that, we'll give ourselves away. It's better if we show up and surprise them."

"But we aren't even family."

"We could be?" His eyes crinkle sheepishly. "How does *cousins* sound?"

I hate this idea with a passion, but my insides flutter at the conspiratorial way he looks at me. Like we're a team. I let out a grumble. "I think the role would be better suited for Victoria Whitlock, master manipulator."

His eyes crinkle as he looks at me, smiling with one side of his mouth. "You'll be perfect."

———

Saturday morning, I fill a backpack and put on cut-off jean shorts and a white tank top with ruffles that May gifted me. I never wear it, and when I see myself in the mirror, shame ripples through me. I can't get dressed up for a day with my nemesis.

But before I can change, I hear the rumble of an engine and look out the window to find Caleb's truck rolling up in front of my house. Nine a.m. on the dot. The nerve of this guy to be so freaking prompt.

Mom is in her bedroom, having her Saturday coffee with a book. The seaside morning fog has yet to lift, so I go to grab a hoodie from my drawer. I pick it up, spotting Caleb's black one below it. I start to take it out too, so I can return it. But for some inexplicable reason, I close the drawer again. Then I throw my hoodie on over my stupid top, tiptoe through the hallway, down the stairs, and through the front door.

Outside, Caleb is making his way to the porch.

"What are you doing?" I whisper-yell. "Get back in the truck!"

"Sorry," he hisses. "I wasn't sure if you'd—"

"It's not a date, Durham! I'm trying to make a speedy getaway here!" Caleb rushes around the front of his truck, and I let myself into the passenger side, slamming the clunky door behind me. "Drive!"

Caleb starts the ignition, and the truck lurches off down the street. Our breathing is heavy in the small cab as he turns the corner and heads onto the main avenue. "What's going on? Your mom doesn't let you out of the house at nine a.m. on a Saturday?"

"Not with *you*, no. She'd kill me faster than Mrs. Blackmore ever could if she found out I'd gotten in a truck with you. She thinks I'm headed to May's house. I told you to park down the street."

"Oh, I—" He reaches for his phone but fumbles it over the cup holder. "Sorry, I didn't see your text."

"Whatever, I don't think she noticed." I gesture to what I now see is a light-gray hoodie. "Glad to see you had a backup. I uh... forgot to grab yours."

"I told you, I don't need it back."

"But you always wear that hoodie," I protest. "You don't actually look right in that *thing*." I feign a shiver.

"Oh, yeah?" He smirks. "How do I look exactly?"

While his eyes are on the road, I venture a better look, treading carefully. His hood has fallen back to reveal a mess of sandy brown hair. His skin is tan from a summer of surfing and soccer. He's impossibly handsome, and it's infuriating. "Even creepier than usual? I don't know."

"Thanks, Eden. So I guess your mom hates me because of my mom," he says in a quieter voice.

"No, of course not. My mom's not a petty jerk like the rest of your parents. She wouldn't hate *you* because of something your mom did." And then it's out before I can stop it. "She hates you because of what *you* did to *me* freshman year."

"What I did—" His head draws back. "What did *I* do to you?"

I roll my eyes. "Please, like you just forgot." I stare out the window, watching the palm trees and the mailboxes whir by as the truck turns onto the main coastal highway. My mind is stuck on homecoming freshman year. On Caleb smiling, and how I thought the smile was meant for me, when he was obviously trying not to laugh *at* me. On how the real smile went to Victoria, looking more polished and glowing than I ever could.

"I just—"

"We don't have to talk about it," I cut in.

He sighs, and after moment, tries in a lighter tone, "So what would you and May normally be up to on a Saturday?"

"How do you know I'd be with May and not…tending to my vegetable garden?"

He laughs. "Apologies. I didn't realize you had a vegetable garden."

"Well, I don't," I admit. "But that doesn't mean I have no hobbies."

"Tell me about these hobbies that don't involve May."

"I play volleyball, of which you're aware." The guys' soccer team has weight lifting right before our team on Thursdays. I've passed by Caleb and Diego every Thursday for the last three years. "I also do an excellent running commentary on Netflix documentaries, and one day, I plan to learn what robotics club is."

"Wow, those are some noble feats, Eden." His lips twist. "Your dad was an amazing surfer. How come I never see you out there?"

An achy sensation spreads behind my eyes. After my dad left, I never wanted to surf again. It was always something we did together. With him and his board beside me, I was never overwhelmed by the wide-open sea or the pounding waves.

"It reminds me of him, I guess," I say quietly. Like so many times over the years, a memory from childhood unfolds in my mind. My father holding me high above the waves. Then the memory twists and morphs into one that never happened. I see myself sitting on a child-size surfboard. I keep floating out to see, trying to paddle in to no avail as my dad swims back to shore without me. "It reminds me that people don't always keep their promises."

Caleb frowns. "I didn't mean to…"

"Maybe I just don't have anyone to go with," I say to push the focus off my father. "May isn't exactly the surfer type."

"Well, I'd go with you. It would be fun."

I allow myself to entertain the suggestion for a moment. A smile pushes onto my lips. Before I can stop myself, I'm thinking of a time that was good, a time that I had fun with Caleb: our eighth-grade field trip to the California Museum. That day, Caleb got separated from Jameson and stuck with me. "Any chance you're still a skilled food fighter?"

He takes his eyes off the road to glance at me. "It's not a skill I find myself in need of often."

"Remember how we ditched our group?" I say, smiling despite myself.

Caleb lifts a brow. "I remember you lied to me about where we were supposed to be, and my mom grounded me for a week."

"Well, yeah, that was part of it. But remember that guy in the business suit? We got bored of throwing food at each other, so we decided to launch stuff as close to that guy as possible without hitting him. But then you accidentally nailed him with something? I can't remember what it was, but it opened and splattered all over his precious suit." I laugh as the picture of Caleb's terrified face passes through my mind, clear as it was that day.

For a moment, a half smile plays on his lips, the memory lighting his face. I hold my breath, waiting for it to come back, to trample all over the haunted air between us.

But his smile falters. "Yeah, sort of." He fiddles with the GPS on his phone, then fixes his eyes back on the highway.

Stunned, I sit frozen for a moment until the anger thaws me. I can't believe I actually tried with him. That I opened myself up, knowing he'd only disappoint me.

"What if we play a game?" he suggests as if everything is fine.

"Pass."

"You're upset," he says, fiddling with the zipper on his hoodie with his free hand.

"Nope." I try to sound disinterested but fail. "To be upset, I'd have to care."

"Come on, Eden. Why does your mom—why do *you* hate me so much?"

"I'm not really sure where to start," I say, scratching at my head in exaggerated fashion. "How about the fact that you and your friends locked me in a janitor's closet for four hours once?"

"I'm the one who let you out of there."

I try to remember back, but all I can see is darkness. All I hear are my fears blaring in my ears, so loud and so violent as my breathing became too shallow. And then I remember waking up in there, after having blacked out. "Well, forgive me if I forgot to award you the principal's medal of valor."

"Eden, I don't—"

"It would be better if we didn't talk," I say, the lump in my throat growing, "about anything."

He sighs. "Yeah."

Then it's quiet. And somehow, it's even worse than arguing.

———

When we reach the house, a two-story covered in soft-green wooden siding, cars fill the surrounding curbside, so we park a few blocks down the street. I start to unlatch my seat belt when Caleb reaches his hand across the center console, placing it on my shoulder. I flinch. But at the concern on his face, I resist the urge to pull away. "I never wanted you to hate me," he says.

"Well, you haven't exactly made it easy to like you," I say, knowing it's a lie. Because even now, I'm fighting to hold on to an ounce of the hatred I should feel for him. Still, I shrug his hand off of me and exit the truck. Side by side, we walk to the porch in silence.

Caleb knocks on the front door, and a moment later, a middle-aged woman with curly violet-red hair and penciled-in brows asks how she can help us, her focus half-set on the magazine in her hand.

"We're here to see Adelina Blackmore," Caleb answers, flashing the smile that charms all the girls at school.

The woman lowers her magazine—*Bird Watcher's Digest*—to squint at us. "Who are you?"

"We're her cousins," Caleb says, rattling off the line we rehearsed. "John and Matilda Sampson. And you are?" He extends a hand.

"The director of this home." The woman lifts her hand tenuously to shake his. "Martha Pearson. I don't remember Adelina having any cousins." Fortunately, I did enough research on the drive over to know that Adelina does, in fact, have some surviving relatives, such as her cousin, Louisa Sampson. I had to gamble on them never having visited her here.

"Well, we're second cousins, really. We never got the chance to meet and thought she might like the company, especially since we're family."

"How's that work exactly?" Martha asks, her guard falling as she steps back to lead us inside. "The second-cousins thing."

"On her father's side." I follow her through the foyer and note a sign-out sheet tacked onto the wall. Beyond us is a living area, where two residents are playing cards, one on a somewhat bedraggled couch and the other in a wheelchair. "We're her cousin Louisa's children. Adelina should remember our mother. Maybe you could ask her?"

The woman's eyes drift to the hallway behind her, and adrenaline kicks up. It's working.

"Unfortunately," the woman says, frowning, "I can't ask her."

"Oh?" Caleb says. "Is she asleep?"

Or dead. That rush is replaced by a sense of powerlessness.

She shakes her head. "Your mother should've told you. Adelina Blackmore left this place years ago."

15

"DID SHE MOVE TO A DIFFERENT HOME?" I ASK.

"No, she was just done with this type of place."

"Done?" I feel a slight sense of relief at the knowledge that Adelina gained back her independence. She must be doing much better. The feeling is quickly replaced by an anxious rush. If Adelina isn't here, she could be our missing link. She could've dropped that note for Henry. The only problem is that this place was our only lead. "Well, do you know where she is now?"

"Unfortunately, even if I did, I wouldn't be able to disclose that information."

"So there's nothing you can tell us to help us get in touch?" Caleb asks.

"I'm afraid not." Martha offers a smile of pity.

We thank her and start back toward the foyer when an alarm sounds from somewhere at the back of the house. Martha lets out a grumble. "Not this again." She glances at us apologetically.

"Can you see yourself out? Some smart-ass set off the smoke detector."

"Sure," I say, the weight of dejection pressing down on my shoulders. As she rushes off, Caleb and I head toward the door.

But we only make it two steps when a voice calls out, "Hey, kids!"

I turn to where the woman in the wheelchair is motioning us toward her. The cards are still out on the table, but her companion is no longer there.

"Did you need something, ma'am?" Caleb asks as we move closer.

"You want to know about the Blackmore girl," the woman says knowingly, leaning forward in the chair. Dressed in a white gown, her feet bare, she looks around forty years old, with long scraggly black hair.

"Yes," I say, startled. "Do you know her?"

The woman smiles, and crow's feet fan around her nearly black eyes. "She's my friend."

"Do you know where she lives?" Caleb asks.

At this, the woman says, "I'll show you." She proceeds to get out of the wheelchair, skirt around it, and take off through the room and down the hall on foot. Caleb and I gawk for a moment, but she turns to wave us on.

Checking that Martha is still occupied, we step past the abandoned wheelchair and follow the woman.

"Why exactly are we following this lady?" I hiss at Caleb, struggling to keep up as she bounds down the corridor with ease.

"Because she knows how to find Adelina."

"Okay, but she doesn't seem…" I pant. "How do I put this?" We reach the end of the hall, which forks off in both directions, only to find that the woman has disappeared. "Where did she go?"

"In here," comes a hushed voice.

We glance toward the sound, and at first, I see nothing. Then, a thin hand protrudes from one of the cracked doors, motioning us inside.

"I don't wanna," I say.

But footsteps sound in the hallway behind us, followed by a low voice. "Hey! You two can't be in here!" Left with no choice, we hurry toward the seemingly disembodied hand and duck into the room. Caleb shuts the door behind us, and breathing heavily, we take in our surroundings.

The white room contains a bed, a desk, and a collection of weird toys from the eighties, all displayed in a bookcase. The trolls, in particular, make me feel weird. The woman, still miraculously on her feet, is searching frantically for something in her desk drawer. A moment later, she strides across the room toward Caleb.

"You'll find what you need in here," she says, her tone suddenly grave as she hands him something. "Take this. Let no one see it."

Caleb blinks, then glances down at the envelope. "Um, okay, ma'am. But I thought—"

She lunges toward Caleb, and I nearly yank her off of him when she whispers into his ear, loud enough for me to hear, "Adelina never lived here." She reels back onto her heels, eyes wide as she adds, "She never lived here!"

"What?" I ask, letting out a frustrated breath as a large man bursts through the door.

"You two, out," he says sternly, holding the door open.

"Wait!" the woman says, snatching something off the desktop. She spins around, places the crinkly object into my palm, cupping her hands over mine like she's bestowed her most valuable possession upon me. "Tell Adelina to come visit me again." A glimmer of hope pulses in me. When she withdraws her hands, backing away, I glance down at the object.

All my hope tumbles to the carpeted floor. It's a disgusting cupcake wrapper of some sort, a familiar green and white swirl pattern on a pleated paper, now barely visible beneath the smears of melted chocolate. I cringe, letting the paper slip until I'm holding it by my fingertips. "Your trash," I mutter. "Thanks so much."

"It isn't trash," the woman says, and when I look up, she grins, a mocking glint in her eyes. "It's everything you're looking for."

The man grunts, and with our heads down, Caleb and I follow him out into the hall.

"I should be calling the cops, you know. What were you two doing with Mrs. Lafferty?"

"She seemed to need us," Caleb says, still clutching the envelope at his side.

"Unfortunately," the man says, "that woman has been having more and more delusions, getting into trouble."

"Stealing wheelchairs, apparently," I say, to which he nods. Beside the front door, Martha stands with her arms crossed, a stern look on her face. Guilt kicks up in my stomach. "Sorry, ma'am," I call out before the worker has to force us out of the house.

"Now what?" I ask as we make our way down the sycamore-lined sidewalk to Caleb's truck.

"I guess I should open this," he says, holding up the envelope.

The wrapper still dangles from between my two fingers, and I hand it to him before he can protest. "Let's trade," I say, taking the envelope and tearing it open. I unfold the card within, my heart hitching at the hasty scrawl. This time, instead of disappointment, I feel a giddy sense of delirium. "Yep. This is going to lead us straight to Adelina Blackmore," I say, showing him the note.

The answer lies in the grounds.

Caleb cuts a glare at me over the note. "That wasn't nice. And it's not nice to laugh at a sick woman."

"What's not nice is leading kids on, pretending to help them, only to shove a crusty old chocolate wrapper in their faces."

He tilts his head. "Fair point. But you have to admit it sounds pretty similar to Henry's note. *The truth is buried in the Village ruins. The answer lies in the grounds.* Maybe it's all connected. Maybe…" Frowning, he flattens out the baking cup, inspecting it.

"Or maybe not," I say. "She didn't give us any information about Adelina." That giddiness twists into frustration as he takes the letter and the muffin liner, and makes to toss them in a trash can along the sidewalk. Only he stops, dropping only the liner inside and pocketing the letter instead.

I arch a brow. "Need a keepsake to remember dear Mrs. Lafferty?"

"I don't know. I just…feel bad throwing it away. I can't explain it."

"Make sure to go over it with one of those invisible ink pens when we get back," I say, and he elbows me in the arm.

"Hey!" I whine, even though my lips are fighting a grin. "That hurt."

"No, it didn't."

"Okay," I say, rubbing my shoulder dramatically, "but it could have."

"You can hit me back if you want."

I purse my lips to ward off that smile. "I'll think about it." This play fighting is much better than the real kind. It feels sort of natural. Sort of *good*, even.

And then I remember that this is exactly what Caleb Durham does. He reels you in and then leaves you floundering like a fish on land. The same way my dad did. This is the power he has over me, and I can't let him use it.

"We could track Adelina down ourselves," he suggests. "Ask if she'll speak to us? Maybe there's something online that we missed last time."

"Guess it's worth a try." I start to pull out my phone when Caleb points down a strip of shops to what looks like a diner.

"Mind if we research in there? I could eat."

"Sure." Why not spend even more time with the boy I once vowed never to think about again?

We head inside the quiet, near-empty diner and take a seat at a booth in the back corner. The place smells of grease, and sizzling sounds drift out from the kitchen. The only other patron is an elderly man reading a newspaper at the counter. After the waitress takes our order, I check my phone, but there's nothing from Mom yet.

"I guess this means that Adelina Blackmore could be behind the note," Caleb says. "She's been out of that place for years."

"We have to find her," I say, already typing her name into the search engine. "If she knows who was really behind Nicolas's murder, she needs to tell the cops. Because telling Henry only got him killed."

"And this person didn't stop with Henry. They killed Diego just for having the video. Which means…"

"Any one of us could be next." On that comforting note, the waitress returns with our food. My stomach starts to rumble as she places a plate with a cheeseburger and fries in front of me, but I can't set my phone down until I find out what happened to Adelina.

Caleb wasn't lying about being hungry. The instant the woman ambles away, he digs into his burger.

I skim the search results, clicking on the occasional post. But while there are recent hits on the Fairport murders, there's no current information on Adelina Blackmore. "It's like she disappeared," I grumble, finally remembering my food.

"Eat. I'll keep looking." Caleb picks up his phone, and I'm too hungry to protest.

But a few minutes later, he puts the phone back down. "Vanished into thin air."

"I guess we could always try to track down our *mother*," I say, to which Caleb's brow furrows. "Good old Louisa Sampson."

"Oh." Caleb picks up his last fry. "I guess you're right. If anyone knows where Adelina is, it would be family."

I search her name on the browser. When an address pops up, my heart lifts. There's a photo too, a thirty-something blond woman with her family. The son and daughter are about ten years younger than Caleb and me, and they look nothing like us. I giggle and show him the photo.

"I mean, Adelina might've bought it. I doubt she had much opportunity to keep up with extended family while being passed around schools and institutions."

"Except she's out now, remember? We have no idea what she's been up to." I click on the address, and my spirits plummet back down. "Louisa lives in Dayton Point. That's another two hours north." In the opposite direction of Fairport.

"It's not that late," Caleb says. "We could make it."

"And all the way back to Fairport before my mom sends the cops looking for me?"

Caleb's lips twist in thought. "Maybe you could say you're with a friend and you'll be back late?"

I give him a dead-eyed stare.

"What? It's not a lie," he says with a wicked grin that almost makes me believe him.

"It's a lie." I pop the lone pickle garnish in my mouth and take out my frustration on it with my teeth. "But it may be my only option. If we're going to do this."

There are way too many Louisa Sampsons on Instagram and Facebook for me to determine the correct one. I do find a phone number along with the address online though. "Maybe she'll tell us where Adelina is over the phone," I suggest. "But...you should call."

"Why me?"

"Old ladies love you. You've got one of those voices."

His brow furrows. "What does that mean?"

"Oh, you know what I mean. I heard you with Señora Márquez last year. *Would you mind if I turn my paper in a few days late?*" I mimic. "*I have important soccer things that will one day improve society for all mankind.* Sounding so harmless and everything. And by the time you realize you're talking to the devil, it's too late. Because you already jumped off a bridge, straight into the mouths of one thousand crocodiles."

Caleb's lips are pressed flat as he lowers his elbows from the table. "You were eavesdropping on my conversation with Señora Márquez?" His voice is level and smooth, but his hazel eyes dance with amusement.

"Can I help it if you choose to have a manipulative conversation with a teacher in the place where I conduct my daily lunchtime loitering?"

"Guess not."

The waitress comes back to check on us, and Caleb asks for the check.

I reach into my backpack, but he waves me off. "I was the hungry one."

I point to my empty plate. "Clearly we both needed to eat." Before he can debate the matter any further, I slap some cash on the table and ask the waitress to split the bill.

When she walks away, I turn my phone around to show him the number. "So you'll do it?"

With a sigh, he starts typing the numbers into his own phone. "What do I say?"

"Coming up with BS stories to get what I want isn't *my* forte. What if you tell her—"

He waves me off. "It's fine. I've got this." He stands up, thanks the waitress again, and starts walking out of the diner.

"Hey," I call out, gathering my belongings. "Where are you going?"

Caleb glances back at me over a shoulder. "Just to get some space. My *manipulation tactics* tend to be more effective without an audience."

I follow him out the door. But outside, I've already lost track of him.

Whatever. Let him have his space. I amble in the direction of the truck, passing a couple of pigeons and a bench advertising some Realtor's face, the teeth Sharpied out. When I reach the end of the block, the wind carries Caleb's voice to my ears.

"Thank you so much, ma'am."

I turn the corner and find him there, triumphant smirk on his face. "Did she tell you where Adelina lives?"

"No, she was a bit odd. Didn't like talking over the phone much. But she agreed to speak with us."

"Really? What did you say?"

"The truth, Eden, if you can believe it." He flicks his head toward the truck and starts walking.

"I…can't, actually," I say, struggling to catch up. "You told her that our friends are being murdered and that we think her cousin knows something about it?"

"Yep."

"And she said, *Sure! Come on up to my house. I'll put the kettle on, and we'll talk about my ex-lunatic cousin alongside a nice spot of tea.*"

"No," he says. "Louisa doesn't have a British accent. And she works until seven and doesn't love the idea of having strangers come to her house. So we're meeting her at the pier in Dayton Point at eight."

"Eight? But that's—"

"Another few hours you're stuck with me. Sorry." He says it like he's not the least bit sorry.

"And my mom?" I ask, as we cross the street. "Who will be extremely disappointed in me should I fail to make it home before my curfew?" As we approach the truck, Caleb's phone rings.

He answers it, his footsteps slowing. "V? Are you ok—slow down." He comes to a dead halt in the road, skin pale. After a moment, he starts to pace in the middle of the road, swiping at his hair with his free hand. When a car starts down the road toward us, I have to tug him out of the way.

"What is it?" I mouth, his fear so palpable that I can feel it clawing into my own stomach.

He doesn't respond but allows me to pull him onto the sidewalk. "Listen to me, V. Did you call the cops? Good, good. You're going to be okay. Stay inside. I'm going to send Jameson over right now."

Victoria's muffled voice answers back, and Caleb chews his lower lip as he listens. "Of course I'll come," he finally says. And even though I have zero context, a sharp pain lashes my chest. "I'm sort of far away, is the thing. That's why I'm going to call Jameson."

"Yeah," he says, letting out a breath, "I know. But in the meantime, the cops are on their way."

He hangs up. Before I can get a word in, he makes another call. "Hey," he says, voice low and direct, "get over to V's place now. She isn't safe alone." He paces away from me on the sidewalk, then spits out, "Just get over there. She'll fill you in. I'm tied up with something right now, but I'll be there when I can." He nods to himself. "Yeah, thanks, man." After ending this call, he lowers the phone to his side and stares down at the concrete.

"What's going on?" I finally ask.

"Whoever's been following us came after Victoria. She was alone in her pool, and she says they appeared when she tried to come up for air, and held her under."

"That's—" *Horrifying.* "How did she escape?"

"Apparently the gardener showed up and scared them off."

"So there was a witness," I say. "That's good. But I guess our plan is off."

"She's afraid to be alone. She's in a panic that it's her turn, and that this person will come back."

"It sounds like Jameson is headed over there though. And the cops."

"Yeah, but she…" He trails off, and I don't need him to finish the thought.

"She wants *you* there." Because, though neither will admit it, there's something between them.

Without answering, he unlocks the truck, pulling open the passenger door before striding to the driver's side. I strap myself in while he fiddles with the GPS. A moment later, we're back on the road, the sage-colored house growing smaller and smaller in the rearview mirror.

But when we reach the main highway, Caleb doesn't get onto the southbound side. Instead, he takes the on-ramp headed farther north.

"Caleb," I say, not wanting to aggravate him any more. "You're going the wrong way."

"No, I'm not," he grumbles.

"But you needed to go south." I shut one eye, like that's going to keep him from scowling at me or from biting off my head.

"No, I didn't. I'm not headed to Fairport."

16

"YOU'RE NOT GOING BACK?" I ASK. "BUT WHAT ABOUT Victoria?"

"*This* is how we save Victoria," he says. "By finding answers. She won't like me going back on my word, but she'll understand when we save her."

"You really care about her, don't you?" I feel that prick in my gut as my memories slide back to homecoming night freshman year.

"She's one of my best friends," he says, to which I can't help but let out a laugh.

Caleb's eyes whip to mine in horror.

"Sorry, I didn't—I find it somewhat comical that after all this time, you're still acting like you're not in love with her."

"I'm not acting," he says, shaking his head. "Victoria is my friend; that's it."

"Here we go again with the denial."

"Eden, I don't know what you want from me."

"Nothing," I snap. The rage bubbles up, a few degrees from spilling everywhere. "I want absolutely nothing from you. You think *this* is where I wanted to be today?" I gesture around the cab, accidentally hitting my knuckle on the back of Caleb's chair. "I had no choice but to come with you. It's not like I'm willing to leave my life in your extremely unstable hands. I've done that before, and believe me, I would never willingly choose to do it again."

"Eden, I'm sorry about the past. I know that we abandoned you after your dad left. We were kids, and we made a mistake. But I tried to fix things freshman year, and you just…blew me off."

"*I* blew *you* off? Are you crazy?"

"Things seemed like they were fine, and then you just started ghosting me one day."

"One day?" I nod, maniacally. "Uh-huh. I see. Just one random day, *I* started ghosting *you*. That's an interesting take, Durham."

"What are you talking about?"

"Just forget it. This is going nowhere."

"You're right about that." Caleb lowers the window, leaning an elbow on it.

His slumped posture, his complete indifference—it all sends that simmering rage to a boil. Before I can help it, the lid pops right off my mouth, words bursting free. "Why did you do it?"

"Do what?" he asks, sounding pompous and irritated.

My fist curls around the shoulder strap, palm itching to spike his face the way I would a volleyball. My heart is beating so hard and fast it feels like it's everywhere—in my hands, my throat, my shoulders. "You went along with that stupid prank. Inviting me to homecoming on Snapchat and then leaving me stranded." Tears press at my eyes, making my voice sound choked and pathetic. "I knew they were like that, but I didn't think *you*... I just never saw it coming."

Admitting this to him—how much his actions that night scarred me—feels like defeat. It feels like carving a giant hole in my own chest and throwing the contents out for him to chew on.

"I wasn't..." he starts, stumbling over the words. Like a liar.

I face him now because it's the only play I have. The only one I haven't completely given up. I take in the way his jaw clenches, the rise and fall of his chest.

His elbow drops from the window and he blurts, "I never did any of that!"

I scoff. "So that's your excuse? Innocence? Or is it forgetfulness? It really just wasn't that big of a deal to you, was it? That you ditched me at the dance to be with another girl. A prettier girl."

His head flops back, windblown hair hitting the headrest. "Don't be ridiculous," he spits, focus still glued to the road.

My lips part, ready to combat whatever excuse he throws at me.

"There isn't a prettier girl."

My lips clamp shut again.

"Someone else must've sent you that message," he says. "Some sort of sick prank, with a fake account. But I swear, I had no part in it. If I'd known you were waiting for me, I never would've—" He grits his teeth, and one hand curls into a fist over the wheel. Finally, he turns to me, hazel eyes shimmering. His gaze slides down my throat and back up to my eyes. "Believe me, I wouldn't have done that to you."

It burns like fire, having his eyes on me. I can't breathe. My vision tunnels, so I turn to face my window again. Is he lying? It's not like he's been this innocent bystander the past ten years. It's not like he had no idea what his friends were doing to me or never participated in any of their bullying. But now, he's using that rugged voice and those pretty eyes to yank at my heartstrings. To make me feel like he's a decent guy even though I know he's one of *them*.

And I hate myself because it's working. I sneak another peek at him, trace the steady line of his jaw, follow the curves of his shoulders down to his arms, imagining them beneath the cotton sweatshirt fabric. Then I imagine what it would be like for him to lean closer.

He catches me, and I'm hit with a wave of red-hot embarrassment. I whip back to the window so fast I bump my shoulder on it. I think he's going to laugh, but instead he says, "I wanted to ask you to homecoming. But Victoria told me you were going with someone else. That's who I thought you were waiting for that night."

"I guess it's no mystery as to who sent me that fake message." An acute pain hits me, and my face heats. I'm such an idiot. "Victoria planned the whole thing." So she could witness my humiliation firsthand.

"I don't understand why she would—"

"She's in love with you. Anyone can see that."

Caleb shifts in his seat uncomfortably. "Like I said, she's a good friend. Though maybe not always *good*. I've never been interested in her like that."

I think I believe him. About all of it. I want to tell him as much. Only the words don't come out. Instead, I keep picturing myself as a toddler, my dad's hands holding me high above the waves. In the real memory, he kept repeating the words, *I've got you. I've got you, Eden.*

He never left me sitting there on a surfboard as he swam back to shore alone. He never dropped me into the frigid water or allowed those waves to knock me over.

But he still let me down.

"Whatever," I say. "Maybe we should stop talking about your love life and strategize how to get Louisa to give up an address."

He sighs, turning on his headlights as dusk settles over us. We spend the rest of the ride silently stewing. Caleb passes it by conducting a series of seemingly innocent moves, like rolling down the window to let the frigid wind turn my hair into a beehive and blasting a soccer podcast—only I know he's doing it all to get under my skin.

I, on the other hand, pass the time recapping his entire denial story via text to May, who irks me even further by suggesting I "give him a chance."

We finally arrive in downtown Dayton Point, and Caleb parks a couple blocks from the beach, just before the no-parking zone. I start to unlatch my seat belt when Caleb's voice drifts over, raw and throaty. "I am sorry, you know."

I freeze, the pain in his voice lancing straight through me.

"Regardless of how it happened, I'm sorry that it did. That you were hurt, and that this whole time, you thought I was the reason."

"Thanks," I say softly, and I might actually mean it. Because it feels like a part of the long jagged crack that's run through me ever since my dad left has been sealed or patched up. Not fixed exactly, but better. "I'm sorry Victoria almost got hurt. That must've been terrifying. Let's get this over with, so you can get back to her."

An inscrutable look crosses Caleb's face. He opens his mouth but closes it again, giving a curt nod. "Yeah, okay."

Together we exit the truck and make our way toward the pier. The path is a straight shot past a graffiti-laden brick wall, overflowing trash cans, and a foul-smelling public restroom. Something skitters in one of the cans, and I jump.

Caleb's arm circles my waist, and he gently tugs me away from the trash. Then he drops his arm like it was nothing as my neck heats and we turn onto the boardwalk, following it until we reach the ramp up to the pier. There's a lamppost at the start of the pier and not another until halfway down. A half-moon glows overhead, reflecting off the surface of the water. I watch my feet as I walk, making sure not to trip on any protruding nails or knots of wood. The wind slaps against my face, and I pull my hood up over my head.

"There." Caleb points to the rounded end of the pier, lit by a single lamppost. A figure stands against the railing, silhouetted black in the hazy light.

"Pretty sure that's the killer and this is a huge mistake," I say, turning around and taking two steps in the opposite direction.

Caleb takes me by the crook of my arm and, this time, not so gently yanks me back. "It's not the killer. It's just a middle-aged woman who's willing to speak with us, so we need to be extremely gracious."

"Fine," I grumble, falling into step beside him. To my surprise, he keeps my arm hooked in his as we continue on, his hold loosening. "Are we...uh, playing a part right now, Durham? Because it would be helpful to know." I indicate our joined arms. "Just so I can pretend to like you."

He glances down and, as if startled, releases me. "Sorry. I didn't mean to—"

"It's fine," I say quickly, wishing I hadn't said anything. But also feeling somewhat relieved that he hadn't done it as part of some bit.

"Do *you* think we need a cover story?" he asks, smirking slightly.

"Nope. Just work your older-lady-charmer magic, and that should be plenty."

"Right," he says, stuffing his hands into his sweatshirt pockets. "Your faith in me is empowering."

"Good," I say, but my nerves are buzzing despite Caleb's close proximity. Because we've been stalked for the better part of two weeks, and we don't know this person who asked us to meet her in an isolated place at this late hour.

At the end of the pier, I taste the salt-spray air and inhale the scent of fish guts. My heart thumps as we near the woman, whose features I can only begin to make out. She's wiry and petite in tight black leggings, boots, and a windbreaker. Her wispy blond hair blows in the wind, and she smiles when we approach her, a disarming gesture that sends a swell of relief through me; it's looking very unlikely that this is the figure who chased me around the ruins and downtown Fairport, never mind the logistics of Victoria's recent encounter. My fears were nothing more than my imagination running wild.

"Thank you for meeting us," Caleb says, reaching forward to shake the woman's hand. "This is Eden."

I wave, and the woman reaches for my hand. "Louisa." At her ice-cold touch, I shiver. "Nice to meet you. I hear you've been looking for my cousin."

"Yes, ma'am," I say. "We think she might know who's behind our friends' murders. This might sound like a strange question, but did Adelina ever mention or blame someone else for her brother's death?"

"Other than Hazel?" Louisa frowns. "No, but she and I weren't exactly close."

Disappointment unfurls in my core. If this woman can't tell us anything about Adelina, this was a wasted trip.

Louisa looks thoughtful for a moment. "Adelina saw and heard her mother that night. That was what she told the police and Uncle Silas. So if Adelina started to invent suspects later on, it was a symptom of her illness."

I give a solemn nod. "We read that she had something of a psychotic break in the wake of her family members' deaths."

In the moonlight, Louisa's green eyes shimmer with beguilement. "Now, that's where the journalists failed to do their homework."

"She was never committed to a psychiatric facility?" Caleb asks, brows furrowed.

"Oh, I'm sure she was committed," Louisa says. "Only the stint mentioned in the media wasn't the first time. Look, I grew up in Fairport. I had to move away after the murder, of course. Couldn't go anywhere without people following me, asking me questions about my family." She tips her head, her smile motherly. "Not people in trouble, like you. People who only wanted to follow the story for the sake of entertainment." Her gaze shifts to the dark water. "When I was little, I actually spent a good deal of time with the family. I went to school with Adelina. We were the same age, had the same teacher. She would get pulled out of school frequently for her appointments. Sometimes she'd miss days on end, even holidays with the family, for one of her *treatments*."

"Treatments?" Caleb asks, his eyes meeting mine.

"Back then, I didn't know. But later, I figured out that she was seeing a doctor. She would have episodes and would have to stay in the hospital. Because Adelina's *sickness* didn't start in the aftermath of her brother's murder and her mother's suicide." She shakes her head. "Adelina was always disturbed. Her parents did their best to brush it off and make her feel as normal as possible. But I remember. She wasn't a normal little girl."

I think of the recording, trying to match the picture Louisa is painting with the timid voice asking for Mr. Hoppy.

"The episodes," I say. "They sound just like the ones I read about her mother having."

Louisa nods. "Those weren't pretty. Fortunately, I never witnessed Adelina having an episode. But I do remember...*incidents*."

A *clank* sounds from somewhere nearby, and Caleb and I spin around. It's only a fisherman, pole knocking against his bucket as he sets up.

"What sort of incidents?" Caleb asks, tugging on his zipper.

"It was so long ago, everything is hazy. But we were all playing on the jungle gym during school recess. There was this boy in our class, and a day or two before, he'd made fun of the gap between Adelina's two front teeth. He was cruel, called her names—you know kids." She clears her throat and pushes a rogue strand of hair out of her face. "At the time, she looked like she might cry, but then she simply walked away. I'd forgotten all about it until that day on the playground, when I heard that horrible scream that ended up haunting my dreams for years. And then I found him, lying there in the sawdust..." Louisa winces, as if living the moment all over again.

"His legs were twisted in this *unnatural* position. And he kept screaming, so loud that all the children came running. Then everyone was crying, and teachers were ushering them away from the boy, trying to help him. My teacher at the time, Mrs. Karavati, took my hand and started to lead me away." She shifts her weight from one black boot to the other. "That was when I heard a giggle coming from somewhere up in the play equipment. When I looked back, Adelina was crouched all by herself at the top of the jungle gym, looking down at that poor boy's body and smiling. I remember that smile, the wide one that showed off that gap between her teeth."

I shudder. "You don't think she—"

"There were no witnesses," Louisa says. "So nobody ever accused her—I certainly couldn't accuse my own cousin of something I hadn't seen. That day, my childhood brain couldn't quite wrap itself around what my cousin was. But I think, deep down, I knew she wasn't like everybody else. And"—she rubs her arms to warm up—"I don't think it was the last time Adelina hurt somebody who'd hurt her."

Caleb's eyes widen. "Do you mean Nicolas? Her own brother?"

"If you'd seen her smile that day," Louisa says, peering out at the water, "while everyone else was screaming, you wouldn't find it such a stretch."

"Oh my god," I say, my mind spinning so fast it could crash. "Louisa, this is important. Do you have any idea where Adelina is right now?"

"I'm afraid not," Louisa says regretfully. "But I have a feeling she's here, in California." Meeting my expectant gaze, she elaborates. "She left me a note on my porch once a few months back, thanking me for staying out of the news. For keeping her safe."

"So she's in the area," I say, breath shallow.

"Most likely." Louisa breathes into her cupped hands for warmth. "And the last thing you kids should be doing is going around looking for her."

"But she—what if we had this all wrong?" I look up into Caleb's terror-filled eyes. "What if Adelina isn't the one trying to get justice for her mother? What if *she's* the one murdering Fairport kids to cover up her own crime?"

October 14

Dear Diary,

I saw her face today. I don't know why she lowered the mask, but for a split second, she allowed me to stare into those too-blue eyes. And I knew then that she must be immortal, because she looked like she hadn't aged a day in twenty-five years.

I followed my Mrs. Blackmore lead to the coroner's office. At first they tried to turn me away. But there was a boy, not much older than me, interning there. He told me to wait around, and when he returned, he let me sneak a peek at Hazel's file and her certificate of death. There were a lot of fancy terms in the certificate like <u>self-inflicted</u> and <u>sharp-force injury</u> that basically lined up with the story we know. She'd slit her own throat in her cell.

Only there was something interesting in the file. Something I never came across in any of my research. Neither the guard who discovered the body nor the coroner could figure out where the razor had come from.

And that day, Hazel had received a visitor. But the person's name was redacted from the log.

If someone else was in that cell, then there may be a killer on the loose.

But if Mrs. Blackmore really took her own life—if it really is Mrs. Blackmore following me—then she must be back from the dead.

17

WHEN WE'RE BACK ON THE ROAD, I FINALLY FACE MY
phone. I've missed four texts from May and seven from Mom.
Apparently, Mom swung by May's house unannounced to drop off
some cookies for our sleepover.

I'm busted. And grounded. And a bunch of other words that
essentially mean *dead*.

I assure May that it's fine since we might actually be getting
somewhere with our investigation. Then I text Mom that I'm on my
way home, because I'd rather die than allow Caleb Durham to listen
in on my blubbery apology conversation with Mom.

Still, when I finally put the phone down in my lap and let out a
huge sigh, he says, "Mother-daughter issues?"

"No thanks to you," I mutter. "Wasn't it your idea to say I was
hanging out with a *friend*?"

"Probably shouldn't have let her assume it was May though."

"Thank you, Mr. Perfect. I assume you've never been in trouble with your parents. They probably throw medals and other accolades at you every time you walk through the front door. *Ooh, our son is so handsome, scholarly, and soccer team captain-y. Aren't we sooo lucky?*"

"I heard *handsome* in there, which"—he shrugs—"is somewhat of a subjective assessment."

I roll my eyes. "Oh please. Like you don't know."

"I didn't know *you* thought so."

An airy laugh escapes my lips. "And when have you ever cared what I thought?"

"Eden," Caleb says, sounding strangely earnest now. "Don't you...?"

"What?" I ask, feigning indifference.

"N-nothing. Sorry you're in trouble. Want me to come up there with you?"

I laugh, because Caleb Durham's presence at my side would make this situation one thousand times worse. But he looks as sorry as he sounds. And I remember that he isn't the person I thought he was before our little road trip. "She never really gets too angry with me."

"No?"

I shake my head. "Not since my dad left. She used to be bad cop, and he was always good cop. Now..." I shrug. "Well, now she's got to be both. But really, there is no bad cop anymore. She'll probably just hug me until I suffocate. For making her worry."

"That's not so bad," he says. "And you kind of deserve it."

"I deserve a suffocating hug?"

He nods matter-of-factly. Then he smiles softly, meeting my eyes until warmth blooms inside me.

———

The next day, I am still in hot—more like lukewarm—water with Mom. When Caleb dropped me off last night, Mom was on the porch before he could even say good night. I had to explain to her why I'd lied, why I was out with a boy past my curfew, and why I was out with *that* boy of all boys.

I did my best to keep things as honest as possible. I told her it was because I knew she wouldn't approve and I was embarrassed. That seemed to tug at her mother's heart. Unfortunately, she's still got a bit of bad cop left in her. After the long hug, she told me to go to bed and made me promise to clean the entire house before church.

That's why I'm yawning on my way to meet Caleb and the others at the wharf to discuss our next move. If Adelina is the one stalking us—if she tried to kill Victoria last night—then we need to stop her.

Mom and her friends went out to lunch and a matinee down-town after the service. She offered to drop me off at the wharf, but I opted to walk. It isn't far, and I didn't want to risk her finding out exactly who my company of late entails. Mom doesn't know every vicious thing Victoria and Jameson have done to me over the years, but she knows enough.

The wind kicks up the hem of my sundress, and I'm suddenly self-conscious. I wish I'd gone home to change first. The sun is starting to burn off the coastal haze, its rays beating against my bare arms and face. This is the postcard-perfect part of Fairport. Tiny wooden-slatted cottages painted bright turquoises and yellows. Manicured lawns fit with tropical vegetation. Palm trees, plenty of them. Bikers roll by as I meet the final stretch to the wharf, soaking up the sunshine and the heavenly salty scent.

The wharf consists of a strand of shops and restaurants, and a series of docks. Seals bark from the large rock a few meters offshore, and seagulls cry overhead. The water slaps against the rocks and the pilings, and children's laughter turns to wailing as the gulls attack their seventeen-dollar ice cream cone from the parlor. It's home, basically.

As usual, I hear Jameson's voice before I see anyone. But when I spot him down the dock, hopping off of his father's fancy cabin cruiser, the others aren't with him. Instead, I find them outside the candy shop, Victoria seated on a bench and Caleb leaning over her, their foreheads inches away from touching.

An unsteady sensation comes over me, like the dock is rupturing and I'm about to plummet straight through it. My steps halt. I turn to flee before anyone sees me, but Caleb's deep voice catches me in the stomach. "Eden?"

Slowly, I pivot back around. "Oh, there you are."

"Why is *she* here?" Victoria asks in a screechy voice. She stands, wearing a short dress that makes me feel suddenly underdressed, and strappy sandals with heels that look like they'd get jammed between the wooden planks of the dock. She flips her long dark hair behind her shoulder as Jameson, wearing his staple jeans and Fairport High Football hoodie, makes it to the edge of the dock, crossing the stretch of walkway to join them. He turns around, chest puffed out as he looks at me like he's assessing the threat level.

"You can call off your dog, Victoria. I'm only here for the salt-water taffy." To be honest, the sweet scent wafting through the air is almost impossible to resist.

"I asked her to come," Caleb says.

"Well, I think she's the one behind all of this," Victoria snaps.

"How?" Caleb throws up a hand. "That doesn't even make sense, Vic. Eden has been stalked by this person too. And she was with us that night in the ruins, remember?"

"She could've tricked us. And last night, that could've easily been her."

"Except," Caleb says, running a hand over the back of his neck, face flushed, "Eden was with me last night."

Jameson laughs. "Good one."

But Victoria's mouth parts, and she gapes at Caleb like he just murdered her pet guinea pig. "What?"

"That's what we—what *I*—wanted to talk to you about. We went to track down Adelina yesterday, to find out if she was the one who left that note in Fairport Brew for Henry. But we found out that she hasn't been in the group home in ages and that she might be the one behind the murders—all of them."

"So then," Victoria says, looking some mixture of hurt and

confused, "you think Nicolas's little sister is the one who tried to drown me last night?"

"It's possible." Caleb leans against the mint-green wooden slats of the shop's exterior, like that explanation sucked all the strength out of him.

"I don't understand why you would go on this *mission*," she says, clearly attempting to belittle it, "without us."

Caleb bites his lower lip. "It was a tricky situation, going to the group home to try to speak with Adelina. We thought a smaller group would work in our favor."

"I see," she says sharply. "So you chose to include...*that* in your plan"—she gestures in my direction—"instead of me."

"She's the one who's been researching the Blackmore family, V. It was nothing personal."

"Oh, it was personal." Her expression is pinched as she looks from him to me. "So what do we do?"

"I think it's obvious," I say. "We get saltwater taffy, and then we tell the police about this lady."

"You know," Victoria says, "I had to sneak out of the house to be here. My mom is terrified after last night. She wants to chain me up in my room until they catch this freak."

"Sorry." My shoulders shrink into my body. "I really do think we should tell the cops about Adelina."

"Except the cops think Diego and Henry died by suicide," Caleb counters. "They'd never spend resources or manpower on something they believe is a closed case."

"Okay…" I tug on the hem of my dress, which keeps trailing upward, exposing more and more of my legs.

"You look nice today, Eden," Victoria says, looking me over like a cat pawing a mouse. "Who'd you get all dressed up for?" Her gaze slides deliberately over to Caleb.

I take a deep, calming breath. "I was at church." I'd ask what her excuse is, but I'm not going to fight with her. We have real problems. "Maybe someone else can help us track her down."

"Someone like who?" Jameson asks, crossing his arms.

"I don't know, O'Sullivan. That's why we're having a clandestine meeting to figure this all out. Which is looking less and less clandestine, if we're honest." I flick my head in the direction of two seagulls and an elderly couple, all bobbing dangerously close to hearing distance.

"We probably should go somewhere more private. How about your dad's cruiser?" Caleb suggests, pushing off the wall.

"Yeah," Jameson says, "we can talk in there."

"I'm…pretty sure I've seen this documentary before," I say, taking a step backward. "Which is why I will not be getting on a boat while a likely intoxicated Jameson drives it around the harbor."

"Don't be such a coward, Stafford," Jameson says. "We're not going to leave the dock."

I clamp my teeth to keep from saying something I'll regret as Caleb nears me with a warning look. He must've noticed how my eyes are fixated on a rock near my sandal and has intuited that I'd like to lob it at Jameson's head.

"We don't really need him, right?" I whisper in Caleb's ear. "On the way to the boat, you follow my lead. When I say *coconut*, we'll rush and knock him off the dock. Got it?"

Caleb's expression is tired. "Can you help me out here, please?" His eyes flick to Jameson. "Anyway, he's a linebacker. He'd barely budge."

I open my mouth, feigning outrage. "I'll have you know that I hold the Fairport Middle School girls record for number of pull-ups. And you're, well…" My gaze drifts down to his torso area, and my face blazes. "I think we could take him."

He cracks a smile.

"Are you two going to flirt all day, or can we go now?" Victoria is waiting at the dock, hands on her hips.

Caleb sighs, and I sidestep away from him, fighting the urge to abandon this entire mission and let the killer get her. Begrudgingly, I follow them onto Mr. O'Sullivan's expensive cruiser.

Jameson leads us down the ladder, and I clutch the railing to steady myself against the rocking. The wind must've picked up while I was busy arguing with those two. In the saloon area, I admire the lush beige upholstery on the wraparound seat. "Have you ever driven this thing?" I ask Jameson, sitting down.

"Duh," he says as Caleb scoots in next to me, followed by Victoria. "I'm"—he rubs a palm over his chin, muffling his voice— "not allowed to at the moment."

"Bad grades?" I ask, grinning.

"Like I'm gonna tell you, Stafford." He pulls a stool out from the wall and slumps down onto it. "So what's the play?"

I shrug. "If the cops won't look for Adelina, we've got to find her ourselves. Maybe we could set a trap."

"That's…" Victoria taps her polished fingernails over the table. "It's not a terrible idea."

"Thank you?"

"Or," she says, "we hire a private investigator to track her down. We know where she lived before, so it can't be that hard. Right?"

"Another decent suggestion," I say, marveling at how well things seem to be going. "Where do we find a PI? Other than TV, of course."

"I still don't understand how that helps us," Caleb interjects. "Even if we find Adelina, how do we figure out she's the one doing this?"

"That's why the trap idea was better," I say as the boat gives a violent heave. I start to lunge off the cushion, face headed straight for the kitchen table. But Caleb stretches his arm out to stop me.

My entire body ignites as he helps me back into my seat. "Thanks," I mumble, locking my eyes on the table.

"No problem. It's getting pretty rough out there."

"Back to Adelina," I say. "I still think we have to catch her in the act. Or find proof that ties her to the murders. If we track down her current place of residence, we could dig around."

Jameson's ginger-colored brows lift. "So what do we have to go on?"

"Her cousin thinks she still in the area," Caleb says, "which would explain how she's been seemingly everywhere all the time." He dips a hand into his sweatshirt pocket. "And we got this from a resident at the group home." He tosses it over to Victoria, who starts to read, her facial expression gradually shifting from intrigued to dumbfounded.

Despite being a little woozy from the rocking boat, I giggle to myself.

She looks up. "In the *grounds*?"

Before I can recount the entire Mrs. Lafferty muffin-wrapper incident, she adds, "Does that mean Adelina's dead?"

"What?" I flinch. "No, of course not." At least I really hope not. "This woman wanted Adelina to visit her again. So she can't—"

"You know what?" Victoria says, waving a hand. "I don't care. Now I'm glad I wasn't invited on your little road trip. It was obviously a waste of time."

"I know," Caleb says, stirring beside me, "it's probably nothing. But she said she was friends with Adelina, so I keep hoping it could be something."

I nod vehemently. "Yeah, we're definitely going to work on that, buddy." Instinctively, I reach over and give him a patronizing pat on the hand.

Victoria's eyes hone in on our hands. She shoves the letter back at Caleb, forcing me to awkwardly pull back.

Jameson stands up and begins pacing. In the small dinette, he looks even more massive than usual. "Maybe we should stick to defense. We've got no play. If we're careful—you know, stay inside, buddy system, food and drinks via DoorDash—this person won't be able to get to us." I want to point out that Jameson would never stick out one weekend indoors, but he nods to himself, like he's just solved this whole thing. "If we can't nail 'em, at least they don't have the advantage. I'd take a tie at this point."

"Okay," I say, looking to Caleb for help, "except it's not actually a sporting event, O'Sullivan. Someone is trying to murder all of us."

"I know that," he growls. "I'm just saying that after last night with Vic, we need to be more careful. This person is clearly a maniac."

The boat continues rocking, and the woozy feeling gets worse. "I think I need to get off the boat."

"You *are* looking a little green," Victoria says, inching back in her seat like I'm going to projectile vomit all over her.

"Not much of a boat person," I say, clambering out of the booth and staggering my way to the ladder.

I start to ascend when a hand lights on my back. I halt, but Caleb's soothing voice prods me onward. "Let's get you on dry land."

I move, not wanting to puke all over him, then remember to grab the hem of my dress so I don't flash him. When we reach the upper deck, he wraps an arm around my waist and helps me onto the dock.

I try to walk it off, to keep my breathing steady. Only we happen to be downwind of a fishing boat containing what smells like a big haul. The nausea intensifies, and I want to lie down in the middle of the dock.

"You okay?" Caleb's hand is still on my hip, steadying me. He's leaning forward like he might have to grab me. And I can see why. It isn't just the world swaying and rocking; it's me.

I find the nearest railing and lay my head down on my folded arms. "I'm sorry we didn't make any progress in there."

"Maybe Jameson has a point. We could just keep from being targets and wait for the killer to make a mistake." He nears me, delicately placing his hand on my back, like he wants to help but doesn't know how.

"But I feel like we were getting somewhere with Adelina. You want to give up now?" I force myself up, wobbling a bit.

"Are you sure you should—" Caleb eyes me warily.

"Yes, feeling much better already. Think I just needed solid ground." I force a smile.

"I don't *want* to give up," he says. "But are we really going to hire a PI to find this woman?"

"You and I could find her. I think if we ditched those two"—I tip my head in the direction of the O'Sullivan cruiser—"we'd have hard evidence in no time. Then we show the cops and have her locked up forevermore."

Caleb's gaze drifts toward the water. "You want to go without them?"

"Well, I don't want to hide out in my house, and they're kind of slowing everything down."

He runs a hand along the bottom of his chin. "I don't know, Eden. They're my friends."

"So? What are you saying?"

"It's just that they really didn't like when you and I went rogue before."

I don't know what I expected, but it wasn't this. That after finally letting my guard down and believing he never meant to abandon me, he'd do just that. "Oh." My chest feels like it's sinking into my gut, and my eyes are sore. The nausea that had temporarily subsided reemerges with a vengeance.

"Let me talk to them, okay?"

"No, it's fine," I choke out, both angry and horrified that I might throw up all over Caleb Durham's shoes. "I just thought…" I thought that after yesterday, he'd feel the way I do. That despite everything between us, we made a pretty good team.

I guess it was all in my head.

"Eden, do you want me to—"

I shake my head, which brings back the rocking movement from the boat, the waves. I shut my eyes, not noticing I'm tipping forward until Caleb grabs me.

"You're not okay," he says, gripping my waist. And even though everything is spinning and my insides might come up, I shiver at his touch.

"I am. Just need to walk it off, is all."

"You're going to *walk* home?" he says, a judgmental edge to his voice. "When someone is hunting us down?"

My hackles raise. Caleb Durham is not telling me what to do—not now, not ever. "I'll be fine."

The water splashes against the rocks as the wind blows, sending a sea-spray mist into the air. Again, I grasp the hem of my dress.

"You do look really nice today, Eden. But then," he adds with a shy smile, "you always look nice. Even when you're a little green."

My face heats, and I wonder if the green hue is mixing with

the red, or if it's a more of a striped situation, like my face is decked for Christmas. "I'm going home now," I say, turning to hide my Technicolor face.

"I don't like the idea of you walking alone," Caleb says. "Even in the daytime."

"Guess it doesn't matter what you like," I say, attempting to inflict some damage, even a microscopic amount, as I edge away from him.

18

"EDEN!" CALEB CALLS, BUT I'M ALREADY PAST THE sweet shop.

I can still smell the vanilla sugar scent, only it's no longer inviting. I realize that in my efforts to clean the house before church, I skipped breakfast. My empty stomach is at least partly to blame for my bout of seasickness.

There's no way I'm stopping anywhere near the wharf; instead, I consider trekking out to Fairport Brew, where the baked goods are even better than the coffee. I think of Miriam's scones, light and airy, not too sweet. Perfect to settle my stomach.

At the thought of her pastries, an image tumbles into my brain. The muffin wrapper, green with white swirls. I thought it looked familiar beneath the melted chocolate but chalked it up to the common pattern. Only now I know where I've seen those cupcake liners before: at Fairport Brew.

The answer lies in the grounds.

As in *coffee grounds*. We should've seen it. It wasn't a mistake at all. Mrs. Lafferty wasn't delusional when she handed me the liner. She was giving me a message—one she wanted to keep secret. Maybe Adelina Blackmore didn't drop that note on the counter for Henry. Maybe, like her cousin Louisa suggested, her intentions were much more sinister than outing the truth. But she must've been to that coffee shop. It would be a desperate attempt, but maybe Miriam or one of the regulars can tell me something about her.

I continue on, past the parking lot, in the direction of the downtown strip. Eventually I reach Fairport Brew, the queasiness slightly better now that I have my bearings. My feelings, on the other hand, not so much.

That scene back on the dock when Caleb chose his friends felt like homecoming all over again. But I walked right into it, didn't I? By trusting him again after I swore I never would?

Fairport Brew is quiet on a Sunday at lunchtime, the weekday chatter giving way to a playlist of modern folk music. Beneath the scent of coffee, there's a faint cinnamon aroma. Likely something in the oven. A woman scuttles past me out the door with her coffee, leaving me the sole patron in the joint. Miriam is alone at the counter today, apparently having given her apprentice the day off. She looks up from wiping the area down.

"Eden," she says with a nod. "Or is it Esmeralda Worthington today?"

"Just Eden," I say, not up for my usual fake-name game.

"Everything okay?"

"Boat incident." At the look of horror on her face, I quickly add, "I got seasick on a docked boat."

Miriam gives me an unamused look over the rims of her purple frames. "Well," she says, setting her rag down, "I've got some tea for that."

"Thanks." At the next ripple of nausea, I add, "I'll take a scone too, if the morning rush didn't clear you out." Quickly, I move to the glass pastry case, seeing one scone left, sugar crystals glimmering beneath the ceiling's pendant lights. Several pastries line the shelf above the scones: muffins, banana bread, cinnamon rolls. I've had them all, and they're exquisite. But when I see the chocolate cupcake, my heartbeat speeds up. Sure enough. It's encased in a pleated liner with green and white swirls.

That baking cup Mrs. Lafferty gave me definitely came from here.

Which means Adelina Blackmore was here in Fairport. She purchased one of Miriam's chocolate cupcakes before delivering it to Mrs. Lafferty. Maybe it was a one-time thing, or maybe she stops in here all the time.

I pull out my phone, clambering for a way to connect the dots. I don't know what Adelina Blackmore looks like as an adult. I scroll the internet for a photo of her as a child, knowing there's no way I can just ask Miriam if she's seen this girl in the shop—but like if she were twenty-five years older and had survived a media frenzy. I stop on what looks like a school photo. In it, Adelina is wearing a striped red dress and smiling at the camera, that big gap in her teeth that Louisa mentioned on full display.

I pay for the scone and tea, too excited to eat or drink at this point. "Miriam?"

"Something else for you?" she asks, placing the cup on the counter in front of me.

"No, it's just… I've been looking for someone. And I think she comes in here and buys cupcakes? I know it sounds weird, but she'd be early thirties. Possibly a gap between her two front teeth." I quirk my lips. "Unless she got braces, I guess. Blond hair, probably, unless she dyed it." I'm rambling, because this is clearly going nowhere, and with the way Miriam is looking at me from across the counter, blue eyes narrowed, I'm wishing I wouldn't have said anything.

"Why are you looking for this woman?" she asks, skirting the counter and moving toward the front windows. She draws the shades before moving to the door.

"Well, to be honest, I think she's connected to Henry's death. I think she's Nicolas Blackmore's sister, Adelina, and…she might be dangerous."

"Adelina Blackmore?" She lets out a laugh. "Back in Fairport? That sounds a bit far-fetched."

A timer goes off from back in the kitchen. Miriam, already headed for behind the counter, taps herself on the forehead. "Sorry. Would you mind pulling the muffins from the oven?" she asks. "I just got a mobile order and my new girl asked for the day off."

"I didn't know you were taking mobile orders," I say, getting up.

"It's brand-new. All of the big chains do it."

I want to tell her that part of the charm of this place is that it doesn't have the same mass-produced baked goods or sterile mobile order system, but instead I say, "Cool," and head through the kitchen door.

The kitchen is small but organized, and the cinnamon scent intensifies inside. I spot the oven mitt on the counter and put it on. As I open the oven door, something clicks behind me. A deep unsettling feeling comes over me as I set the first of two muffin trays on top of the oven.

"Thank you, Eden."

At her voice, I startle. I turn around to find Miriam smiling at me. When I notice the gap between her front teeth, an icy chill spreads through me.

She's already moving by the time I put it together.

The little blond-haired, blue-eyed child from the newspapers. She's all grown up, and she's headed straight for me.

19

I BACK UP, TOSSING THE OVEN MITT TO THE GROUND. I pull out my phone and attempt to text Caleb an SOS. But before I can hit Send, Adelina Blackmore snatches the phone away.

"Just to make sure you don't do anything stupid," she says, and then I notice the set of knives on the counter within her reach.

"Why are you doing this?" I ask, stepping away from her. I guess this means there are no mobile orders. Between this creepy woman and her oven, I'm just hoping to make it out of here without her baking me alive.

"Doing what?" she asks, closing the gap between us again. "Keeping you from making a huge mistake by blabbing to everyone that I'm Adelina Blackmore?"

"Why are you killing kids?" I ask, peering past her to the door. I can undo the lock. The challenge will be getting past Adelina and her knives.

Her brow furrows, the glasses inching down the bridge of her nose. "Killing—is that what you think?"

I take another step back. "I know you've had some…issues over the years. That you nearly killed a kid on the playground, and he might not have been your last victim."

"You've been talking to my cousin. What else did dear Louisa have to say?"

"I, uh, think maybe you should talk to her," I say, moving behind the steel prep table. "This definitely sounds like a family affair." I search for another knife lying around on this side of the kitchen, but the island is immaculate. There's a mixing bowl wedged into an electric stand, and I pick it up by the handle, thinking maybe I could hit her with it. Instead, I slam it onto the tile floor. It lands with a clang, and batter spatters the floor, distracting Adelina momentarily. When she refocuses, attempting to follow me on one side, I skirt the island on the opposite side and sprint to the door.

"Eden, I didn't kill any kids!" she calls after me.

I flip the lock and grasp the handle, my pulse blaring in my ears when Adelina's voice punches through. "Please, you can't tell anyone that I'm Adelina Blackmore."

I twist and pull on the handle, then freeze in the doorway. Hesitantly, I crane my neck to glance back at her. "Why not?"

Her head lowers. "Because it's taken me years to get to this place." She gestures around the kitchen and to the open door. "Somewhere all my own, where nobody knows who I really am.

Where no one hounds me for interviews about the worst day of my life, or asks about my time in the hospital or at the academies."

She seems desperate to keep this secret. It explains why her friend Mrs. Lafferty had to point me here through that cryptic message. "I'm really sorry about everything that happened to you, but I need to get home to my mom, who knows *exactly* where I am right now."

"Please," she says, looking much older than her thirty-three years, "just sit down. Drink your tea, and let's talk."

I stretch my neck to peer at the tea on the counter. "Oh, sure. I drink the tea and never wake up. Sounds like a plan."

"I didn't put anything in your tea," she says with a sigh.

"You did steal my phone," I say, still hovering on the balls of my feet. "Why should I trust you?"

"I didn't want to do that." She glances down at my phone in her hand. "I just…couldn't risk you telling anyone about me. Not until you heard my side of the story. Eden, I didn't kill anyone, but"—she shuts her eyes—"I did leave that note for Henry."

"What? You did?"

She nods. "Right out there on the counter."

I think about the video, how Henry zoomed in on the note while searching the creepy cottage. *The truth is buried in the Village ruins.* He assumed it was left by a customer, because he had no idea who his employer really was.

"All right, I'm listening," I say, moving backward into the shop so I can keep an eye on her. "But you can keep your poisoned tea."

She rolls her eyes, following me. "Thank you." Taking the tea and the scone off the counter, she places them on the table nearest her. Then she gestures to a chair before pulling out one for herself. "You won't mind if I take them then." She brings the cup to her lips and takes a sip. "See? No poison."

"Bet you spent years building up a tolerance," I say, "for this very moment." She sighs, rubbing at an eye, and I snatch the scone back. "I'm going to eat this," I explain, "because you made it before I figured out your identity."

"And because my scones are irresistible," she says, a glint in her blue eyes.

"And that." I weave through the tables to sit across from her, then hold out my hand. "I'll need to text a friend my location or no deal."

Her expression remains impassive, fist clutched around my phone.

"I promise I won't text anyone your real identity," I say as a burnt scent wafts into the shop. "But that's the trade-off. Also, I think your fire alarm is about to go off. I left a tray in the oven."

Adelina's spine stiffens, and she glances back toward the kitchen. "Fine." With a huff, she slides my phone across the table and scurries off.

I look to the front door, still thinking of bailing.

But I have so many questions, and she may be the only person with answers. While she's dealing with her baking disaster, I pull up May's name on my contact list and start to type. I erase it though, finding Caleb's name instead and typing out a message: At Fairport

Brew. Urgent. Please come. I hit Send before I can talk myself out of it, even though he proved less than an hour ago that he doesn't care about me.

But part of me will always hold out hope that he'll prove me wrong.

I set my phone in my lap and look up at Adelina. "Okay, talk. Why did you leave that note for Henry? A note that got him killed, by the way."

"I never thought something like that would really happen," Adelina says, tears brimming in her eyes. "I thought searching the ruins was the only way to bring the truth to light."

"The truth about Nicolas's murder?"

She nods. "It's taken me years to remember what happened that night. And now that it's finally come back—now that I understand—it's too late for me to do anything about it. Now, I'm this *crazy* woman whose version of events holds no merit, who doesn't even own the property or the land."

"Adelina," I say, treading cautiously, "what Louisa said about your childhood. Was it true? Were you in and out of psychiatric facilities?"

She lets out a long breath. "Louisa is remembering appointments, but they weren't psychiatric evaluations. When I was small, I had some developmental delays. I couldn't read as well as the other kids, was always bumping into things. My parents were, understandably, concerned. So they sent me to specialists, who discovered a tumor on my optic nerve."

"Wow," I say, picking at my scone.

"Treatment required surgery after surgery. My parents didn't talk about it to other parents, because they didn't want other children to accidentally let it spill that I could go blind. Or you know, die."

"But what about that kid on the playground?" I pick at what's left of my scone. "The one Louisa says you were smiling at while he was lying on the ground, hurt?"

"I'd been playing with Sam—that was the boy's name. But I didn't have my glasses, and back then, my vision was terrible. So when he fell, I thought he was playing. I thought the screams were a big joke until one of the teachers came up and got me. I tried to tell Louisa all of this years later. But she has this idea stuck in her head that I was this *bad seed*."

"And the psychiatric hospital?" I ask, instinctively drawing away from her. "That was after Nicolas?"

"Yes, after his death I was dragged into the police station." She sets the tea down, wrapping her arms around herself. "I never should've been interviewed in the first place. By then I'd had a couple of surgeries and was seeing better, but I was so shaken from the murder—from seeing my mother covered in his blood and being dragged away in handcuffs. The way she screamed." Adelina shivers. "They wanted a closed case, and I wanted to get out of that tiny box of a room. So I told them what they wanted to hear. I told them what I thought I'd seen. I'd heard Nicolas arguing with my mother, and then I'd seen her holding the bloody knife. There was blood all over her, and then"—she inhales and lets the breath loose slowly—"I saw Nicolas's body, lifeless on the floor. I heard my mother screaming my name, searching for me, and I thought she meant to kill me too. That's what I told the cops, and that seemed to make them happy. Only it didn't make *me* happy. I was left with my father, who didn't know how to help me through the trauma, especially after my mother died. Hell, he didn't even know how to help himself.

"So," she says, adjusting her glasses, "we didn't work through it. Not any of it. My grief and trauma began to consume me until I simply couldn't function. And my father eventually had me committed. I did improve at Saint Christopher's Hospital, but by the time I was ready to come home, my father's health had begun to deteriorate. Before he figured out what to do with me, he passed away."

"I'm so sorry." I want to mention that I'm also without a father, to show her that I understand. But it's not the same thing. At least my father is alive out there somewhere. "Is that how you ended up at St. Andrew's Academy?"

She nods. "Straight out of the facility, Louisa's parents became my guardians. But they wouldn't take me in. They sent me off to a school for *troubled* kids. And when that school shut down, they shipped me off to another. I stayed there until I aged out."

"That's when you moved to the group home?" I ask, moving the crumbs around on my plate.

"Yes, my first job," she says brightly.

"Job?" My arm wrenches back, causing the ceramic plate to clank along the table. "You *worked* at the group home?"

She nods. "I'd spent so much time around troubled individuals. After I completed my training, they hired me on the spot."

Embarrassment streaks up my neck as the words bounce back. *Adelina never lived here!* Once again, Mrs. Lafferty was trying to help, and I dismissed her words as the deluded ramblings of a sick woman. Adelina never lived in the group home because she was on staff.

"The director said you left the home a couple of years ago." I brush the scattered crumbs back onto my plate and think back to when Miriam—Adelina—first took over ownership of Fairport Brew. "What made you come back here? To the place where everything happened?"

"I still owned Fairport Village," she says. "Back then, I was only the manager of this shop, not the owner. I didn't have any money, so my plan was to sell Fairport Village. I figured it would be impossible, but maybe if I could find some investors to turn it over and make it shiny again, some interested party might come along." Her eyes go distant. "But then, I saw the place again, and I couldn't do it. I remembered my mother's words—her proclamation—on that horrible night, and I decided to leave it there. Just like she wanted. Whether you believe in the supernatural or not, that ground is *cursed*. It's been a place of death and misery ever since the first founders set foot on the land. I couldn't make money off of its existence.

"So I worked and I worked until finally, I was able to own this shop. I tried not to think about all that money sitting in Fairport Village." She purses her lips flat, brows lifting. "But then Starlight Developers came along."

"Starlight?" I ask, the word stirring up the dust coating some long-forgotten memory. The nursery rhyme my dad used to recite with me whenever I asked for something. *Star light, star bright, first star I see tonight…*

"The developers were nice at first," Adelina continues, "sending me typewritten letters, asking if I'd be willing to sell them the property. Claiming they would make me rich. But they didn't like my answer. Then they got pushy, saying that I was keeping Fairport from reaching its potential by leaving that eyesore there. I knew they had a point, so I promised I'd clean it up if they'd simply respect my decision."

She picks up a polka-dotted napkin from the holder. I think she's going to wipe tears with it, but instead she begins to fold it. "They didn't. They performed background checks on me, hired private investigators, harassed me, until finally, they threatened me and my place of business. They learned who I really was and threatened to tell everyone in town. I knew that I'd lose the life I'd created. I'd only been able to live in Fairport as Miriam Delacroix. I could never be Adelina Blackmore. Not here, not anywhere. So I had no choice but to sell them the property."

My phone dings in my lap, and I startle. "Sorry," I mumble, relieved that Caleb hasn't completely blown me off. He must be on his way.

But my heart sinks at the text from my mom. Everything ok? We're all headed to the farmer's market. See you there?

Practically everyone in Fairport spends Sunday evenings at the farmer's market. Each family has its own niche—knitted scarves, hand-painted dolls, wood carvings. Somehow, Mom became the town's resident jam maker. I usually go and help out.

I text her back. Everything's great. See you there! I check my message to Caleb, seeing that it's marked *read* before looking up at Adelina. "That's horrible. But I still don't understand why you left that note for Henry. After everything you heard and saw, what made you change your mind about your brother's murder?"

"It was after I sold the property." She continues to make delicate folds on the napkin, her fingers working even as she looks at me. "I'd never met any of the developers in person. When I signed documents, it was with some assistant. But I spoke to one of the executives on the phone a few times, and I kept thinking that his voice sounded so familiar. Unfortunately, it wasn't until after I'd signed all the paperwork with the assistant that I remembered the voice. It was Nicolas's friend from high school. And I'd heard it the night he was killed."

At this, my chest tightens.

"It was common knowledge that there'd been a gathering of Nicolas's friends that night, but everyone assumed they'd left long before his death. My brother didn't want me hanging around, so he instructed me to stay put in my room. That's why I'd only heard him arguing—I didn't see it. And the more I thought about it, the more the memories came back. I recalled that Nicolas had gotten in an argument with one of those boys—the executive who'd spoken to me over the phone. My brother's shouting had never been at my mother at all. It was directed at this boy—one I hadn't seen because Nicolas hid me away.

"And suddenly, this boy—a man now—was coming around

looking to buy the place? It didn't make sense. In twenty-five years, no one had ever come looking for me, asking to buy that land. It was tainted by history, a stain on Fairport. Even if someone had restored the resort to its former glory, or even started over with an entirely new development, they would've had too many challenges finding buyers. No one wants to own a cursed piece of property. So I started to wonder why this company had been so eager to take this *burden* off my hands."

I think of my father and Nicolas and their matching tattoos. The fight over the surf tournament only a week before Nicolas's death.

The nausea threatens to rise again.

"That was part of the story I'd never told anybody. Not the police, not the journalists who hounded me for years. I never reported a false story, but I never corrected the police either. They said that my mother must've thrown the knife into the ocean after she killed my brother. But I know that's not what happened." She clears her throat, then finishes off the dregs of her tea. "Before the police arrived the night of Nicolas's murder, I was terrified. My mother was screaming Nicolas's name. She was screaming my name, searching for me, and my father was still out, checking on the guests after his evening away. I stayed hidden until I heard my father's voice. I peeked out my cracked bedroom door long enough to watch him enter the foyer and find my mother drenched in blood, holding the knife that killed Nicolas. He pulled her from the scene, and I couldn't watch anymore. I didn't see what happened to the knife."

"What do you think he did with it?"

"A couple of years later," she answers, "in one of my fits, I asked my father about that knife. And he said not to worry. That he knew simply wiping it down wouldn't be enough to save my mother. So instead, he'd buried the knife in the Village, beneath the foundation." She looks at me, pleadingly. "But you see, his act didn't vindicate my mother. It *condemned* her. Because she never killed my brother. Someone else did. The real killer's fingerprints and maybe even DNA are on that knife. And I realized it too late." Her shoulders roll. "Now my father—the only soul on the planet who knew the location of that murder weapon—is dead. And I don't own the property anymore."

"That's why someone wants to build over the land," I say. "They must know about that knife and can't find it. So they're trying to bury the evidence, once and for all." I consider this, unable to help the way my father's face, the features blurred with time, keeps popping into my mind. Is he the owner of Starlight Developers?

I type *Starlight Developers* into my phone's browser and get a hit. But the website only contains a home page, a vague company description, and a gold four-pointed star logo.

There's a phone number at the bottom of the page, and when I dial it, a generic robotic voicemail thanks me for calling Starlight Developers headquarters and asks me to leave a message.

"Don't bother," Adelina says. "Once I realized the mistake I'd made in selling the land, I tried doing some digging into the company. No one ever calls back."

"So Starlight Developers is…what?" I ask. "Fake?"

"Some sort of private LLC, from what I've gathered. Whoever's behind it is virtually untraceable."

Just like my father. What if he killed not only Nicolas but the others as well? "There could be more evidence buried on the land. We all know your mother didn't kill Farah Palmer or Esther Lamb." Or the most recent victims.

Adelina nods solemnly, finally setting the napkin down on the table to reveal a polka-dotted flower with six pointed petals.

"But how come the developers couldn't just sneak onto the property to search for the knife? Just like the seniors sneaked in?"

"You think they never tried? I'm sure they've looked many times, only without the hint about the foundation, that knife was a needle in a haystack. All that rubble? And," she says, leaning in closer over the table, "even if they'd known about the foundation, they would've only searched beneath the main house. They wouldn't have known about the *other* crawl spaces."

"What other crawl spaces?" I ask as her eyes dart to the corners of the shop, like the developers could be listening in.

"Only my family knew that the cottages were built with crawl spaces. Most of the homes around here weren't back then. But my father wanted to do things his way. And since the town wouldn't have signed off on the plans, those crawl spaces aren't even included on them. The entry is hidden, accessible only beneath the porch. I was able to search five out of the six, but I never made it to Sea Glass Shore before the developers started keeping close tabs on me. I couldn't risk them finding the access points. And of course, I never could bring myself to check beneath the main house." Her head lowers. "Couldn't even get within yards of the place."

"What about the police?" I ask. "Maybe they could go in there and—"

"I can't go to the police," Adelina cuts in. "Not with my history. That's why I dropped the note in front of Henry. I needed someone to bring attention to the place enough to convince the police to search it before it got bulldozed. Henry was so interested in the town history and in the curse. I knew that if I could just get him to start searching, the truth about Nicolas's murder might finally come to light." Tears well in her eyes, and she wipes them away with the back of her hand. "But believe me," she says, voice breaking, "I never meant for anything to happen to him. I never thought the killer would be hovering there in the ruins, ready to keep anyone from discovering the truth."

The killer, I think with a shiver.

Who may be my father.

20

"MAYBE YOU CAN'T GO TO THE POLICE," I SAY, CHECKING my phone again for a text from Caleb, only to find none. "But I can. They might not listen to a kid, but I can try." Henry's death delayed the demolition a few weeks. Once the yellow tape is removed though, the bulldozers will show up. The evidence will be cemented over forever.

I say goodbye to Adelina, promising to keep her identity safe. As I set out for the Fairport police station, I text a quick update on my location to Caleb. Not like he'll even read it.

On Sundays, apart from the farmer's market held in Fairport High's parking lot, everything in town shuts down at 4 p.m. Since it's 6:15 now and dusk is approaching, I'm basically walking a ghost town. Palm trees shiver in the breeze, and ahead, the fluorescent bulbs of a motel sign attempt to light before crackling out again.

Fortunately, the farmer's market—and Mom—stand between me and the police station.

I pass the small parking lot, edging along the chain-link fence until I reach the end of the building. When I make a right at the corner, a shadow catches my eye up the street—a figure leaning against the chain-link fence.

My heart skids. I keep walking, head down, and cross to the opposite side of the street. Trying not to be too obvious, I make a U-turn and continue on past this street. I can always get to the police station the long way.

The jingle of chain link cuts through the evening air, and I speed up. Caleb's words from the wharf flicker in my head: *I don't like the idea of you walking alone.*

He had a point, but it's his fault I'm in this situation. I sent him an SOS, and he completely ignored it. Even if he doesn't care about *me*, he should care about finding his best friend Diego's killer. Caleb acted like he was so concerned with getting justice and protecting Victoria—who he's totally obsessed with. Yet I'm the only one out here doing any real investigative work. *I* found Adelina. Meanwhile, he and his buddies are probably still on that boat, drinking beers and singing about it, no clue that everything's about to fall apart.

I should've texted May. She would've dropped everything and come running.

I take a right on the next street, where the high school parking lot lights are in view at the end of the block.

At the sound of footsteps, my mouth goes cotton dry. I'm being followed again, just like that night after the library.

I turn around in an attempt to scare this person off, but no one's there. No hooded being, no ghost.

Breathe. I'm fine. All I have to do is pick up my feet and sprint two hundred yards, and I'll be surrounded by people.

Suddenly, I feel silly. I keep moving at a decent pace until I reach the edge of the parking lot. Then I thread between the rows of vehicles, picking up the chatter from the farmer's market, along with the scents of kettle corn and pan dulce.

At a grating sound, like a sharp tool scraping a car—though which car, I'm not sure—I sprint toward the crowd.

The booths are set up on the next stretch of asphalt. They form a square, with rows of stands facing each other all the way around. Shoppers stroll through the center, tasting samples and talking with the vendors. Kids run between legs and beneath booths, fruit juice dripping down their chins. Parents chasing after them.

My plan five minutes ago had been to pass the school and get to the police station; now I want to find Mom. Her homemade jam booth is at the opposite corner of the market. I pass the frozen lemonade stand, the Kaur family's handcrafted candles, and the booth where Naomi Lamb and her parents sell handwoven goods. As I hurry past some fruit stands, a shoulder bumps me, knocking me off-balance. I whip around, finding it's only a shopper with his head in his phone.

"Sorry," he mumbles, glaring at me like *I'm* the one not paying attention.

When I start through the path between the booths again, I freeze. A black hood bobs along through the crowd toward me, face hidden within the fabric.

I take a sharp left in between the next two booths, ducking

behind the crates of fruit piled up behind the vendors. I peek to make sure I'm not being followed, but between the tables and canopies, it's hard to get a clean view. The only thing I can do is keep moving along the outside of the market until I reach Mom's booth.

There's a gap before the corn dog stand, so I crouch low and peek through, checking for the hood. But a number of dark hoods dot the market-goers now; the sun has set, and the sea breeze makes a chilly tunnel of the market. I check behind me, finding the coast clear.

The corner is up ahead, which means Mom's booth isn't far. A couple of vendors give me dirty looks as I pass behind their booths, but I keep my head down and push forward. I reach Amy Park's beaded jewelry booth with a whoosh of relief. No one is going to attack me. For all I know, no one has been following me. She greets me with skewed brows, either because I'm still wearing a dress or because I'm creeping around the back of her booth.

I start to move around to the front when my phone dings in my purse. I pull it loose and find a message from Caleb.

Caleb Durham: Hey, sorry I didn't have my phone. Are you okay? The police station??

I grit my teeth and type out a message: I'm fine, no thanks to you

CD: I'm really sorry. I'll explain in person. Are you home now?

Eden Stafford: No, farmer's market

CD: Good. Me too. Meet me somewhere?

Mom's booth is only a few yards away, and I don't want her asking why I haven't learned my lesson about this boy yet. Plus, I can't risk anyone overhearing the truth about Adelina Blackmore. I promised the woman she could trust me.

ES: We should talk somewhere less packed

CD: Outside the weight room?

I glance across the blacktop in the direction of the gymnasium, but the parking lot floodlights only extend another few yards. Beyond that, the campus is dead on a Sunday, not a single light on in any of the buildings. The locker room and weight room are tucked behind that gymnasium, shrouded in darkness.

ES: Headed there now

"Everything okay, Eden?" Amy asks.

"Oh, yeah," I say, finally looking up from my phone. "Sorry, I just remembered something I've got to do for my mom. See you later." Giving her a wave, I slip back behind her booth to cross the blacktop. I wrap my arms around myself for warmth, keeping my steps quick. Unlike the rest of this crowd, I didn't bring a sweater, and my legs are exposed to the elements in this dress.

Once I leave the glow of the floodlights, something stirs in the darkness. "Caleb?" I call out.

But there's no answer, so I continue my trek. Reaching the path that splits the gym from the athletic wing, I pause, unsure if I should wait for Caleb here or move closer to the weight room.

I push a little farther up the path, turning on my phone's flashlight. "Caleb?" He should be right behind me. I finally reach the locker room, and alarm streaks through me. Instinctively, I take a step back.

The door is cracked open, the light within spilling onto my feet. I take a breath and inch closer to peek inside. "Caleb?" I hiss.

My phone chimes in my hand, startling me so much I fumble it.

CD: Inside

I'm about to text back, asking what the hell he's doing inside the weight room on a Sunday, when I hear the clank of weights.

That's what he's doing. I've heard of the football coach letting his athletes in here after hours so they can keep training; I didn't know the soccer players also had that type of access.

I push inside, eager to escape the cold and the creeping darkness. "I'm here," I call out, searching for him among all the equipment. He's not at any of the machines, which means he must be in the attached locker room, just through the door at the back.

The hallway light is off, and as I pass through it, my elbow knocks into the water dispenser. "Damnit!" I grumble. Why is he making this so difficult?

A sudden memory from seventh grade hits me: being locked in the dark janitor's closet for hours. If this is a prank, I will tie up

Caleb and the rest of them with jump ropes from this room and let
Nicolas Blackmore's killer have at them.

The locker room door is parted, the sound of the shower drifting out. Seriously? "Durham, you better hurry up and come out of
there!" I yell into the room. "Clothed," I add as sweat beads on my
forehead.

There's no answer; he can't hear me above the water. I inch
inside the room. It's identical to the girls' locker room, apart from
the fact that ours smells like Victoria's Secret body sprays and theirs
smells like Axe mixed with body odor. Cautiously, I tread toward
the showers at the back. Steam fills this part of the room. The closer
I get, the more a sense of guilt spreads up my core. "Caleb?" I say,
expecting him to hear my voice and freak out.

Instead, I hear nothing but the constant rush of water. The
steam is so thick, I can barely see. I'm about to call out again when
a *clink* sounds from the weight room.

A chill winds up my spine.

I look over my shoulder at the empty locker room, then peer
back into the steam.

I force in a calming breath. Maybe Caleb asked Jameson and
Victoria to come. Maybe I triggered some sort of school alarm, and
the cops showed up. Still, I tiptoe back toward the locker room door
to investigate, scanning the area for something I can use as a weapon.
But there's only a plastic water bottle and someone's balled-up practice shirt.

I take two more steps toward the door when I spot a baseball.

It'll have to do. I bend over to retrieve it when a shadow shifts into the doorway.

A hood.

My heart seizes. The figure takes a step into the room, the familiar features finally visible.

It's Caleb.

Confusion ripples through my head as footsteps sound on the tile behind me.

I look at Caleb, whose hazel eyes grow wide. He opens his mouth to say something, but movement whips in my periphery. A flash of silver as a hand swings around my shoulders, gripping a knife.

I hear my name from Caleb's lips, but it's too late.

The blade halts high in the air, long enough for me to glimpse the tattoo on the inner wrist of the person holding it. A shark fin tattoo.

Then the knife swings down, headed straight for my throat.

21

MY EYES SHUT AGAINST THE PAIN, AND I CRASH TO THE ground.

At the sound of my own scream, I force my eyes open. My hand darts to my throat, coming away bloody.

But I can scream: I'm still alive. The knife only grazed me.

My attacker is moving to the door now, long hood flapping like a caged beast in the small locker room. I stagger to my feet, unsure where Caleb went.

The person—this *man*—has a shark fin tattoo. Just like my father.

A moment later, I hear a grunt, followed by a loud crash.

I hurry to find Caleb and the figure on either side of a fallen exercise machine. Caleb sprints behind another machine, attempting to push this one on top of our attacker. But it holds firm, and Caleb turns to search for another weapon.

He grasps a foam roller, tossing it at the attacker in desperation.

The roller bounces off the figure's chest and falls to the ground. Caleb dashes toward the power rack, reaching immediately for the weighted bar. He grunts, attempting to lift it once, before opting to remove one of the weights on the end.

As our attacker skirts the machine, Caleb chucks the weight at his head. The man dodges it, letting out a growl and barreling around the machine with renewed purpose.

I reach for a kettlebell from the rack against the wall and, hefting it, rush toward them.

Caleb removes another weight from the bar, but when he throws it this time, he misses completely. It clanks against the machine, bouncing back to throttle his hand. He cries out, the sound shredding my nerves.

I cross the room, kettlebell held at my chest. Caleb starts to lift the bar with his good hand, but our attacker is already in front of him, knife held high.

"Hey!" I call to distract him.

As he turns, I heave the kettlebell with all of my might, letting it swing back and ricochet forward into the attacker's head.

The knife clinks to the floor, and the man wobbles, stunned.

I'm torn between taking another swing and reaching out and removing the hood.

Caleb has no such hesitations. He pulls the weighted bar back, eyes narrowing as he aims.

"Wait!" I scream.

Caleb halts, stunned. His hazel eyes shift to mine.

It's all our attacker needs. He gathers his bearings, bulls past me, and makes a crooked sprint out of the room. Caleb starts to pursue him, but stops, gripping his injured hand, breathing labored. "Why did you do that?" he huffs, holding on to the machine as if for dear life.

"I-I'm sorry. I don't know." Except that's a lie. I know exactly why I did it. Just like Jameson always says, I'm a coward. I couldn't let Caleb kill my father, even if the man did try to kill me minutes before.

Remembering the door still swinging in the night breeze, I rush to shut it. "Does this thing lock automatically?"

"I think so," he says with uncertainty.

Of course Caleb doesn't know. He's not the one who unlocked this door.

"I'll call the cops." I grasp at the fabric of my sundress, noting the utter lack of pockets and trying to remember what happened to my phone.

"Wait." Caleb wipes the sweat from his brow, looking at me with some mixture of concern and relief. He lowers his injured hand to his side and strides across the room to me. Before I can take a step backward, his arms enfold me. I flinch, but as he holds me close, my muscles ease.

When he pulls back, his eyes don't meet mine. "Sorry," he mumbles. "I just—I thought I saw him kill you back there."

"I thought I saw him kill me too," I say, suddenly conscious of the tickling sensation running down my clavicle and inside the front of my dress. I bring a hand to my neck and hiss at the pain. My fingers come away wet.

Caleb touches my arm. "You're bleeding."

"I'm okay," I say, remembering what I'd been certain had been my last moment. "But I have no idea how I escaped. He had a knife to my throat." *My father.*

"I must've distracted him," Caleb says.

"We need to call the cops."

"Are you sure?" Caleb asks. "We're not supposed to be in here."

"He's the one who broke in. We can say we noticed suspicious activity." I retrace my steps back to the locker room, where my blood speckles the floor.

Then I see my phone on the ground. I pick it up, finding the screen shattered. I try to unlock the home screen, but it won't turn on. Leaning my head out into the corridor, I yell, "Can I borrow your phone?"

"I don't have mine," he calls back. "Try the one in the office."

The athletic department office is at the back of the building, nestled deep in shadows. I hurry down the hall and yank on the door handle, finding it locked.

Grasping at my temples, I return to Caleb, who's holding on to the machine for support.

"No phone. I'll go out to the market and see if anyone's still there." I'm already heading back toward the door.

"No," Caleb says, the firm edge to his voice blurred by panic. "This maniac could be out there, waiting for us. We'll stay here until it's safe." He touches the quickly blooming bruise on his jaw with his good hand, shutting an eye.

"What happened there?" I dip my shoulder beneath his arm like a crutch and help lower him to the ground.

"That machine." He points to the one that was already laid flat by the time I followed them in here. "He got me with the bar."

I kneel beside him, gesturing for his hand. "Can I take a look?"

Hesitantly, he allows me to cradle his injured hand in mine. "It's not a big deal. Just a smashed finger."

"You're going to need an X-ray, and someone to make sure your face is okay." I shrug. "I mean, it's not; we've always known that. But now you can get an official diagnosis."

He cracks a smile that turns into a grimace. "I guess I'm a mess."

"You are. And lucky you've still got all your teeth." Gingerly, I set his hand down and mumble, "But thank you…for showing up."

"No," he says, looking straight into my eyes and forcing me to meet his, "thank *you*. I'd be a dead man if you hadn't clobbered him with that kettlebell."

His gaze stirs up a million feelings, followed by questions. I tear my eyes away. "I'm still confused about everything. You texted me to meet you outside, so how did you end up behind me?"

Caleb shakes his head, then winces again, his eyes falling shut. "No, I never texted you. Someone took my phone from the ice cream parlor." That explains why Caleb never came to Fairport Brew while I was with Adelina. "I set it on the table next to Jameson while I went to order him an ice cream—I lost a bet on the boat. It's a long story.

Anyway, when I came back, Jameson had gone to the bathroom, and while he was up, someone stole my phone."

"Not *someone*," I say. "The killer. But what made you come here to the locker room?"

"I went by your house to apologize about the way we left things. And when you weren't there, I got worried. I knew you sometimes help your mom out at the market on Sundays, so I went there. That's when Amy Park told me she saw you headed toward the gym."

"I really need to buy a beaded bracelet from that girl," I say, getting up. "I'll grab some ice for your jaw from the first aid room."

I walk to the trainer's room, which is graciously unlocked. As I fill a bag with ice, I consider telling Caleb about my father. That it's possible Greg Stafford is even worse than any of us imagined. Not only did he cheat his friends and abandon his family, he's a murderer. And tonight, he may have been willing to kill his own daughter to cover up his crimes. My stomach turns at the thought.

"Look," I say, lowering beside Caleb and delicately pressing the ice to his jaw, "about that whole letting-the-killer-flee-the-scene thing…"

"Eden, you don't have to explain. You had compassion. It's human. And it's very *you*."

"It is not," I argue, still holding the ice.

"Right." His lips curve in a half smile. "Of course not."

I shiver, maybe because it's cold in the weight room and I'm holding a pack of ice. Maybe because of the way he's looking at me.

"Here." Caleb pulls away, tugging off his hoodie. He cringes as he glides his mangled finger through the armhole before draping it over my shoulders.

"Before long," I say shyly, setting the ice down, "I'm going to own your whole closet."

"You can take whatever you want." His eyes drift down to pause on my lips before sliding lower. "Not sure I've got a replacement for that though," he adds, indicating my dress covered in blood spatter. He leans back against the machine with his legs stretched out.

"My mom's going to be pissed. She loved this dress."

"It is a nice dress," he says, looking away suddenly.

"Everything okay?"

"Yeah, fine. But I was wondering if…" He chews the inside of his cheek. It's endearing and makes the barrier between us waver slightly. I wait for him to say something, but he seems to be struggling. I start to wonder if, somehow, he knows about my father. If that's what has him so tongue-tied. But before I can blurt the truth about everything, Caleb reaches over with his good hand to touch my cheek.

His fingers roam down to my neck, walking ever so slightly into my hair. It sends tingles down my spine. "There's something I've thought about since eighth grade."

My mouth goes dry. "Oh?" I say, trying to swallow, a joke lingering on my tongue. One about how he's been thinking and plotting up ways to prank me. To humiliate me. But I don't say any of it. Instead, I ask, "What's that?"

His fingertips are still threaded loosely through the hair at the nape of my neck, and reflexively, I tilt my head, pressing my cheek against the warmth of his hand.

But a sudden doubt grabs hold of me. "Why are you doing this?" I ask, forcing his hand down. I shift to face him, folding my legs beneath me.

"Doing what?"

"This!" I gesture between the two of us. "Being..." I nearly say *flirty*, but more doubts come rushing in. "Being nice to me," I finally say. "Ever since the homecoming debacle, you've avoided me like the plague that killed our founding fathers." He quirks a brow, but I barrel forward. "You never spoke to me, never noticed me before that night in the ruins. Even today, you refused to come with me to find Adelina."

"And I told you I came to apologize! I didn't—I couldn't stand knowing you were upset with me."

"But I..." I still can't wrap my head around any of it. "I really believed you hated me."

His head wrenches back. "I believed *you* hated *me*! Look, yesterday you asked about the field trip in eighth grade. If I remembered hitting that guy in the suit. I said I forgot, but the truth is that I remember he tried his hardest to ignore us, but we kept badgering him anyway. It was my yogurt container that opened up and splattered all over him. I remember you slipped and fell on the concrete when you were trying to dodge my sandwich, and you ended up tearing your jeans."

His lips twist into a nostalgic smile. I'm not sure where he's going with this, but before I can ask, he adds, "I tried to help you, but you took advantage of my distraction and chucked an orange at my head. Your hair was tangled, and you kept pushing it out of your eyes while you ran. Your T-shirt was this perfect shade of green, like a tropical sea, and by the end of our fight, there was barely an inch of green left, it was so splattered with mustard and orange juice. You had a single peel stuck in your hair, and when I pulled it free, you blushed."

He reaches to tug the strings of his hoodie together around my collarbone, drawing me closer to him in the process. I don't resist. "You were formidable and beautiful, and I realized that as long as you were around, I'd be hopelessly lost. I didn't forget a single moment of that day. But when you asked me about it, I…well, I knew you hated me and felt too scared to admit that the last thing I could ever do was hate you back. But I tried to tell you in my truck yesterday—I've been trying to tell you ever since that night in the ruins that I *notice* you. I think about you. Constantly."

I want to pull his hoodie up to cover my face, which is undoubtedly blushing worse than it ever did back in eighth grade. "I always thought you were staring at me because you hated me."

"I know that. You were never exactly quiet in the halls when you'd tell May that I was contemplating ways to murder you. But the truth is"—his head tilts in reminiscence—"I was probably imagining what it would be like to kiss you right there in front of the lockers."

I try to swallow, but my throat is bone-dry. "But you—but—but you…"

"Sorry, what?" He arches a brow teasingly.

His gaze hovers again on my lips before moving up to my eyes. For some reason, his words pour into me, pulling and twisting at my heart more than if he'd spat abuse. And I can't decide whether to shush him before my heart along with my whole worldview explodes, or if I should just let him talk until it kills me. "So"—my eyes lower—"we're not nemeses?"

"We," he says, reaching out to gently lift my chin when I refuse to look at him, "are not nemeses."

I should tear my chin away and end this, but those hazel eyes have me entranced. Caleb peers down at me, that little smirk playing in his features. He smells like bonfires and surfer—a dash of salt water mixed with a dab of coconut sunscreen. I press my lips flat together, determined not to give away the fluttery feeling in my stomach or the chills coursing down the sides of my neck at his touch. Despite how much I try to squash it, hope stirs in me. It hovers at the edge of my heart like a tightrope walker, and I have no clue whether I'm about to fall all over again. "Then...what are we?"

The smirk falls, replaced by a look of wanting as he leans closer. "I know what I'd like us to be," he says, breath warm against my throat. He pushes the bedraggled hair off my face, and when he tugs me closer, my pulse quickens.

He lets go of the strings, sliding his injured hand carefully around to the small of my back. I feel lightheaded. Maybe it's the blood loss, or maybe it's how I'm struggling to manage my breathing with his hand on me. Still pulling me toward him, Caleb's other hand threads through the hair at the nape of my neck as his head tilts toward mine. My eyes fall shut, my breath growing shallow and uneven as it becomes one with his.

When his lips meet mine, my breath hitches. The worries and fears I had about him, about how to do this—all of it is quickly replaced by a sense of urgency as he shifts to pull our bodies flush and he kisses me like I'm his only lifeline.

Then a *thump* sounds, and we pull apart.

22

MY HEARTBEAT MIMICS THE THUNDEROUS SOUND. ALL
I can see is black fabric rippling in my mind.

But the image fades, and the sound rings clear. Someone knocking on the weight room door.

"Caleb?" The muffled voice is blanket soft, even while shouting.
I recognize it from my childhood immediately.

"It's your mom," I hiss.

But another voice hollers, "Eden? Are you in there?"

"And yours," Caleb says, confusion etched on his brow.

"I guess this means it locked," I say, picking myself up off the
ground. "And that we're saved." I extend a hand to help Caleb, who
takes it, only to tug me down for one more quick kiss.

My insides melt, but I give him a quick jab to the gut for tricking
me. "Coming!" I yell, rushing to open the door.

"Eden," Mom says, her eyes widening in horror as she takes in my bloodied and battered appearance.

"I'm okay, Mom. It's just a nick. Promise."

Cecelia Durham pushes past us to Caleb. "Oh my—what happened to you?" She makes as if to touch his bruised jaw before clutching her hands together. "Who did this?"

The answer to her question sits at the back of my tongue, so heavy I nearly choke on it.

"We don't know," Caleb says. "His face was covered. But we think it's the same guy who killed Diego."

"And Henry," I add.

"Have you called nine-one-one?" Mom asks.

"Neither of us has a phone," I admit. "Mine was destroyed when this freak attacked me."

Mom whips out her phone and steps aside to make the call.

"This finger's broken," Cecelia says to her son. She disappears back into the hall, returning a minute later with a medical wrap, which she uses to secure his hand to his body. "It was good thinking with the ice. Do you need an ambulance?"

It isn't until she moves to stand directly in front of me that I realize she's speaking to *me*. "Eden," she says, lowering to inspect the gash on my neck, "you might need stitches. Should your mother ask for an ambulance?"

"Oh." I blink. "No, I think, well…my mom can drive me."

"I got a ride here," Mom whispers, still holding the phone at her ear.

"Then we'll take my car," Cecelia says with finality.

Mom tells the cops to meet us at the hospital, and then the four of us head to the parking lot.

"How did you find us?" I ask my mother, who's holding on to my arm even though she knows I'm perfectly capable of walking.

"When you never showed up at the booth, I started asking around. Amy Park mentioned that you and Caleb had gone into the school. I called Cecelia to see if she knew what was going on. But I guess she'd been trying Caleb's phone all day with no success."

I struggle to picture my mother calling Cecelia, even out of desperation. Mom was never part of the original Fairport High clique, but when she moved here and started dating my father, she became an honorary member. Most of the memories I have of Mom from when I was little involved Cecelia—CC, as the group called her. She and my mom were best friends before everything took a dive.

"That's because this creep stole Caleb's phone." I slow my steps so that we fall behind the others. "Since when do you speak to Cecelia Durham?" I whisper.

She side-eyes me. "Since you decided to fall for her son."

"Fall for—I did not do that."

"So that's not your blood all over his T-shirt?" Mom's expression is stern, but a smirk lies beneath it.

"I wish May was here," I say, sulking now like a five-year-old. "I need a real friend, one who doesn't make wild accusations or try to perform CSI bloodstain pattern analysis on me."

She wraps an arm around me and kisses my matted hair. "I'm going to talk to Cecelia."

As she drops back with Cecelia, Caleb and I fall into step beside one another. "What are we going to tell the cops?" he whispers.

He drifts behind me, and I start to ask if he needs us to slow down when he switches to my other side, taking my hand in his good one. A fluttery feeling swims in my stomach. "Let's stick to the truth," I say. "They might find your phone, and then we'll have to explain all those texts."

We reach the area of blacktop where the market used to be. It's completely cleaned up now. "And what about the murders?" he asks. "Do we tell them that we saw this person the night Henry died? That they've been stalking us, and it's all connected?"

Suddenly, I remember that I haven't shared anything from this afternoon with Caleb. He doesn't know that I found Adelina or that she believes Starlight Developers is behind the murders. Or that the face behind that group could be my father, the man with the tattoo that matches Nicolas Blackmore's.

I really don't want to do it. If Fairport found out that my father is more than a cheat and a coward—that he's a murderer—it would ruin Mom's life. She'd be completely run out of this town.

Then again, I don't have much of a choice. I can't stay quiet and let my father continue killing kids. Just when I think I've worked up the guts, there's a beep as Mrs. Durham's SUV unlocks.

A moment later, we're all piled in, our mothers up front and Caleb and me in the back. Cecelia starts the drive to the hospital, and I keep hoping the women will strike up a conversation again like they did in the parking lot. Instead, silence settles over us, as solid and impenetrable as a wall. It's crushing, and despite my fingers still entwined in Caleb's, tension seizes my every muscle. The former friends must've said all they have to say.

Cecelia parks the car and turns off the ignition. Seat belts unlatch, but before anyone can exit the SUV, I blurt, "Our attacker had a tattoo!"

Everyone turns to me, and I point at my right wrist. "Right here. It was a shark fin." I force a swallow through my dry throat. "Just like Dad's."

The women exchange a look of shock. After a moment, my mother clears her throat. "Eden, are you sure? It's been years since you saw that tattoo. There must be others like it, especially around here."

Am I sure? It was so fast. The blade was about to strike my throat. Could I have imagined it?

No. I push the doubts back. That tattoo was identical to the one on Nicolas Blackmore's wrist. I knew the moment I saw it on the computer screen, and even in my panic, I knew it in that locker room. "I'm sure. It had to be Dad."

"Except there are two other men with that tattoo," Mom says grimly.

Cecelia shakes her head. "No, it can't be Arturo. He hasn't left the house since Diego passed away. And Jim is out of state on company business. I booked the trip and drove him to the airport myself."

"Wait," I say, looking at Caleb. "They *all* have the same tattoo?"

"Yes," Cecelia says. "They got it together, senior year."

Caleb nods. "They were all friends with Nicolas, like Bianca said."

"*We* were all friends with Nicolas," his mother corrects. "Arturo and Jim are like family to me. They would never hurt Caleb."

"Well, it wouldn't be the first time those men have turned their backs on supposed family," Mom says sardonically.

Cecelia inhales. "Please, Alice. There has to be some other explanation."

"Like Nicolas Blackmore back from the grave?" I ask, anger gathering in my core at the way my mother and I are having to listen to her defend those men.

"No." Cecelia grabs her purse. "Look, tell the police what you saw. I'm confident Arturo and Jim have alibis." She opens the door, but her gaze slides over to my mother, and her eyes—hazel irises that match Caleb's—flood with sadness. "But I'm not sure any of us can say the same for Greg."

I flinch back into my seat. "Are you threatening me? Trying to scare me into keeping silent about what I saw?"

"No," she says, looking truly taken aback. "I didn't mean anything by it, other than what I said. If Greg really is hurting people. If he"—her breath catches—"if god forbid he tried to lay a hand on you or Caleb, than he deserves to be locked up for good. But I just—well, I hope there is some other explanation."

In the passenger's seat, Mom is quiet. Her focus remains on the windshield, and I hate not knowing what she's thinking.

"The Greg I knew was a good kid," Cecelia continues, "who used to help me with my chores and homework. He was always making me laugh. Believe me, I was deeply shocked by everything that happened back at Surfside Cleaning. He was a good man."

"A good man?" A bitter laugh slips past my lips. "Didn't you catch him cheating and fire him?"

She sighs. "I did fire him, yes. But it was the last thing I wanted to do. And I wasn't the one who caught him stealing."

Beside her, Mom finally stirs. "Then who did?"

"I think it was Jim," Cecelia says. "He caught Greg in my office, changing the numbers in the books. Transferring funds from our account to his own."

"Jim?" Mom says, frowning.

"Look," Cecelia says, "it was years ago, and I still feel terrible about the way everything went down. It was wrong of us to cut you and Eden out of our lives. We were just...so hurt by Greg that we didn't know what to say to you."

"So you treated us like *we* were the criminals," I say. "Makes sense. Oh, and telling your kids to make my life hell was a nice touch too."

Cecelia turns around to look me in the eye. "I won't make excuses. I know those kids believed they were acting on our behalf, but it was wrong. I'm so sorry." She faces Mom now, who's still staring out her window. "And, Alice, I don't expect your forgiveness or your friendship. But I need you to know that I'm sorry. I guess it took my son to show me the error of my ways." Her gaze flicks momentarily to Caleb, and she smiles somberly. "I was the worst friend to you when you needed me the most."

I see the slow rise and fall of Mom's chest. Caleb's hand tightens on mine, and I know he's hoping for a miracle. I must be too because I haven't taken a breath since Cecelia stopped speaking.

Mom turns to Cecelia. When her lips part, it feels like my lungs are going to burst. "Let's get these kids fixed up," she says, opening the passenger door. Then she gets out, leaving us with only the sound of her door slamming.

23

AFTER OUR MOTHERS GET US SETTLED IN THE EMER-
gency room waiting area, they check in at the desk. I spot two
police officers entering the double doors and turn to Caleb. "I found
Adelina today."

Caleb's eyes widen. "What? Where?"

"It's a long story. She lives in town, and she doesn't believe her
mother murdered Nicolas anymore." As quickly and as hushed as possible, I tell him about Starlight Developers, how she recognized the
voice of the executives as one of Nicolas's friends from high school. How
I'm afraid it's my dad out there, pretending to have some development
company so he can cover up the evidence of what he's been doing.

Caleb takes a too-long moment to absorb it. The officers
have already spoken to our mothers. Now their gazes light on us.
"Starlight Developers?" he finally asks, eyes shifting from me to his
mother at the desk.

"Yeah, like I said, my dad always used to repeat that 'Star Light,

Star Bright' rhyme when I was little."The emergency room is frigid, so I zip Caleb's sweatshirt up as high as I can, careful to avoid my neck wound. "It's got to be his company."

"I don't know, Eden." Caleb rubs at his clammy forehead with the back of his hand. "It's a common nursery rhyme. You saw the tattoo, but your father isn't the only guy who has it. He wasn't the only friend whose voice Adelina could've recognized. What about Arturo Rodriguez?"

"If everything is connected, that means our attacker from the weight room killed Diego. Why would Arturo murder his own son?"

"Yeah." Caleb looks lost in thought. "And my mom says Jim O'Sullivan is away on business."

I can't help wondering if Cecelia Durham is telling the truth about Jim. If she knows more than she's said. Of course, I can't say this to Caleb. "Some football players have keys to the locker room," I say quietly, looking down at the tile. "You don't think Jameson—"

"I don't know," Caleb says. "Maybe his dad took it?"

"But your phone." My stomach knots. "Jameson was with it last."

"Let's leave Jameson out of it," Caleb says, his voice pleading. "At least until we know more. When we speak to the cops, let's focus on the facts."

Only I *am* focusing on the facts. We know Jim O'Sullivan has the tattoo. We know that twenty-five years ago, Jim was in love with Bianca. Then, as soon as they broke up, who did she start dating?

Nicolas Blackmore.

It sounds like a motive to me.

When I open my mouth to say more, a woman's voice calls out, "Eden Stafford."

Over at the doors to the triage area, a nurse with a clipboard looks out at the room expectantly. "I guess they heard, 'Knife to the throat,'" I say to Caleb with a shrug.

"Pretty badass." He smiles proudly.

"Definitely more badass than getting hit by a weight you threw yourself." I wince. "You might be here a while."

"I'm never going to live that down, am I?" He leans in, his lips grazing my cheek.

"Never," I say, a tipsy, buzzy feeling coming over me at his kiss as I head over to the nurse.

———

When I'm finally bandaged up, the doctor allows the two police officers into the room.

"Hello, Eden," says the first officer, a woman with blond hair and a kind smile. She turns to my mother, seated in the corner. "Mrs. Stafford," she adds. "I'm Officer Schultz." She looks barely older than me. "This is Officer Salazar." She gestures to the older man, who offers a curt nod as he readies his notepad.

"Hi," I say, my voice hoarse.

"We're going to ask you a few questions about tonight's ordeal," Officer Schultz says.

"Oh," I say. "Shouldn't we get my friend? He and I were there together."

Officer Schultz smiles again. "We'd prefer to interview the two of you separately."

Despite the affirming look on her face, my chest tightens. This is already starting to feel like an interrogation. "Okay."

"Officer," Mom says, "my daughter has been through a lot tonight. Why can't she have her friend with her?"

Schultz's lips tighten. "It's a small room."

"Then we can go somewhere else," Mom says, starting to get up.

"I'll be up front with you," Officer Schultz says. "We're trying to get the facts straight. Your daughter and her friend were trespassing on school property, and we'd like to understand why."

"My daughter was attacked tonight. Someone tried to *kill* her."

"And why were you on campus tonight, Eden?" Officer Schultz asks as if my mother weren't there.

"Everyone was," I say, "for the farmer's market."

"In the parking lot," she corrects. "Not the classrooms."

"Technically, we were in the weight room," I say, immediately regretting it. This woman, who seemed so kind moments ago, doesn't give up the faintest smile. "I got a text to meet my friend—eh, Caleb—outside of the weight room."

"You keep referring to Mr. Durham as a friend," Schultz says, lifting a brow. "Sure that's all he is?"

"Yes," I say too quickly. "I mean, I don't know. Maybe we're something—we haven't exactly had the *talk*, okay?"

Across the room, Salazar scribbles in his notebook furiously. My stomach clenches.

"Why did Mr. Durham need you to meet him outside the weight room?"

"Well, he didn't. It wasn't actually a text from him. I mean, I didn't know it at the time, but this person who attacked us, they'd stolen his phone and used it to text me."

"I see," Schultz says, her voice drenched in skepticism. "And how, uh, did you draw this conclusion?"

"Because this person has been following us for days. They—I mean *he*," I correct, still struggling to comprehend how we could've all believed the person who chased us that night in the ruins was female. "He attacked Victoria Whitlock in her pool yesterday. We think he killed Diego Rodriguez and Henry De Rossi. He set Caleb and me up tonight with the intent to *kill* us."

Schultz and Salazar exchange an inscrutable look. "Diego and Henry? The boys who committed suicide?"

"No," I say, gritting my teeth. "They didn't…"

Before I can hash out my thoughts, Schultz asks, "And how did you and Mr. Durham end up inside the weight room?"

I shrug. "I saw a light on and thought Caleb was inside. Some of the athletes have keys to the room, so they can work out after school hours."

Schultz frowns. "I see. But Mr. Durham wasn't in the room?"

"No, our attacker was. I don't know how he got in."

She scratches at her hair. "Eden, we were just speaking to Mr. Durham in the triage room where he was being treated. And we found his phone in his sweatshirt pocket. His mother moved his pile of clothes so she could sit down, and"—she shrugs—"the phone fell out."

"What? No, that's—it doesn't make any sense. He didn't text me. He followed me to the weight room when this other person texted. My attacker."

"And did you get a look at this person's face? Your *attacker*?" Schultz says it like there never was any attacker, and my blood starts to simmer.

"I didn't slice my own throat!" I shout, immediately struck by a wave of dizziness.

Mom stands and moves to me. "Eden, calm down. Do you want to end this?"

"No," I say. "I want them to listen to me. I want them to find this guy before he kills again."

"A description would help," says Salazar, whose voice is jarringly soft for his strong build and stoic face. "You keep saying *he*? Did you get a look at this guy?"

"I mean, no, not really," I admit. "They wore a dark mask. And a hood, pulled tight." I demonstrate what I mean.

"Why do you refer to the attacker as male?" he asks.

I freeze, caught. "I, uh, I guess because of the way he fought Caleb," I say, not sure I should say it. "And…because of the tattoo. He had a tattoo that I've seen before."

I explain the tattoo, the list of suspects. The officers promise to look into it, but they seem far more concerned about whether or not the school will press charges about the breaking and entering and property damage in the weight room.

As they're about to leave the room, Officer Schultz stops in the doorway. "We'll be in touch. Until then, try not to trespass at night. That'll help."

I don't respond. I'm too frustrated, too confused. Caleb's phone was in his pocket? They're acting like it's our fault that we were nearly killed tonight.

The longer this goes on, the more apparent the solution becomes. It sits at the forefront of my mind, a hulking thing of dread. A thing of wreck and rot.

If the police aren't going to intervene in this—if they're not going to find the killer—then I'm going to have to find the truth the only way I can. I know this person is worried about whatever's hidden in the ruins. That they believe it will lead to their capture.

I'll have to do the very thing the cops just forbade.

I'll have to trespass on the Fairport Village ruins one last time.

October 17

Dear Diary,

I'm going to fight. I found someone a few towns over, a mystic of sorts. He told me I could perform a cleansing ritual over the place where Mrs. Blackmore cursed the town. He sold me some herbs and beads to aid in the ritual, and gave me the words to chant.

Tomorrow night, I have to go back to that place of rot and ruin. The only way out of this curse is to break it myself. If I don't try, I'll never be free.

24

THE NEXT MORNING, I WAKE UP AT 10:53 A.M. WITH aching muscles and a stinging pain where I was cut. Mom must've decided school was a bad idea.

On my bedside table is a note from her. *Had to go in to work. Use Mrs. Napoli's phone if you need anything. Love, Mom*

It would take a pretty massive emergency for me to venture over to Mrs. Napoli's house and risk getting sucked into one of her tales. Like the one where an earthworm singlehandedly decimated her vegetable garden.

Without a phone though, I can't call Caleb. I wonder how he's doing, if he went to school. I feel a warm flush as last night's kiss rushes back.

But it's quickly followed by a feeling of unease. Last night, I never got the chance to ask Caleb how his phone ended up in his sweatshirt pocket. By the time I'd been released by the doctor, his mom had already taken him home. I guess Mom had made it clear that we'd be getting an Uber.

The phone had to be the killer messing with us. He must've planted it on Caleb. Though…I am wondering how this guy managed to pull it off.

It couldn't hurt to swing by Caleb's house, just to make sure the doctors didn't have to amputate that finger.

And to ask him some questions.

———

An hour later, Caleb greets me at the door, looking battered and bruised, his hair disheveled in a sleepy, hot kind of way. "Hey," he says, looking surprised to see me.

"Hey." I already regret coming here. Things might be weird now, after everything last night. "How'd your interview go?"

"Terrible," he says. "Didn't help that my main injury came from, well, *me*." He holds up his left hand, showing off the splint on his index finger.

I shake my head. "That was never going to look good."

"No, and it definitely didn't help that the cops found my phone in my things while they were in my hospital room. With all those texts luring you to the weight room."

"Yeah, they might've mentioned that and used it as a reason to discredit everything I said. What the hell happened?"

"They made me change into a hospital gown, and then had me leave my clothes in the room while the nurse took my mom and me down the hall to do an X-ray." He glances down at the splinted finger. "That had to have been when the killer snuck it back in there. I just don't know how this person slipped past the hospital staff. For all we know, the cops planted it in there themselves."

Maybe because, like everyone in this town, the cops are friends with Jim O'Sullivan. If he's the guy who attacked us, maybe he called in a favor.

"But how are you?" Caleb asks, concern in his expression now.

"Fine, mostly. My head didn't fall off last night, so I consider it a win."

"That's good, I guess?" He clears his throat, his eyes lowering to the welcome mat. "I know I consider part of last night a win."

"Oh yeah?" I'm fighting a smile so hard my face hurts. "Which part?"

His lips quirk. "You know which part," he says quietly.

Before I can tease him any further, he leans in to kiss me on the cheek. Stunned into silence, I let him tug me along into the house I haven't been in since I was a child. It smells the way I remember it—jasmine and vanilla—back when the five of us kids were running around, shattering Cecelia's vases and dripping sticky Popsicle juice onto the furniture.

"Is your mom at work?" I ask, looking at the family photos on the wall.

"Yeah, she'll be out for a while."

"That gives us time to do some actual research on Starlight Developers. Get to the bottom of it."

His shoulders slump. "That was the first thing I did when I woke up. I can't trace them back to an actual human being."

"Damn," I mutter, wondering if I should bring up that horrible plan that keeps niggling at me. It may be the only option. And I could use his help breaking back in—*if* I can convince him.

"Can I get you some water?" he asks. "Tea?"

I blink, still stunned at times by his behavior. How it contradicts everything I thought I knew about him. "Tea would be lovely. But are you sure you can manage in your condition?"

He presses his lips flat. "Funny, Eden. It's a broken finger. You make yourself at home. We do have Netflix. I know how much you like true crime documentaries, so I added a bunch to my watch list."

I can only stare with my lower jaw hanging open. He's starting toward the kitchen when the doorbell rings.

"Oh," he says, doubling back. "I hope it's okay that I asked Victoria to join us."

"What?" He might as well have brewed the tea and tossed it at me. Did everything last night mean nothing to him? "Why?" So much for this guy getting me.

"Just to talk strategy," he assures me.

"But she didn't bring Jameson," I say, worry spiking as I race past him to block the door. "I know he's your friend, but we can't ignore the fact that his dad might be involved."

"No Jameson, I promise." He takes my hand in his good one, squeezes it, and keeps it as he turns the lock and opens the door.

Victoria moves to throw her arms around Caleb but halts, her gaze slipping to our entwined hands. "You could've told me about last night," she bites out, and my fingers loosen in Caleb's grip. "I had to see the cops all over the place, yellow tape around the whole athletic wing, and then put it together with the fact that you weren't at school."

"I'm sorry, Vic," Caleb says softly, and my heart sinks at his use of this nickname, spoken like a term of endearment. "It was a late night with the cops."

"So are they going to find this guy?" She shoves right between us into the house.

"Not likely," I say. "They didn't seem to believe our story."

She rolls her eyes and helps herself to the couch. "What the hell is wrong with this town? That's exactly how I felt when I was nearly murdered in my own backyard. What are we going to do about it?"

"That's what we need to decide," Caleb says.

"And we're really going to keep Jameson in the dark?" Victoria asks. "I mean, I get the whole tattoo thing with his dad, but he's our best friend."

"He's *your* best friend, who stole Caleb's phone yesterday," I correct, "which the perp then used to try and lure me to my death."

"You can't prove that," she bites back.

"This is the safest way," I say.

She crosses her arms, and I think she's going to argue the point further when she says, "So then what are we going to do?"

"The first thing *I'm* going to do is make tea," Caleb says, motioning for me to take a seat on the cushiony chair across from Victoria. "You want some, V?"

"Coffee would be amazing, thanks." She smiles sweetly.

Caleb glares at her, and I have to hold back a laugh. The moment he exits the room, Victoria turns on me like an eagle ready to rip a worm from its comfy hole in the dirt.

"So you and Caleb, huh?" Her tone is anything but casual.

I look down at my hands fidgeting of their own accord. "Mm-hmm." I start to get up. "Maybe I should go help him."

"Guess I always saw it coming," she says.

I lower back onto the chair. "You did?"

She presses her lips flat. "Even as kids he was practically obsessed with you. Don't you remember how he would always steal an extra cookie for you and hide it in the disgusting pocket of his shorts?" She cringes.

"I forgot about that," I admit, combating a smile.

Victoria sighs. "He's always been in love with you. Even when the two of you weren't speaking, he was always watching out for you. This one time, in U.S. History, you left your study guide for the final exam on your desk." She rolls her eyes. "He thought he was being so covert about it, but I saw him pick it up. Then later that day, he snuck it into your backpack."

My mouth falls open. I remember that day. My class notes were always tucked within my binder, so when I saw the study guide loose in my backpack, I assumed May had put it there.

"Look," she says as the kettle starts to whistle in the kitchen, "I was a brat. I kept telling myself that I was allowed to be that way with you. That I could treat you like crap because of all the drama between our parents. Only that wasn't why I did it. Not really. It was because..." Now she's the one struggling to maintain eye contact. "I was jealous," she says quickly. "I hated that Caleb looked at you like you were this rare autographed soccer jersey or something. Like he had to get his hands on it. And I was just—well, I wasn't *you*. I ruined homecoming freshman year for both of you because I couldn't deal with any of it. But I wish I hadn't. I wish I'd realized that my selfishness was keeping him from being happy. That I was hurting one of my best friends. And I wish"—her voice lowers to a barely perceptible mumble—"I'd understood that you weren't the enemy."

She glances up at me, waiting for a response. It wasn't an apology exactly. But whatever it was, it was very *Victoria*.

"Wait a minute," I say, a memory emerging like the sun through the clouds. "Caleb had to steal an extra cookie for me...because you always ate mine!"

She blushes. "Pretty sure that was Jameson." She tucks her elbows in tight and smooths a strand of hair.

There's a shuffle from the doorway, where Caleb hovers with two mugs. I don't know how long he's been standing there. He joins us, placing both mugs on the coffee table in the center of the set-up. "So, you two hashed out a game plan, I presume?" he asks coyly, and I know he heard way too much.

"We were getting to it." I reach for my tea.

"You guys," Victoria says, leaning in, "something weird happened at school this morning. Naomi Lamb stopped me before first period." She sits back now, a sly smile on her lips.

"And?" Caleb says, taking the bait.

"And she said she heard about what happened to you two last night, and she was babbling about the curse being real. She said we never should've gone into the ruins for the senior overnighter. She claimed she can prove that Mrs. Blackmore is back from the dead. She actually tried to get me to come with her to her house, like right then." Victoria throws up a hand. "She's a lunatic, right?"

"Her sister was murdered," I say, keeping my voice steady as my hand quivers around the mug handle. "She's obviously still traumatized. I doubt Henry's and Diego's deaths are helping." I look to Caleb. "I'd like to know what she's talking about though. This proof."

"But you saw a flesh and blood human in the weight room," Victoria says. "You don't think she could actually have anything worth our time?"

"I don't know." I blow on my tea. "Probably not. The best thing for us and our possibly *short* time is the cops looking into my tip about the tattoo. But that's not seeming likely. Which is why I think we have to handle this ourselves."

"What do you mean?" Caleb asks. "Like, track down the killer?"

"No, like go to the Village and find whatever smoking gun—or in this case, knife—is buried there. Whatever has this guy scared enough to kill kids in order to keep them out of those ruins."

"That's a terrible idea," Victoria says. "Like, horrendously awful. If we don't go into the Village ruins, there's a chance we could live. If we go into the ruins, there's a one hundred percent chance of death."

"I know," I say, burying my face in the steam. When I come up for air, they're both looking at me like I'm as far gone as Naomi Lamb. "Okay, hear me out," I say. "Ten years ago, seniors went onto the land, and Farah Palmer died. With a whole class full of seniors, word was bound to get out to Nicolas's killer that kids would be on the property snooping around. Same with our overnighter. Right, Victoria? You and Diego weren't even supposed to be there."

"And Esther Lamb?" she asks smugly. "She didn't die at an overnighter."

It's a good point. I'm not sure how the killer found out that Esther was sneaking around the property. "Hidden cameras?" I suggest. "It makes sense, doesn't it? If this person is so anxious about someone finding that knife, then he'd be monitoring the place."

Caleb tilts his head. "And how come this developer hasn't ever managed to find the knife?"

"Because Mr. Blackmore hid it beneath one of the foundations. Maybe beneath the main house, but more likely in a secret cottage crawl space that only the family knew about. Adelina's searched all of them except Sea Glass Shore. So that's where we need to look."

"Before the evidence is gone for good," Caleb says.

"Right." I take a tentative sip of tea, finding the temperature perfect. "Do we have any idea when the place is getting knocked down?"

"The police tape has been gone since last Thursday," Victoria says. "I noticed on a morning run."

"So then it's no longer a crime scene. That means it could happen any day."

"Any minute, really," Caleb mutters.

"Then we should go tonight," I say. "Just the three of us. We tell no one." I look at Victoria. "And I mean *no one*. Especially if their father might be involved."

Victoria crosses her arms. "Technically, *your* father might be involved."

I start to rub at one eye, getting the distinct urge to claw it out and end up the town's new one-eyed ghost lady. But Caleb takes my hand from my face and laces his fingers through mine.

Victoria gives a dramatic eye roll. "I have to get back for a student council meeting."

"Okay, so tonight?" I let go of Caleb's hand to put her at ease. "Are you in?"

She starts to twist her long hair in front of one shoulder. "I don't know. It's a bad idea, like I said. What are we supposed to do if this freak comes after us?"

"We'll go prepared," Caleb says, his fist tightening. "I'd love a rematch against this bastard."

"Okay, relax," Victoria says. "We could fight. Or"—she lets the twist go, and her hair falls back into perfect shape—"get in, get out, and not get caught."

"Yes, that." I attempt to salute her with my mug, but it knocks into the armrest. Lukewarm tea cascades onto my jean shorts. "Damnit." I right the mug, but it's too late. My shorts are soaked. Luckily, the drops avoided Mrs. Durham's nice chair.

"Are you okay?" Caleb asks, already on his feet.

"Yeah." I wave him off. "It wasn't hot. Just managed to ruin another piece of clothing my mom actually approved of."

"You can save them," Victoria says. "Go to the bathroom and soak them in cold water. Add a little of the hand soap; add hot water. Let them soak for five more minutes."

"And should I just walk around here in my underwear?" The instant the words are out, my cheeks burn.

Caleb chuckles, and I avoid his eyes when he says, "I'll bring you some shorts."

"I think I'd rather stick with this brown stain on my shorts than talk about this for another second."

"Just do it," Victoria says, like that's the end of it.

"Fine. You, uh, must spill tea on yourself often." I never thought I'd be taking laundry instructions from Victoria Whitlock, but here we are.

Inside the bathroom, I follow the queen's commands, soaking the shorts in the sink. Then I'm left standing and waiting, praying I don't have to call out a reminder to Caleb to bring me some shorts. As I alternate between checking on the shorts and listening for

Caleb, my eye catches on something hanging on the wall beside the mirror.

It's a framed poem, much like the one Mom has up in our bathroom, "The Road Not Taken" by Robert Frost.

Only the author of this one is CC Durham. In the top-right corner is a hand-painted gold four-pointed star.

And the title of the poem is "Made of Starlight."

25

THE KNOCK ON THE DOOR RATTLES ME.

"Eden?" Caleb calls. "I found you some shorts. They'll be big, but—"

"That's great, thanks!" My voice comes out much too loud, too squeaky.

My brain is still trying to puzzle together how Cecelia Durham could be involved in all of this. She could be one of the developers. She wasn't the caller, since Adelina said it was the voice of one of Nicolas Blackmore's *male* friends.

But even Cecelia admitted she'd been *a* friend. She could be part of this somehow. She definitely had access to Caleb's sweatshirt in the hospital. Is there any chance that Caleb's entire showdown in the weight room was staged?

Caleb must've known his mom was involved in the development company, at the very minimum. I saw the look on his face when I mentioned Starlight Developers. But he didn't say anything—even when I threw my own father under the bus.

Everything is spinning as I crack open the door to retrieve the soccer shorts from him. He's right; they're enormous. I roll them a few times and ask for another minute to wring out my own shorts. Then I prop myself up against the wall and watch the room flip.

Could everything with Caleb be fake? Just as I'd feared from the beginning?

No. I didn't tell him about Starlight Developers until after he confessed his feelings for me. Until after we kissed. I have to confront this now. If I don't trust him, there's no way I can show up at the ruins tonight.

"How do they fit?" he asks when my vision finally clears enough to open the door.

"Like a glove," I say. "If you could stuff all your fingers into one of the glove fingers. Told you I'd own your whole closet eventually."

"You were right." Caleb grins and takes both of my hands, pulling me closer.

I stretch my neck to look past him down the hall. "Where's Victoria?"

"She went to that student council thing. But she's coming tonight. We'll meet before the Village to fine-tune some of the details of our plan." His eyes narrow as he peers down at me. "What's wrong?"

"You never told me your mom was a poet." I push the bathroom door open to point to the wall hanging. "Why did you keep the Starlight thing from me?"

His face falls. "Because I know my mom has nothing to do with this. And I didn't want you to worry that she did."

"Which is *exactly* what I'm worried about now! And that my boyfriend had something to do with this!" My stomach drops. I want to hide. "I mean, that you, Caleb, have something to do with this."

He blinks, and when his blue eyes gleam, I know it's not because of my relationship-labeling blunder. "You're really worried that my mother is killing kids and that I'm trying to cover it up?"

"No," I say, even though that's precisely what I was considering a moment ago. "Of course not. I just want to know what's going on. Why does your mom's poem have the same logo as the Starlight Developers website?"

"I'm trying to figure that out. I really did wake up and dig for information on Starlight Developers." He nibbles his lower lip, gaze shifting to the floor. "Only I did some of it in my mom's home office."

My head draws back. "You did?"

"Yeah. I even searched her computer but couldn't find anything. She either has no knowledge of the company and the Starlight thing is a coincidence, or every trace of it is at work. My theory is that she might've helped start the company at Jim or Arturo's request, not knowing exactly why they wanted to move from the cleaning side of things into property development."

"Unless…" It's too much of a stretch. "You don't think your mom could secretly be in contact with my dad, do you?" Caleb frowns, but I press on. "Out of everyone, your mom is the only person who still seems to care about my dad. Maybe it's because she never stopped being his friend. Or maybe he reached out to her about this new venture, and they reconnected."

"No." He shakes his head. "That's not…"

"She wouldn't have known she was doing anything wrong. The opposite, actually. She'd be thinking she was going rogue, helping the outcast get back on his feet. She's a saint when you look at it from that perspective."

He's quiet now. "Do you really think your dad is capable of murder? Of trying to murder *you*?"

"I can't say," I answer honestly, sadness thickening like syrup in my chest. "I don't really know my dad."

———

At 11 p.m., dressed in long layers to brave the cold beachy night, I inch my door open and peek down the dark hall. The house is still, Mom's bedroom door shut as I tiptoe past it and down the stairs. I reach the landing, running a mental list of everything I packed: candy, water, garden spade in case "buried in the Village ruins" requires actual digging, and the hunting knife complete with a leather sheath I stole from my dad's old gear.

Then I'm out the door and into the cold night. I get down the porch steps and cross the driveway, backpack bobbing as I make my way toward the street.

"Hey." I leap at the low voice. Caleb emerges from the shadows, and I glower at him.

In the fading porch light, he smirks. "You're more scared of *me* than you were of our attacker."

"What are you doing skulking around in the dark, Durham?"

"I came to get you," he whispers. "I ended up having to park down that way. There was a nosy neighbor poking around where you told me to wait."

"Mrs. Napoli. Good at making pasta from scratch. Better at talking your ear off." Together we head down the sidewalk, past the clump of bony-branched trees at the end of the street to his truck.

He opens the passenger side door to let me in, and I find Victoria in the back seat. Once I'm settled, backpack heavy on my lap, we make the drive and attempt to discuss the plan. But we're all on edge, all undoubtedly contemplating the fact that we're going inside the one place we should never enter.

To avoid any trespassing calls, Caleb parks the truck downtown, and the three of us walk the rest of the way to Fairport Village. The last time I passed through here was with Henry at my side, and I feel his absence as I brave the dark alleyway.

Beside me, Caleb accidentally kicks a pebble, which clinks unnervingly off a metal dumpster. Victoria is surprisingly quiet, though she keeps asking to use her phone as a light. We agreed on a no-flashlight policy until we get deeper into the ruins, so only the moonlight guides our way. I scan the area for any sign of life. The coast seems clear. There's a breach in the chain-link fence, and Caleb opens it so I can crawl through. The cool, briny air turns stale and smells of rotting vermin as I emerge inside the Village. I grab my throat, struggling to breathe.

But just as fast as it started, a fresh gust of wind kicks up. I'm left wondering if I imagined it. One by one, Caleb pushes our backpacks through the fence, the jagged metal jaws snagging the nylon fabric. The second he and Victoria are through, the clouds smother the half-moon. Darkness engulfs us.

We start to shoulder our packs when a voice—eerily soft—stops us all dead.

October 18

Dear Diary,

I'm writing from the Village, crouched in the corner of the cottage Hazel called Sea Glass Shore. I tried to perform the ritual, but she appeared and stole all my herbs and my beads. Though now I'm not sure she is a _she_ at all. I don't know if it's human or monster. All I know is that it wants me dead and there's no escape.

    It's everywhere I look. Behind me. Before me.

    Even now, I hear the swish of fabric outside the door. I won't be able to tell my family goodbye in person, so this diary will have to do.

    That black cloak that stalks my dreams is about to carry me into the next life.

    Take care. I love you all so much.

                          Love,
                          Esther

26

"STOP," THE VOICE REPEATS AS A SHADOW DRIFTS toward us through the alleyway.

"It's a ghost," I whisper to Caleb, who silences me with an elbow nudge.

Naomi Lamb steps up to the chain-link fence, her pale skin nearly translucent beneath the moonlight. Her white-blond hair shivers in the wind. Eyes an icy shade of blue as they stare through me. "You shouldn't be in there."

A viselike terror grips my chest. "Naomi," I say, "you can't tell anyone we're here. This isn't a senior thing; this is important. If you tell, more kids will die."

"What are you talking about?" Her fingers move to thread the chain links, but she pulls back, lowering her hands to her sides.

"There's a killer out there," I explain. "The man who really killed Nicolas Blackmore. The cops won't listen to us, but the evidence that can pin this guy to the crime is buried somewhere on the land.

If we find it, we get him. If we don't—and *soon*—this whole place will be bulldozed and the killer will get away with everything. Even your sister's death."

"No." She shakes her head. "It's not a man. It's that evil woman. My sister saw her. She"—Naomi pulls something from her cross-body bag—"just look at this. Please." She passes a small book through the opening in the fence.

Caleb and I exchange a nervous glance, but I take it, opening it to the first page. It's too dark to make out anything, so Caleb motions us along behind a palm tree and clicks on his light. "It's a diary," I say as Victoria and Caleb push in to read the first entry over my shoulder.

We skim each entry, following as Esther descends deeper and deeper into the Fairport Village curse lore. Further and further into seeming madness.

Only I've been this girl. I know she isn't mad, because I've been stalked by the same cloak-wearing devil Esther claims was following her.

When we finish the final entry, dated October 18, the day Esther Lamb was killed—Caleb shuts off the flashlight, and we near the fence.

"Look, Naomi," I say hesitantly, "all three of us understand how your sister got to this point. We're headed down the exact same trail, and at times, we've believed we were being chased by a ghost. But I saw this guy with my own two eyes—he is made of flesh and blood."

She holds the diary tight against her stomach, gaze lowering to the trash near my feet. "You really think this person killed Esther?"

"Yes," I say.

She sucks in a breath, and for a moment, I think she's about to cry. "Because I'll admit, I had my doubts about the ghost. But at least some supernatural version of Mrs. Blackmore explained how she knew my sister had stepped onto the property."

"We think this psycho has some sort of surveillance set up," Victoria says, "and the moment your sister set foot on the land, he came and—"

"He hurt her," Caleb cuts in, and I sling him a grateful look. Esther's murder isn't as fresh as Henry or Diego's; still, that kind of thing can't ever really go away. Not when it's family.

"We can't say if it was because Esther got too close to his secret," I add, "or if it was simply to use her as an example. Something to keep the legend alive."

"And you're going in there to prove otherwise," she says, sounding unconvinced.

"Yes," I say. "To get justice for your sister, and for Henry and Diego. For Nicolas Blackmore and Adelina, whose brother was killed and mother committed suicide. This monster ruined so many lives, and we need to keep him from hurting anyone else."

"Then," she says, putting the diary back in her bag, "I'm coming with you."

"You what?" I look to the others in panic. I can't be responsible for one more person in this beachfront deathtrap.

"No," Victoria says, already turning away from her.

"Please." Naomi's lips purse, and now she really looks like she's going to cry. "I have to do this, for my sister."

Victoria continues striding in the direction of the first cottage.

I shut my eyes and take a deep, calming breath. "Wait, Victoria," I hiss into the dark.

"Oh my god," she groans. "Don't fall for this. She's a liability, and you know it. Plus, she's not in on the plan, so we'd have to waste even more time briefing her."

"She has as much stake in this as the rest of us," Caleb offers. "Maybe more."

"Wouldn't hurt to have more hands to dig," I say.

Victoria rolls her eyes. "Whatever. You were the one who wanted to keep this operation small. Now it's on you if she tells someone and either gets us arrested or killed."

"I won't, I promise," Naomi says. "I just want to help you search." She makes to duck through the breach in the fence but stops. She licks her lips, studying the fence and then peering past us into the ruins.

"Any day now." Victoria puts her hands on her hips.

"Sorry, I just…I know you said the curse isn't real. But up until a moment ago, I believed it killed my sister. That if I set foot on that side"—she flicks her chin in our direction—"I would be next."

Victoria flashes a saccharine grin beneath the moonlight. "This is great. Because we're not on a time crunch at all. You take your time. And you know what? Go ahead and put that call in to the killer too, while you're making up your mind."

Naomi's features draw taut. She stares down the fence one last time, tucks her hair behind her ear, and lowers herself to slip through the opening.

As I help her to her feet, she's shivering. "It's okay," I say, but she glances back at the opening like she just left the land of the living for good.

I only hope she isn't right.

Together, the four of us head into the shadowy wasteland. We take to a path stitched with greenery and cluttered with debris. Naomi's presence won't change our plan to stick to one location at a time, since no one will want her as a search partner. We can use her as an extra lookout.

The wind rustles every leaf, every crumpled piece of trash scattered over the terrain. The loose beams groan and creak. I can't keep my eyes from darting in every direction, my heart from seizing with every sound and flutter of movement.

Caleb reaches for my hand, and I instinctively swat it away.

"Sorry," he says. "It's going to be okay, Eden."

"I know that. But I don't need a bodyguard."

"I wasn't trying to be your bodyguard," he says quietly. "Can't a guy hold his girlfriend's hand?" There's a smirk in his voice.

I keep looking dead ahead, speechless. "I didn't—I mean I—"

"That is, if you want to be my girlfriend." We stop on the pathway, facing each other now as moonlight filters through the palm leaves in claws of white, close enough for me to feel his breath on my skin. "I know I'd really like that." A few strands of chestnut hair peek from beneath his hood.

Half of my hair is still in its ponytail, the other half blowing in my face—very Beach Sasquatch Barbie. "I mean, I guess so. If it would make *you* happy."

"It would." He grins, running his fingers from my chin up to my cheek, sending a million sparks through me. His other hand moves to my hip, pulling me flush with him. I let my eyes fall shut as his head lowers, lips nearing mine.

"Hey," whispers Victoria from up ahead, and we freeze. "Where'd you guys go?" She turns on her flashlight, and Caleb and I part just before the beam hits me in the face.

"We're coming," I say. "Got my shoe caught in a…sinkhole."

We turn on our own lights and rush to catch up, taking the sharp left to cross the courtyard. "That's where I would've looked." I point to the headless mermaid fountain. "Mr. Blackmore could've shoved it down that sculpture's throat. Back when it had more than a throat."

Caleb lets out an uncomfortable laugh that means we're getting close. We follow Victoria's light onto the narrow path that leads to the beach-facing cottages.

Our lights click off one by one; we can't risk detection by anyone out for a late-night stroll down on the beach. The path is dense with overgrown foliage, making mere shadows of Victoria and Naomi at the end of it. The waves crash, rhythmic but smothering. I can barely hear my own brain telling me to abort this mission. Leaves hang black and fang-like before us, slivers of moonlight trickling through. It's like walking straight into the jaws of an enormous beast when we step past them into the open.

There, at the back of the throat lies our destination: Sea Glass Shore.

27

SEA GLASS SHORE IS BETTER KNOWN IN FAIRPORT AS
Hazel's Lair, the location of one of her infamous episodes. In my
research for the documentary, I learned that Hazel Blackmore liked
to add tiny decorative touches that coordinated with the cottage
names. Daisies for the Darling Daisy, bouquets accented with palm
leaves for Palm Villa. They say she came into this particular cottage
to place a vase of colorful sea glass on the kitchen table. Only by the
time Silas Blackmore dragged her out of here, Hazel had smashed
dozens of vases over every inch of the place, covering it in tiny sharp
fragments of glass.

"Where to?" Victoria asks.

"Adelina said the way beneath the structure was under the
porch," I say, leading the way around the cottage. We reach the front,
and I check our surroundings, moving closer to the rock wall to get
a clean shot down the front of the resort. There are no signs of life,
apart from the crustaceans skittering over the boulders.

I start to turn when something flaps in my periphery. It's only a gull landing on the Founder's Slab a few yards away. I scan the area in the opposite direction, toward the cliff. Satisfied, I hurry back to where the others are investigating the sides of the porch.

"This thing is boarded up," Victoria says, touching the panel and flinching back.

I reach out to feel, and my fingertips sink into the rotted wood. "Maybe we just knock it down?"

"It's not like Mr. Blackmore had time to knock it down and rebuild it the night he frantically hid that knife from the cops," she argues. "This can't be the spot."

"Hold on," Caleb calls from the other side of the porch. "Will someone help me out here?"

I head around, finding him kneeling before the panel.

"Can you hold this?" he asks, handing off the flashlight.

I aim it toward the porch slat and click it on. In its glow, Caleb's finger draws a line down one side, where the board meets the wooden frame. He digs until something falls free: a handle, tucked inside the frame. He tugs and jiggles it, but nothing happens. I shine the light closer to get a better look as he attempts to move it to the left with no luck.

But when he pushes it to the right, sure enough, the panel moves.

Adelina was right. The entrance beneath the foundation was here all along. Hidden from the eyes of the police and the new developers.

"So who's going under there?" Victoria asks.

"I'll go," Caleb says, still crouched by the opening.

"I can go too," I offer, fear planting itself in the center of my chest. I shrug off my backpack, letting it drop to the ground. "You two can keep watch, I guess."

Victoria throws a nervous glance in Naomi's direction. "Great," she mutters, like *she's* the one in danger.

"Or you could crawl into the pit of hell with Caleb," I grit out, unzipping my pack to find that spade. Even if no digging is required, I might need to shoo away a rat or two.

"We'll be good," she says.

Caleb is already ducking beneath the porch when Naomi whispers, "Guys, what's that?"

I glance in the direction she's pointing. The shadow is tall, moving swiftly along the rock wall toward us.

I tug on the back of Caleb's sweatshirt. We scramble to our feet, backing away from the figure clothed in black.

"Let's go!" Victoria calls, already yards away, headed for the cliff.

Only there's nothing that way except a long drop into the ocean. "No," I shout, taking the path back through the resort, Caleb and Naomi right behind me. "Come on, Victoria!"

We only make it a few yards when another voice—one entirely too familiar and too loud—calls out, "You invited her but not me?"

Nooo. I freeze in my tracks, hoping this is a dream and I'll wake up. "Pinch me," I tell Caleb. "Actually, knock me out with this." I push my spade toward him.

Caleb swats it away. "How the hell did you find out about this?" he asks as Jameson bumbles his way across the small front yard toward us.

"The better question is why you left me out of the loop. I forgive you though. You've been through a lot lately. Hitting yourself with a weight and all."

"Why on Earth would you tell him that?" I whisper. When I spot Victoria wandering back in our direction, head lowered, I rush to her. "We agreed not to bring Jameson in on this."

"It wasn't me!" she says, lifting her hands.

"I followed you guys," Jameson admits, stepping on an aluminum can, which gives a resounding crunch. "Vic's been dodging me all day. So I monitored the house, and when Caleb came to pick her up, I followed."

He seems far too motivated to keep tabs on us. "Don't you have to wake up early for preseason tackling sessions or something?"

"Funny, Stafford. How's your throat?" He drags an index finger over his neck.

Caleb slings an arm around my waist and pulls me close before I can go feral on the guy, who's twice my size.

Jim O'Sullivan is big, like the guy who attacked us. He has the tattoo. He had the motive to kill Nicolas Blackmore twenty-five years ago. Jameson must be here as his spy.

Victoria begins scolding him, and I pull Caleb to the side of the cottage. "Now what do we do?" I mutter. "We were so close to finding that knife. But we can't tell *him* the plan. He was probably sent here to find that knife and cast it into the sea."

Caleb shrugs. "I guess you and I could check the cottage, and V could take him on some made-up mission. He doesn't know about the knife."

"That's not a bad plan. Only we can't put Victoria in danger."

"I could do it," he offers.

"And leave me alone with those two? Look, if he's really a part of this, then our plan is already dead in the water."

"That leaves us two options," he says. "Abandon the mission or let him help."

"I choose neither," I say, rubbing at my face hard enough to leave a mark.

"I really don't think he's involved," Caleb says. "But I'll talk to V, see what she thinks. In the meantime," he adds, "you get to distract Jameson." With the cottage roof blocking the moon, I can't see his face. But I have a strong feeling he's smirking.

"Perfect. But I'm taking the spade." I follow him across the soggy patch of grass that used to be a yard. "Hey, Jameson," I say. "How's your dad's business trip going?"

This diverts his attention enough to allow Victoria to slip away. Naomi soon wanders after them, leaving me alone with Jameson. "How the hell would I know?" he says, stomping straight toward me. Suddenly, the ten yards between the rock wall and me aren't nearly enough.

I see Henry's body dashed upon the rocks and get a surge of nausea.

I start to move, hedging the cottage, and he follows me onto the covered path. "I assumed the two of you video chat every night with a mug of hot cocoa. Where, uh, did he go?"

"Why are you asking about my dad? And how do you even know he went on a—" Jameson grunts and clobbers a stray branch with his fist. "Damnit! Can we get some light yet? You know what? Screw it." He takes out his phone and turns on flashlight mode.

"And you wonder why we didn't invite you."

"Why do you have a shovel?" he asks.

"It's a spade, and it's for protection from creeps." Since he's taken the liberty and there's nothing we can do now if a neighbor spots his light, I turn on my flashlight. "Why are you here?"

"I want to help get this guy."

"What makes you think it's a man?" I ask, that suspicion crawling around the forefront of my mind.

He lets out a sigh of frustration. "Because the bastard got the best of my guy last night. Durham is a tough son of a bitch. Look, I know you think my dad is involved in this. And if it turns out he is, I want to help anyway."

It catches me off guard. I keep forgetting that Jameson isn't always a complete moron. "Some things just aren't adding up for me. Like the tattoo I saw on my attacker, for example. A tattoo your dad has on his forearm. Or the fact that this guy had a key to the weight room."

"We both know my dad isn't the only dude from Fairport with that tattoo," he says pointedly. "And as for the key, last year some idiot made copies and passed them around. There could be dozens of them floating around out there."

I grit my teeth. "You were alone with Caleb's phone when it was stolen."

"And like I told him, I'm sorry about that. But a super-hot girl was flirting with me in the ice cream parlor. I wasn't exactly keeping tabs on Caleb's phone."

"Well, I don't trust you," I bite out.

"That's your problem, Stafford. This whole mission, on the other hand, it's *all* of our problems." The words are low but come out in a gush, fast and forceful. "Someone is trying to kill everyone who knows about that note left for Henry. And I happen to be one of those people. My friends," he says, voice strained, "happen to be those people. So you know what? You need to back off and let me help, because I'm part of this."

I'm too stunned to answer, so I let him trudge away from me, back toward Sea Glass Shore. His phone's light dances over the cottage and the night sky like a firefly.

Or a signal.

"Hey, Eden," whispers a voice from somewhere near the shrubs.

I check that Jameson is still out near the rocks, then wander to the others.

"So we talked," Caleb says.

"I know you're afraid of him," Victoria says. "But I'm not, Eden. He's my best friend. If you want, I can tell him we're on guard detail while you guys search. But I think it's a waste of manpower."

She may be right. Even if I'm not completely convinced that Jameson can be trusted, we can't afford to waste two sets of hands.

I'm about to say something I know I'll regret when Naomi cuts in, "Or we could test him. If the killer has surveillance, then he's already on his way, regardless of Jameson tipping him off. So then what are we worried about? That Jameson's going to wait around until we find that knife and then snatch it, right? So let's give him a different job. One that might actually help us if he's on our side. One that would get him away from the knife if he's not. See if he goes for it."

There's one problem with this idea: should Jameson *not* go for it, he could decide to trap Caleb and me down beneath the cottage and light the whole place on fire. "What do you suggest?" I ask, keeping this horrific image to myself.

"I've got this," Victoria says without letting Naomi answer. "Hey, Jameson," she calls, hurrying to catch up with him. We follow, backpacks bobbing. "We've got to split up. We need you to keep watch around the perimeter. See if the killer shows up."

His shoulders roll back. "I'm on it," he says, sounding proud to be given the guard role.

"Make sure you text us the moment you see anything weird," Caleb adds.

Jameson nods and salutes him. Just like that, we've gotten rid of him. For now.

"There's your answer," Victoria says, looking at me smugly.

"We'll see if he actually roams the perimeter or sneaks up on us wearing a hood," I say, dropping down to the ground in front of the porch opening. "After you," I tell Caleb, who's shining his light into the endless black void beneath the house.

"How generous of you." He stares at the space another moment, then crawls into it. I watch as it eats him whole.

"Last chance to volunteer as tribute," I say, glancing up at the girls.

"Good luck," Naomi whispers. Beside her, Victoria looks down at me like I'm about to throw myself into a flaming fire. Like I'm headed straight to my death.

I inch myself forward into the dark space, giving Victoria the okay to slide the board shut behind me. "Leave it open a crack," I instruct her. We need to be able to get out on our own, but we can't risk leaving it wide open.

I only make it two inches before crawling headfirst into a spiderweb. I yelp and bat the sticky strings away, shivering.

It's awkward trying to move with the light in one hand and the spade in the other. It gets even trickier when the porch ends. Here, the hollow triangular space converts to a lower, flat space. I get down on my stomach and army-crawl through. This really is the pit of hell, only colder and mustier. Beneath me is some mix of dirt, rocks, and loose cement pieces. I manage to avoid a wire strung from one side of the space to the other, only to hit my head on a hanging pipe. In front of me, Caleb's light arcs around the space, pinging off the boards overhead and to the sides.

I prop myself up on my elbows and use my light to scan the ground. Every few yards, a small brick pillar supports the structure, so I move slowly, checking both the ground and the area ahead of me. Using my spade, I push aside the debris. If I were a knife, where would I be?

Something brushes my ankle, and I jolt, nearly hitting my head on another pipe. "Caleb, stay on *that* side."

"I am on *that* side," he calls, his voice distant.

My body freezes. Then what the hell just touched me? I kick behind me, and something lets out a hiss. I skitter forward so fast I rough up the elbows and knees of my clothes.

"Caleb, there's something down here."

"I heard." He shines his light in my direction. "What do you—oh."

"What was that *oh*? That didn't sound like a good *oh*." It's a venomous snake, or something else that's going to kill me dead for kicking it.

"Come this way," he says, which doesn't make me feel better at all. "It's just a rat."

"*Just* a rat? Just a descendant of the plague-carrying rodent likely responsible for killing off our founders?"

"It's already gone," Caleb says.

"I can't do this," I say, my breathing too fast, bordering on hyperventilating. "I thought I could, but I can't."

"Yes," he says slowly, "you can. It's got to be here somewhere. It doesn't make sense to put it beneath the main house. The developers would've known about that crawl space. They would've looked there."

"Only we've checked just about every inch of this space."

"Not really." He flicks his light to the slats above us, and it hits me: Silas Blackmore could've tucked it on top of one of these low-hanging beams. Or maybe even tied it to a pipe.

"See anything?" Caleb asks.

"Nope," I answer, checking the sides now for some irregularity.

Caleb's phone dings. I hear him shuffling around, reaching for it. "It's Jameson." He comes closer, holding up the phone so I can read the message. When I see the fluorescent green screen, my stomach pushes into my throat, the spade sliding from my grip.

Jameson O'Sullivan: Something's coming.

28

"WE HAVE TO GET OUT OF HERE," I RASP, ATTEMPTING to turn around in this tiny space.

"Right behind you," Caleb says.

I swat my hand through the dirt, trying to find where I dropped the spade. My knee bumps it, but my elbow lands in a puddle. Shuddering, I continue on, my elbows and knees screaming out.

I reach the panel and call up to the girls. "Hey, help us out here!"

No answer. The lever Caleb used is only accessible from outside of the crawl space. I try to dig my fingers into the crack Victoria left me, but it isn't wide enough. I try the spade, but it doesn't fit either. *Damn you, Victoria Whitlock.* I reach around me for something to pry it apart. "We need a stick."

"How about this?" he asks, digging something from his pocket. He moves his thumb around one side, releasing a blade. I startle, but take it from him, jamming the tip into the narrow space. "Here," he says, moving alongside me. "You push from there, and I'll pull from this side."

"One, two, three." I throw my entire weight onto the knife, and at the opposite end of the panel, Caleb grunts.

The panel moves. Just enough so that Caleb can reach past me and pry it open the rest of the way.

I'm about to wiggle out into the open when Caleb's hand falls on my back. "Wait," he whispers. "Turn off your light."

My pulse speeds up. "Why?"

"The girls were supposed to be out there keeping watch. Only they're not."

My heart catches in my throat. "Oh," I breathe. "Jameson." Victoria trusted him. She was so convinced of his innocence that she let him stay, and he must've… I can't let my mind wander to that place. Not now. "Do you think that text was meant to lure us out there?"

"I don't know," he says. "But we can't stay in here. The girls might be in trouble."

"Here." I hand him the knife. "Better get it ready."

Carefully, he peeks his head through the opening. My heart hammers loud enough to drown out the waves. "I think it's clear," he says, holding the knife in front of him as he inches forward through the hole.

I follow him through, spade in hand. Everything is too dark, and it's not just the lack of light. It's like I'm too afraid to take a full breath as Caleb helps me to my feet. He tugs me along to the front of the cottage, where we press our backs against the facade. I try to stay as still as possible, but I begin to tilt, my shoulder bumping Caleb's arm.

"Are you okay?" he whispers.

I nod. "Just lack of air down there and, you know, mold spores. Must've got to my lungs." He can't know that it's actually my fears that have me suffocating. That Jameson was right about me all along.

Jameson, who's out here somewhere in the dark and mist, waiting for us.

"Should I text Victoria?" he asks.

"I don't know. What if the killer hears her phone?" I think about Naomi next and realize that no one bothered to get her number. She could be hiding somewhere, helpless and alone.

"Damnit," he growls, arm muscles tense at my side. "But we can't help them if we don't know where they are."

"Yeah," I say, knowing we have to make this impossible decision. "I just—I think—"

Then a scream cuts through my words, rattling me to the core.

"V," Caleb says, eyes wide with terror as he pushes off the wall.

I follow him. The panic, the scream ringing in my ear— everything echoes the night we found Henry's body down in the water.

We tear across the yard to the rock wall, scanning the area in every direction.

"Where the hell is she?" he asks, panting as he scales the boulders.

"I don't know." I want to tell him to be careful, but I don't. Victoria is one of his best friends, and that scream… He steps onto the Founder's Slab, tiptoeing out until he's on the edge. One gust of wind could knock him off, sending him over a hundred feet down onto the beach. He clicks his light on to shine it over the shore. "I don't think she—"

He spins the light around in a full arc, then halts, head flinching back. I follow the beam until I see it too: Naomi Lamb, up the wall, in the direction of the cliff.

"Naomi," I call out, rushing toward her while Caleb scrambles down from the rocks.

But when I get within a few yards of her, I get a sudden uneasy feeling. Like those crabs from the rocks are scuttling up my spine. She's just standing there, staring out at the sea the way she did the night of the overnighter. Like she didn't hear that earth-rattling scream moments ago.

Like a killer isn't on the loose somewhere nearby.

I stop so fast that Caleb slams into my back.

"Whoa. What—why are you—" He looks from me to the girl whose white-blond hair sweeps through the air, mimicking those glimmering peaks on the waves below. "Naomi, where's Victoria?"

"I think we should go," I whisper. I don't like this. Not one bit.

But Caleb pushes past me, looking ready to wring Naomi's neck. "Where is Victoria?"

Naomi finally pivots, looking up to meet his eyes with her ice-cold ones. "She's gone."

That's when I notice that she's holding something. In the beam of Caleb's light, it looks like a piece of old rusted pipe.

And it's covered in blood.

29

"WHAT DID YOU DO?" I CROAK OUT, TRYING TO MAKE sense of this. Naomi was there the night Henry was killed. He died moments after harassing her for an interview. She was likely at school the day Diego was killed. And tonight, she insisted on accompanying us into the ruins.

I back up, tugging Caleb with me by the elbow.

"Where is she?" he asks, voice frayed and desperate. He moves toward Naomi cautiously. "Please, I just want to see her."

Naomi stirs, her gaze meeting mine without seeing me. "I'm sorry," she says quietly, almost to herself. "I didn't want to do it. But she forced my hand."

A sick feeling roils in my stomach, threatening to come up. "Oh my god." I tug Caleb harder, but he stands his ground. My fingers slip free of his sweatshirt fabric. "Caleb, we have to go."

"No, she's going to tell us where Victoria is." He pulls his pocketknife free, releasing the blade. "Did you hurt Jameson too?"

Naomi blinks, then looks at Caleb like she's seeing him for the first time. "Jameson?" She glances down at the bloody rod in her hand and drops it. It clanks on the ground, and she flinches. "No, I-I didn't hurt anyone. I mean, I did, but…"

"Damnit, Naomi," I spit. "Just tell us where they are!"

"Victoria is up at the cliff," she says, pointing. "And I have no idea where Jameson is."

Not wasting another second, Caleb motions me along. Together, we race past Naomi along the rock wall. Then her voice carries on the wind, soft as the clouds overhead but pointed as a blade. "Wait! You shouldn't go up there!"

But Caleb either doesn't hear or doesn't care; he keeps barreling up alongside the main house, to the cliff's crest. We're nearly to the back of the house, passing the battered garden shed, its door still screeching with the wind like it did the night we found Henry.

I barely begin scanning the area when I see her, sprawled out at the edge of the cliff like a sacrifice to some ancient sea god.

"No," Caleb says, rushing to her.

Footfalls sound behind me, and I spin to find Naomi there, peering past me at the horrible scene. "I'm sorry. So, so sorry."

"Why?" I ask, glancing from her to where Caleb kneels beside Victoria's body. "Why did you do it?"

Naomi shakes her head. "I told you, I didn't want to."

Up this high, the wind slaps hard, whipping loose hairs into my face. Tears sting at my eyes, making it even harder to see as I fight my way through the fog. I get closer and hear the retching sound before I see Caleb hunched over the edge of the bluff.

My insides twist. It's real. She's actually gone. Another victim claimed by the ruins.

And then, it's as if I'm watching Victoria's spirit pick up out of her body as she gets up, walks closer to the edge of the cliff with her arms extended, like she's about to give Caleb a hug.

Except it isn't a spirit. It isn't a ghost.

Victoria herself, pristine outfit drenched in blood, is up and on her feet, walking to the edge of the cliff. And I don't think it's a hug she has in mind.

"Caleb, look out!" I scream, already running toward him.

But I know it's too late.

30

HIS NAME LEAVES MY LIPS, FOLLOWED BY A STRANGLED SOB.

At the sound of my voice, Victoria stops, momentarily distracted.

I sprint toward her, legs pumping hard, all further cries, warnings, or pleas caught in my throat. *No, please no.* Only this silent prayer, thrown up to the heavens. That's all I have.

At the cliff's edge, Caleb cranes his neck to look back and spots Victoria. "What the hell—"

"Get away from him!" I manage to blurt, only yards from them now.

"Eden," Victoria says, suddenly wobbly. "What are you—" And then she doubles over, clutching her side.

"Vic," Caleb says, rushing to her. "Are you okay?"

"I don't feel so good," she mumbles, toppling over just as he slides onto his knees to catch her.

I help him lay her down, so we can check for a pulse. "Victoria," I call, lowering my ear to her heart next. To my relief, there's a thrum, faint but steady. I cup my hand over her face and feel her breath. "She's alive," I say, my eyes roving to her clothing, saturated with blood. "But we need to get her to a hospital. Did you call for help?" I ask Naomi, who's skulking up behind us.

"No, I-I was too scared to think. And she was dead. I *know* she was."

"Yeah, she's the walking talking freaking dead." I reach for my own phone, then remember I don't have one. "Does anyone have a signal?" The others check, then shake their heads. "We'll have to call when we're farther inside the ruins. For now, let's try to slow the bleeding." Before I can figure out what to use, Caleb is unzipping his sweatshirt and tearing off the lower half of his T-shirt. As he wraps the scrap around Victoria's waist, I turn to Naomi. "How the hell did this happen?"

Naomi stops a few feet shy of us, head lowered into her shoulders.

"Are you going to tell us, or do I need to hold you out over the cliff?"

"Sh-she was chasing us."

"She?" Caleb asks, pushing the hair out of Victoria's face.

"*It*, I don't know. That thing with the hood. The thing my sister saw before she died. It was here, chasing us."

"So Jameson really did see something." I shine my flashlight back down the rock wall, then at the center of the Village. The mist is too thick to make out much of anything.

"Except..." Naomi says solemnly. "Look, we were running as fast as we could. Victoria tried to speak to it, to get it to stop. But it wouldn't. It kept coming, forcing us to keep going. Then we got separated somewhere in the center of the ruins. I could hear... Victoria's footsteps, but I couldn't see her. When I heard her scream, I finally found her, in bad shape. She said she'd tripped and"— Naomi shivers—"fallen on a metal rod sticking out of the ground, over in that part of the restaurant with the missing roof."

At this image, I shiver. I never made it to the restaurant the night of the overnighter, though it had been on Henry's agenda for the documentary. It wasn't a murder site. But ever since a storm blew off half the roof, it's basically been the pinnacle of haunted lore cinematography. "And right before she went down," Naomi continues, "she said, 'No, Jameson. Please.'"

I wrap my arms around myself. So Victoria identified the killer before she fell. She was wrong about Jameson O'Sullivan, and she paid for it. "Are you sure it was only one person, Naomi?" If Jameson is involved in this, Jim O'Sullivan must be too.

"I only saw one, but...I don't know."

There's something else I don't understand. "Why did you keep saying you were sorry?"

Her head lowers. "I'm the one who pulled out the metal rod. It broke free from the ground when she fell, and when she got up, the other end was stuck inside her." She motions to the left side of her abdomen. "I didn't think I could or even *should*—I've heard you should leave that kind of thing to the professionals. But she kept screaming and begging me to do it. So I did." She takes a deep breath. "Then she was out."

"And you thought you'd killed her." Only she's alive, and Jameson would rather have her and the rest of us dead. "We're sitting ducks here at the top of the cliff. We'll have to move her."

Caleb glances down at Victoria's pale face and nods. "Get our things."

Cradling her in his arms, he lifts her with a grunt and moves away from the cliff. Naomi shoulders her pack, using my flashlight to guide us. I gather the rest of our belongings and follow the others to the doors of the big house. "Maybe we can hide her somewhere inside until help comes."

"Guys," Naomi whispers.

"What?" I ask, nearly tripping over a water spigot and dropping everything. My arms are leaden weights and my back aches. I just want to make it to the door. Caleb's expression is pinched, and I know his injured hand must be in agony.

"It's coming," Naomi says.

My hands start to sweat over my precariously piled load. I attempt to look back, but it's too dark. "How do you know?"

"I saw it—*him*." Naomi is running now, passing us by as she heads up the porch steps to the main house.

I try again to get a glimpse of the assailant, but Caleb says in a low voice, "Keep your eyes on me."

Then a crunch sounds, and dread rises in my gut.

Caleb and I continue with our small labored steps. I grunt against the pain in my arms and follow Naomi. She drops her things onto the porch and tucks her flashlight beneath her arm, keeping it trained on the door handle as she pushes. "It's stuck," she cries out.

Behind me, footsteps pound the gravel. Closer and closer. I keep my eyes on Caleb, even though every sore inch of me begs to get a peek.

We reach the steps where Naomi still contends with the handle. "Help me with her," Caleb tells us.

Naomi looks past me, and her eyes widen. She concedes, looking powerless, and I abandon everything in my hands to help. We get a tenuous grip on Victoria as I take her upper half and Naomi lifts her feet. But the instant Caleb gets to work on the door, Naomi falters under the strain.

My knees start to buckle. In front of me, Victoria's shoulders are slipping from Naomi's grasp. Behind me, the footsteps grow closer.

Caleb throws his shoulder into the door. "Damnit!" He starts to kick at it next, and my hopes take a dive into the rubble.

"Lower her!" Naomi screams, her gaze on the person racing toward my back.

I start to bend, but Caleb lets out a loud growl as he shakes out his injured fist, and the door swings open.

"Come on!" he yells.

A rush of adrenaline floods me, giving my wobbly arms new life. Caleb takes over for Naomi, ushering her inside. The footsteps are so close behind me now, I can't resist a peek as I race toward the open door.

The figure cloaked in black lunges for the first step on the porch, knife raised.

"Eden!" Caleb yells from beyond the threshold.

I snap to, bulling forward with every ounce of oxygen and strength until Victoria and I are inside.

The door slams behind me, and Naomi shoves her weight up against it. "Help me!" On the other side, our attacker throttles the door so violently that Naomi shrieks.

Caleb and I set Victoria down and rush to the door. As they fight to keep it shut, I maneuver the dead bolt into place.

The door seemingly secure, I double forward, completely out of breath. "Will it hold?"

"I don't know," Caleb pants, taking a cautious step back into the foyer.

The overwhelming scent of mildew hits me, reminding me of where we are. Reminding me of what we've resorted to making a sanctuary.

I turn to take in the place, with its fading sea spray print on the peeling and moldy wallpaper. My first thought is that, beneath the rot, it doesn't look like a horrible murderer's mansion. Then I remember that Mrs. Blackmore was a mother and a beach village owner. It explains the chipped and dust-covered ceramic gulls near the front door. It explains the rotting side table pushed against the wall where, beneath the cobwebs, you can still make out the seashells carved into the wood. Once upon a time, this house would've maintained a relaxing, beachy vibe, perfect for a family of surfer kids.

I inch farther inside. Compared with the six bungalows, the inside of the house has remained fairly intact, succumbing only to the effects of salt and water. Looters were likely too worried about the legend to make their way to the tail end of the property. Too scared to enter this cursed ground.

Naomi steps beside me, shining her light on the tiles beneath our feet. We take a few steps, and the dingy white morphs into large burgundy stains. Just like the legend says. Though the truth behind it has all gone completely hazy. Cringing, I scan the room for Caleb and call his name.

"In here!" he calls back from one room over. "Checking for another way in!"

A draft kicks up the threadbare curtains at the broken front windows. There's definitely another way in. Possibly several.

A thump sounds above us, and I flinch. Naomi and I exchange a horrified glance, and Caleb hurries back to us.

"What the hell was that?" he asks.

"Someone else is in here," I whisper, eyes latched on the staircase leading to the second floor.

Another thump, followed by a rattle. This one from around the back of the house.

"The back door," Caleb says, reaching for my trembling arm. "I didn't get to it."

Naomi lowers her head into her hands. "What do we do?"

Caleb looks down at Victoria, who's starting to stir but still very much out of it. "Maybe we can hide her and then—I don't know, fight?"

"We don't have much of a choice." I crouch down beside Victoria. "Hey," I whisper. "Are you there? We've got to move."

She moans softly, but her eyes stay shut despite the hammering from the back of the house.

"We'll have to carry her," I say, though even in this heightened survival state, my energy is down to dregs.

When Caleb lowers himself near Victoria's feet, the staircase creaks. The sound cuts straight through the pounding and the whistling wind. Naomi's light swooshes up to it, landing on a tall faceless shadow.

My breath catches. Caleb's lips are moving, but all I hear is the sound of my own heartbeat, so fast and hard it might explode.

The shadow steps down, and the ancient wood groans.

"Eden!" Caleb yells, but I can't take my eyes off of the figure.

Naomi's light flits up to finally land on the face.

"It's you," I say.

And of course it is.

31

"GUYS?" JAMESON O'SULLIVAN CONTINUES TO THE bottom of the stairs.

"Stay right there," Caleb tells him, pulling the knife from his pocket.

"What are you doing?" Jameson steps onto the tile. "Why are you—"

"He said stay back!" I shout.

Jameson turns his head in the direction of the pounding noises at the back of the mansion. "I don't understand." He glances back at us, his eyes lowering to Victoria on the floor. "Oh my god. What the hell happened? Is she—"

"She's alive, no thanks to you," I snap. "Now stay there, or we'll end you." He's big, but there are three of us. Then I realize with a sudden sense of panic that Naomi dropped our backpacks outside. Apart from my flashlight—which I gave to Naomi—I'm defenseless.

"Are you all insane?" Jameson's hand goes to his head. "Are your ears working? The killer is the person trying to break down the door back there."

Except I've suspected this was a two-man job for a while. "We know that's your father out there," I say, "and that you've been helping him." I can't believe I let him fool me earlier tonight. That I ignored my instincts and let Victoria talk me into letting him play *lookout*.

"My father?" Jameson throws a hand into the air. "That lunatic out there who tried to *kill* me?"

"We're not falling for it, Jameson," I say.

"Victoria knew it was you," Naomi adds in a timid voice, "before she fell."

"It wasn't me! I'm the one who texted you guys that someone was coming! Why the hell would I do that if I was the killer?"

"To make it look like it was someone else," Caleb says with a mixture of shock and hurt. Like he finally sees his friend for who he truly is. "You had my phone last. You had the key to the weight room. Your dad has to be Starlight Developers and Nicolas Blackmore's killer."

Jameson grips both of his temples, pushing in hard with his meaty fingertips. "You are all completely off base here. And this is a waste of time." He steps forward, and Caleb releases the blade on his knife. "Because the person who killed Nicolas Blackmore and tried to kill V tonight was not me!" he snarls, punctuating the last three words.

On the floor, Victoria stirs. And though I keep my eyes trained on Jameson, I hear struggling. "Ugh," she moans. "This hurts like hell."

Caleb moves to her, and I take a lightning-fast peek to watch her sit up.

"Then why didn't you help her?" I shout up to Jameson as something shatters behind the house, sending a gust of terror through me. "Why are you inside this house?"

"I was being chased, damnit! I think you're right about one thing. There have to be two killers. Only I'm not one of them. I was doing my perimeter sweep on the other side of the property when I saw someone sketchy. I texted Caleb and V, and then this guy spotted me and started chasing me. That was when I heard Victoria scream from way over here." He shakes his head. "There was nothing I could do."

"Hey," Naomi whispers.

But Jameson ignores her soft voice, pressing on. "This guy almost had me—and yes, I thought it was a dude because he was almost as big as me. I did what I had to do. I came in here through a busted window on the side. Look." He shows his hands, sliced and caked with blood.

"Guys," Naomi tries again, her posture stiff as an animal on alert. Immediately, I know why she needs our attention.

The banging noises…they've stopped.

The shadow, large and hulking, so different from the lithe, ethereal being I swore I saw the overnighter, fills the doorway at the back of this grand room. Then its hooded head flicks in Caleb's direction.

"Caleb, watch out!"

The figure holds the knife high as it rushes Caleb, who ducks out of the way. In the process, he leaves Victoria unguarded. Our attacker moves to her, knife still in hand. Victoria screams, throwing her arms up to shield her face.

Caleb hurls himself forward, plunging his pocketknife into the figure's back. The figure lets out a deep howl, dropping his own knife. Spine arched, he reaches back, grasping for the handle. He drops down onto his knees, groaning.

We waste no time helping Victoria to her feet. Naomi is already at the door, undoing the dead bolt.

I glance back at the staircase where Jameson stands frozen, staring at our attacker. *His father*. For years Jameson has called me a coward, but he won't even budge to help his own father pull the knife from his back.

As Naomi finishes with the dead bolt, Jameson yells, "Wait!"

"Hurry up!" I heft Victoria's arm over my shoulders. Caleb is on her other side, looking torn between helping Naomi and turning back to fend off our attackers.

I look again, spotting Jameson racing across the stained tiles toward us. "Take her," Caleb says to me, attempting to shift Victoria's full weight onto my shoulder.

"I've got her," I say as he turns weaponless to face Jameson.

Only someone else gets to me first. The hooded figure, on his feet now, has Caleb's bloody pocketknife in one hand, his own blade in the other. He swipes at me, the sharp edge so close I hear the whip of wind as it passes my arm.

It's too late by the time I see Jameson coming at me from the other side. I throw my hands up in defense, knowing I'm done for.

Except Jameson doesn't rush at me. He barrels into my attacker, who manages to slice open Jameson's stomach with the knife in his right hand.

Behind me, the others cry out.

Jameson glances down at his stomach, his eyes wide. He staggers, his foot landing in his own pooling blood as the attacker swipes again with his left hand, slashing Jameson's chest.

Victoria screams, a sound so deafening, I lose hearing altogether.

Then a moment later, I hear a voice. My own, repeating the most horrible of truths like a battering ram to my skull.

No, no, no. I was wrong, wrong, wrong.

"Oh my god," Victoria chokes out. "Oh my god."

Before us, Caleb stands on in horror as blood spills from his friend's wounds. Jameson stares at the faceless figure in confusion, then collapses onto the floor.

His blood seeps down onto the tiles, covering the stains already there. He gasps for a breath, and Caleb moves toward him, but the specter steps in front of him, bloodied knives raised.

Beyond them, Jameson's eyes fall shut.

"No!" Victoria cries, reaching out for him, still trying to break free. Even if the path were clear though, she's lost too much blood to make it on her own.

Our attacker moves for Caleb now.

"Let's go!" Naomi calls out, remembering the door. She pulls it open and starts onto the porch, feverishly motioning us along.

I help Victoria outside as Caleb breaks free from his trance. He spins around on the blood-slick tile and sprints to us. Once he's through, Naomi pulls the door shut.

Only there's no way to lock it from this side without a key. "We need a weapon," I say as Caleb grabs the handle, pushing his feet against the doorjamb for leverage. "We can't outrun him, not with her like this. Naomi, get my backpack. Find the spade and hunting knife."

She nods, heading down to where she discarded everything. As she scrounges through my belongings, our attacker starts yanking on the door handle from his side.

Naomi returns a moment later, out of breath.

"Good," I say, taking the spade from her as she hands off the knife to Caleb. "Victoria, can you make it down the stairs to wait for us?"

"I think so." Hesitantly, she ventures a step and then teeters across the porch.

When she reaches the last step, I motion for Naomi to move to the wall. "Your back against it," I whisper as the attacker tugs on the door handle again, this time opening it a crack. But Caleb pulls it shut again, just barely. "Get the flashlight ready."

Naomi does, lifting it high. The next time our attacker pulls, Caleb eases off. The attacker shoves his foot through, then pulls hard.

We let the door go and move backward.

When the figure steps forward, Naomi swings the flashlight. It meets skull, letting out a *crack*. Stunned, our attacker wobbles onto the porch.

It's enough for Caleb to pin him to the ground and press the blade against his throat. "Get the hood," he tells me. "Let's see who this son of a bitch is."

I hurry to them, noticing the man's sleeve is cinched back, revealing the back of his wrist. Whoever's beneath the mask can't be Jim O'Sullivan. He can't be Arturo Rodriguez. Neither would've killed their own son. That leaves only one man, and before I see his face—meet the eyes that match mine—for the first time in ten years, I have to see that tattoo.

I grab his wrist and attempt to turn his arm over, but he struggles. Before I can react, his arm is free and swinging in my direction.

Caleb's fist connects with the side of the man's already bloody face, and he goes still. I flip his wrist over, exposing the delicate flesh and the black shark fin tattoo.

The tattoo that's now faded and smudged.

All of my rapid-fire thoughts converge, crashing like a twenty-car pileup on the freeway. I don't understand.

I push back the hood and reach for the mask. As I grasp the black fabric, I hear Victoria's voice, commanding as ever despite her weakened state. "Stop."

32

I TURN TO FIND VICTORIA LOOKING OFF INTO THE MIST.
Something out there moves, like a glitch on a screen. One of the
shadows breaks free to push into the moonlight before the porch.

A second hooded figure. Just like I thought. Only if the pair
isn't Jameson and his father, who the hell are they? As the dark form
moves toward Victoria, willowy and unearthly, I know it's the same
someone I saw the night Henry died.

And just like that night, I'm hit with the pulsing sense of fear
that this isn't a flesh and blood being at all that approaches Victoria
as if floating on air.

"P-please," Victoria begs. "No."

But it only drifts closer to her.

Caleb leaves the unmoving attacker there on the porch and
races down the steps.

Out of the corner of my eye, I spot Naomi tiptoeing down on
the far side, along the decrepit porch railing. She moves into the

shadowy mist, slipping past the figure, who turns from Victoria to Caleb now.

The specter moves at him like a flash, arms stretched out, long fingers gleaming white beneath the moonlight.

Fingers made of flesh and bone.

"Hey!" I yell, waving my hands. "Your partner's in pretty bad shape." I point to the masked man lying on the porch. "We should call an ambulance."

At this, the figure pauses, covered face tilting in the direction of the fallen man. A muffled cry escapes from beneath the mask as our attacker lifts a very real sneaker. Before they make it two full steps, Naomi slides free of the shadows and leaps onto their back.

Caleb rushes to them, helping bring the assailant down.

This time I'm not hesitating to unmask this ghost. I march down the steps to where Caleb has this new figure face down, arms pinned while Naomi wrestles with the legs. I kneel, grabbing the mask along with whatever hair or skin I should happen to take with it and yank.

Naomi's flashlight finds the figure's face, illuminating disheveled brown hair and a gray eye rimmed with smeared mascara.

"Oh my god," Caleb says.

We're staring down at Bianca Nielsen—Victoria's mother.

Immediately, the hairs on my arms stand straight. *Victoria.*

I turn to face the mansion, finding that Victoria has made it up the porch steps. She's crouched beside the other assailant, who lies still before the door. The black mask is in her clenched fist. "Sam?" she whispers, the name crumbling to pieces in her throat.

I venture up the steps, peering past Victoria to the man on the ground. He's in bad shape, still face down, but with his head tilted to face Victoria. His eyes are cracked open, tears spilling from them. Victoria's stepfather, Sam Nielsen.

"Why?" she asks, voice barely rising over the waves that crash against the bluff.

"I'm sorry," he groans. "I didn't...I didn't want to."

Was Victoria really unaware that her parents were the killers?

Yes, of course she was. I saw the devastation in her eyes as she watched Jameson die. I know she'd never let anything happen to Caleb or Diego.

And yet...

"Check if you have service," I tell Naomi, keeping an eye on Victoria. "If not, head to the fence. Call nine-one-one. We need police and an ambulance."

She nods, moving toward the center of the ruins with her phone to her ear as Caleb hauls Bianca to her knees.

"Why did you do it?" Caleb demands, tears in his eyes. "You killed Diego and Jameson! They were like family to you!"

"They got too close," she says softly.

"To finding that knife," I say. "The one you used to kill Nicolas Blackmore twenty-five years ago."

Her gray eyes spark, and an eerie smile creeps onto her lips. "So you found Adelina then."

"I did. She said you threatened to ruin her life in order to buy this place, and that knife was the reason."

"Did she?" Bianca struggles, attempting to get free. "I don't suppose she told you where that knife was buried?"

I take a deep breath to calm myself. I only have to last until the ambulance gets here without murdering this witch.

"I don't understand," Victoria says, clutching the wound at her side. "You told us you loved Nicolas. Why did you kill him?"

Bianca's gaze goes to the front door of the mansion, though it's like her mind has gone elsewhere. Past all of us, past the door, into the foyer where Nicolas's body was found twenty-five years ago. "It was an accident, sort of." She starts to settle onto the cracked cement with her knees to one side, making Caleb visibly nervous.

"When I started working here, my goal was always to earn enough money to leave Fairport with Jim. He was working a crummy job too, over at the boardwalk surf shop."

"What about the inheritance?" Victoria chokes out, face pale.

"There never was any inheritance, no money to speak of. My family was poor." Bianca looks my way disdainfully. "I kept moving through the ranks, from cleaning to the restaurant. Getting promotions but never making enough. Then one day, Mr. Blackmore learned that I was acing calculus, and he put me in charge of the bookkeeping." She pauses, as though deliberating sharing this next part with us. "I thought about it for months before I actually added that first zero to one of my paychecks. I always cashed them out monthly to avoid suspicion from the bank."

Behind Bianca, a crunch sounds, putting us all on alert. It's

Naomi, holding up her phone. "They're on the way. Cops, ambulance. Should be soon."

"Thanks," I say, nodding for Bianca to continue.

"One day, Nicolas discovered my little trick. I tried to talk him out of reporting me. Only it didn't work. At least, not until I used one of my *other* tricks."

"You pretended to like him," Victoria says. When her mother only looks shamefully off at the cliff, she adds, "You pretended even after his death."

"I'd always been in love with Jim. But I needed Nicolas to believe he was the only one for me. I brought him into our group, convinced the guys to accept him. Eventually, they really did. When lunchtime hangouts and parties turned into matching tattoos, he finally trusted me.

"But then came the night of the party. The night everything went wrong." A whistle rings through the trees, and my heart lifts in hopes that help has already arrived. But it's only the wind howling. It picks up sand and gravel, and I bat it away. "A couple of us were already here, finishing up shifts. Nicolas was going to be running the place alone, so we decided it wouldn't hurt anything to invite the others over. The guys brought drinks. We all had way too much. Well, one thing led to another, and I ended up kissing Jim out on the cliff." Her eyes fall shut. "Nicolas saw us. I never realized how much he liked me until I returned to the house and saw the way he looked at me. Like I was worse than a monster."

Nicolas was right about that. I shiver against another gust, shielding my eyes with a hand.

"He was devastated," Bianca says. "He called me a liar, a witch. Jim tried defending me, arguing with Nicolas."

The voice, I realize. The male voice that Adelina heard all those years ago that belonged to one of Nicolas's friends. It was Jim O'Sullivan. He—and maybe even the whole Surfside Cleaning company, Cecelia included—really are behind Starlight Developers. The question is, do they know why Bianca wanted to purchase this property so badly?

"Was Jim there?" I ask. "When it happened?"

Bianca shakes her head. "I tried to defuse the situation by telling him and everyone else that the party was over. I stayed. I had to make Nicolas believe I'd made a stupid mistake and that I loved him. I had to make him keep my secret." She twists her lips to blow a strand of hair out of her eye. "Only he was done falling for my act. He told me that as soon as his mother got back, he was going to tell her about the money. I panicked. We were in the kitchen, and I grabbed a knife and threatened to cut myself. I thought that, maybe, if he saw my desperation, he'd have to forgive me.

"Instead," she says, "he looked at me like I was insane. He actually backed away and told me he was going to call the police. He said that I needed help." She tilts her head. "I guess he was right, because I followed him with the knife into the foyer. And when he turned around, I sliced his throat."

Over on the porch, Victoria moans—from pain or from hearing her mother's cool, collected voice as she recalls taking another human's life, I don't know.

"I stayed beside him while he died. Even though I was never in love with Nicolas, I still considered him a friend. But when the life went out of him, my first thought was that I was all alone in the Blackmore house. If I could find the key to the cashbox, it would be mine. The cops would assume a burglar had broken in and Nicolas had ended up a casualty." She rolls her eyes, reminding me so much of her daughter. "Stupid me, I never realized his little sister was home in her room the whole time.

"I left the knife there by Nicolas's body, washed my hands, and found the key to the office. By the time I heard the Blackmores' car coming up the driveway, I'd already broken into the office and stolen everything in the cashbox."

The cash. Bianca must've used that stolen money to fund Surfside Cleaning's entrepreneurial endeavors. All that talk about five friends being these young business geniuses was utter bull. They never earned the money. There was never any inheritance, like Bianca must've told her friends.

Bianca glances over at her daughter, who seems to be growing weaker by the minute. She wriggles again in Caleb's grip, trying to contort her limbs to freedom; it's no use.

Behind Victoria, her stepfather isn't moving. Where the hell is that ambulance?

"You never thought to wipe down the knife?" I ask to keep Bianca talking.

She frowns. "I got spooked by the Blackmores' car. I wasn't thinking about fingerprints or DNA. I just wanted to get the money and get out of there. It wasn't until later, when I got home, that I realized I'd nicked the palm of my hand with that knife at some point. I knew I'd left more than my fingerprints behind."

"So you took the money and fled," Caleb says.

"Maybe I should've," Bianca says with a sigh, "but no. I hid in the bushes outside the front window, where I could watch. I saw Hazel arrive, saw her kneel beside the body, saw her hold her son until she finally stood, covered in his blood."

"That's horrible," Naomi says softly.

"She never called anyone—no police, no ambulance. She picked up the knife and started screaming for Adelina. She was desperate to find out if she'd lost one child or two. Then her husband arrived, and I saw him take it all in. I watched him mourn his son, make sure his daughter was alive, and then switch into the role of his wife's protector. He took the knife and walked off into the ruins with it. I tried to follow him, but I lost track in the dark. Then his wife grew more and more hysterical, and the guests started coming out of their cottages to see what the commotion was about. I had to get out of there."

"Nothing he did to protect her worked," Caleb says grimly. "She couldn't live with any of it."

"Naomi," I say, my chest growing tighter, "why aren't the police here yet? Are you sure you told them exactly where we are?"

"Yes," she says somewhat defensively. "But the Blackmores' old driveway entrance is blocked off. They won't be able to get an ambulance through the place, so they're probably on foot."

We would've heard sirens though.

I start to press her further, but my mind gets pulled back to Bianca's story. Something about it doesn't add up. "You went to all of this trouble—purchasing the land, killing teens who might happen to stumble upon the knife—but you never actually saw Mr. Blackmore hide it. What if he'd thrown it into the ocean?"

Bianca's lips curve into an unsettling smile.

"What are you not telling us?" I ask, my fist tightening around the handle of the spade.

She shrugs. "Maybe that's the part of the story I'd like to keep for myself."

"Or maybe we drag you over to the Founder's Slab, tie you down, and let the seagulls feast on your flesh until you talk."

"Eden," Caleb says, sounding exhausted. "It's not worth it."

"It's worth it to me," I say as something shifts in my mind. It's like a groove sliding into place. The long rock dating back to our forefathers is called *the Founder's Slab*.

"The foundation," I say. "What if—what if, in Adelina's eight-year-old mind, she only thought her father said that the knife was buried beneath the foundation? Over the years, maybe that's the word that keeps repeating in her head. She remembered it sounded *like foundation*, and it *meant foundation*. But it was never actually the word *foundation*. Because what Silas Blackmore actually said was that the knife was buried beneath the Founder's Slab?"

Caleb's eyes grow large. "Because a slab *is* a foundation."

A wave of dizziness throttles me. "The knife that killed Nicolas

Blackmore isn't hidden under one of the cottages, or under the big house. It's buried in the rocks beneath the Founder's Slab."

"Guys!" Naomi says, her voice shrill. She's pointing at the porch.

Immediately, I see what's wrong. Mr. Nielsen isn't passed out near the door anymore.

He's lurching past Victoria on the steps, headed straight for me.

33

"EDEN!" CALEB SCREAMS BEHIND ME.

But Mr. Nielsen is already leaping at me from the bottom step. I go down hard, all of his weight knocking me straight to the cement pathway. My spade falls from my grip to skitter across the ground.

He jumps on me, reeking of sweat and blood. Grabbing the neck of my sweatshirt, he slams my head against the cement.

Pain spreads through my skull. My vision goes bright with stars. I strike and claw at his hands to no effect. Then I hear him grunt, and through cracked vision, I see Naomi, whaling on him with her flashlight.

He releases my sweatshirt and spins on her. I try to get up, but everything is spinning. Mr. Nielsen catches Naomi's flashlight and tears it from her grip. Then he swings it at her, missing her head as she turns but nailing her in the back. She cries out, dropping to the ground.

Mr. Nielsen faces me again. He lifts his shoe and steps down hard on my foot. It gives a sickening crunch. I scream, writhing on the cement. When he goes to step on my arm next, I shut my eyes against the next bout of agony.

Only it doesn't come. Caleb tackles him, knocking him off-balance. He takes my spade off the ground, but Mr. Nielsen manages to right himself. He dodges Caleb's blow, only to careen into a lamppost. He makes a horrible wheezing sound, then straightens his shoulders.

I force myself upright, wincing at the pain in my head and foot. I put all of my weight on my good foot and scan the area for the rest of our weapons.

I spot Naomi, attempting to get to her feet. Over on the porch, Victoria sits slumped to one side like a rag doll, barely able to keep her eyes open. Then her gaze shifts from the fray between us to something beyond me.

Cold fear slithers up my back. I spin around as a blade slices through the air, headed for my chest. I flinch, and it only grazes my sweatshirt, tearing right through the fabric.

When I land on my bad foot, pain rockets up my entire leg. Tears flood my already blurred vision. Bianca rushes at me again, steel glinting in the moonlight. I dodge this blow, frantically searching for a weapon to use against her. A collection of wooden boards and debris lies in a pile a few yards away. I'll never make it there. "Naomi!" I call out. "I need a weapon!"

Bianca is in terrific shape and could likely play this game for hours. And with the way the authorities are taking their sweet time, she may have that long.

"Eden!" comes Caleb's voice behind me. "Take—"

I try to look, but Bianca comes at me again at full speed. There's no time to move out of the way. Instead, I drop down. Bianca doesn't see it coming and hurtles over me, her feet taken out.

I check on Caleb, who's busy with Mr. Nielsen. There's no way to those wooden boards without going straight through Bianca, who's already getting back up on her feet.

"Eden, run!" Caleb yells.

But where? I can't escape in the opposite direction, straight off the cliff. *And how?* I can't run in my condition. Instead, I limp as fast as my busted foot will allow, headed along the side of the house.

When I spot a loose board on the ground, I pick it up. But it's so old and waterlogged, it starts to disintegrate in my hand. I drop it and press on, clenching my teeth against the shooting pains in my foot.

Behind me, Bianca's steps crunch over the gravel. I have to hide. I can't fight this woman, not when I'm injured and without a weapon. But I can stay hidden until the cops arrive.

Up on my left, I search the shrubbery that hedges the mansion. It's weedy and dense. And it's my only option.

I dive in, pushing through sharp branches and spindly leaves. They snag and tear my clothes, but I bury myself deep inside. When Bianca approaches, I stay still, holding my breath.

A light swings over the path, skimming the bushes. Either she's using her phone or she got hold of a flashlight.

My heart hammers. In this crouched position, my wounded

foot fires such sharp pains that I think I might pass out. I try to shift my weight off of it, but I wobble. A twig snaps under my palm as I catch myself.

Bianca's light zips to me, falling a few inches to my right. I don't breathe, don't move a muscle as her footsteps inch closer. When I start to believe she can't see me through the foliage, the beam of light slides right to my eyes, blinding me. "There you are."

I stiffen, panic crystallizing like ice through my veins. There's nowhere to go. By the time I shove my way through these shrubs again, she'll be on me. I blink away the blurriness and look to my left for a clear path out.

That's when I see it. In the weak moonlight filtering through the leaves. The door to the mansion's crawl space.

I don't have enough time to get inside though. Grabbing hold of a branch, I snap it off. Then I wind up and throw it as far as possible. It falls to the ground behind Bianca, causing her light to whip in that direction.

I scramble to the crawl space door, ignoring the pain in my foot. I'm making as much noise as a large boar back in these bushes, and Bianca immediately changes direction. She charges through, slashing at the foliage with her knife.

I reach the steel door and feel along the edges for some sort of latch. I find the handle and yank, but it sticks. Frantically, I run my fingertips along the surface again, this time locating a sliding latch. I shove it inward and tug on the handle again.

The door opens.

I drop it in the dirt and crawl inside, engulfed by complete darkness. Bianca is thrashing around out there, getting closer. With her light, she'll figure out exactly where I went. All I can do is press on, deeper and deeper into this cramped and dirty pit.

"Eden," she whispers, sending a shiver up my spine. Her light is off, but she's in here with me.

I stop, lying flat to make myself small. The stench of mildew sits heavy in the air, along with a sickly-sweet layer of rot. My cheek is pressed against the damp, disgusting ground, and I force myself not to gag.

The light clicks on, and my chest constricts. The glow bounces around the space, illuminating bricks, pipes, and mounds of dirt.

It lands on me, and Bianca lets out a growl. I get back onto my hands and knees, and race through two pillars, trying to lose her.

She skitters toward me like a giant rodent. "Eden!" she screams.

I hurry forward, but there's nowhere to hide. I press on, her breath behind me propelling me forward. With zero visibility, I can't go at full speed or I'll knock myself out on a pillar. I feel the ground quake as she crawls closer, followed by a grunt.

Bianca slashes at me, nicking the bottom of my sneaker. I kick my leg back, and my foot strikes her. She shrieks, and I scamper ahead, trying to create some distance between us.

I don't hear her behind me right away. Instead, there's a sound like digging or shuffling. I must've knocked the flashlight out of her hand. The glow is either buried in the debris or the light shut off. That means Bianca's as blind as I am—at least until she finds it.

"Hey, Bianca!" I call out. Maybe it's a stupid gamble, but if I can get her to abandon that flashlight, we're on even ground.

Minus the whole knife thing.

I consider doubling back while she's in the dark. It would be risky, but if I can pass her and that blade, I could trap her down here. The cops must be out there by now. I could hold that door to the crawl space shut until they take over.

I have to try. I start to turn around when the light lashes at the pillar in front of me before swinging back to the dirt. *Damnit.* I'll never make it past her now. Not without a fight.

I pick up a chunk of loose cement and chuck it back in her direction. It misses, only making her angrier as she speeds up.

I keep moving, searching for a pillar to hide behind. If I can find another piece of cement, I might be able to land a blow hard enough to slow her down.

The beam bounds in front of me, this time skimming a rock. I grasp it, still moving, but adjusting my grip.

Only it isn't a rock, I realize with a shiver.

It's a bone.

At first, I nearly drop it, the idea of something dead in my hands so repulsive. But then I remember that it's Bianca Nielsen and her knife…or me.

I feel the bone in my hands, short and slender. I touch the ground to find more bones. Maybe a possum carcass.

But as I feel my way over the terrain beneath me, the bones become longer. Much too long for a possum or a raccoon. My fingers light on a large round shape next. It only takes finding the small holes for me to comprehend that this is no rock. No, I've just crawled on top of a human skeleton.

I suck in a breath. This body doesn't belong to Nicolas or any of the victims: all of their corpses were recovered and buried. So then who is this?

"Come here, Eden!" Bianca growls, hitting a pipe as she slashes wildly through the air.

Her light skips over the mound of bones again, landing on a dark object that nearly blends into the ground, save for the brightly colored letters stitched over it. By the time I process the letters, Bianca's light is darting dangerously close to me.

I flinch my head back, my mind reeling. The letters were *SF*. The object is a black baseball cap. Confusion and horror tangle in me, followed by a crushing wave of sorrow. This person, whose body was discarded beneath this mansion like trash, is my dad.

An involuntary cry escapes my lips.

It's all Bianca needs to zero in on my exact location. She's within a few feet, coming at me full speed, flashlight shining in my eyes. "Come here, Eden!" she screams again. "I only want to help you! To help take you to your father!"

Anger floods me, overtaking all other emotions. *This* was the part of the story Bianca refused to tell. Her last secret. The reason she had to purchase the land. It was never just about the knife. The real reason she decided to destroy the entire place was that she'd hidden my father's corpse down here.

It takes Bianca a moment to switch the flashlight to her non-dominant hand, replacing it with the knife. As she does, I pick up the longest bone in the pile.

She lunges for me, and I swing with everything left in me. The bone connects, the sound nauseating.

Bianca crashes to the ground, the glow of her light spinning and landing on a pillar in the center of the crawl space.

I don't wait. I simply grab her light and crawl as fast as my injured foot will let me. Tears start to fall, and my nose runs. Between sobs, I wheeze, oxygen failing to reach my lungs. My arms and legs start to tingle, and it's like moving on phantom limbs. I'm crying so hard and moving so fast, I can't tell if Bianca is following me.

I reach the door and wiggle my way out, not stopping until I'm through the shrubs. They claw at my hands and face, nearly ripping my clothes off my body.

Then I'm out, met with the faint moonlight and a silence cold enough to frost over. I don't know which way to go. New fears about Caleb and the others pour in, joining the anguish writhing in my chest.

And then I hear it. "Eden!" His voice.

I turn to see him running, two uniformed officers at his sides. I wait until he reaches me and collapse in his arms.

34

TWO WEEKS LATER

I HAD ANOTHER NIGHTMARE LAST NIGHT.

Just like all the others, I dreamt of bones. Some clean and ivory colored, some brittle and chipped, others coated in rotting flesh. Piled high, the bones shivered and shook. They moved like one living skeleton with the pieces all out of place.

Only they weren't alive at all; they were full of worms. The slimy creatures wriggled through the eyeholes, over the sinewy, rotting tissue, and between pointed fingers.

And then I became the worm, all alone and trapped in a labyrinth of bones.

Mom shook me awake, the way she has every night since the ruins.

It took a few days for Mom and me to piece together what must've happened to Dad. We may never know every detail, but we know a couple of things for sure: Dad never stole anything from his friends. He never skipped town. He never abandoned Mom or me.

Our best theory is that Dad discovered that Bianca's money had come from the Blackmores and that she'd killed Nicolas to cover it up. Maybe Dad confronted her, or maybe she stumbled upon him digging into her finances. Either way, she decided the only way to silence him for good was to take his life. Just like she'd done to Nicolas.

Having worked with my dad, she must've had access to his email account, which allowed her to send that goodbye letter to my mom. Then she probably figured that beneath the crawl space in an abandoned house in a forsaken beach village was the best place for a corpse. Better than a body of water, where it could wash ashore. Better than in the dirt, where the elements and nature would unearth it over time. But then the Fairport youth decided to make a game of coming onto the condemned property. They started digging around. They got too close.

Bianca must've considered going down there and moving the body. Only she would've faced all those obstacles in disposing of it again. So she committed one last atrocious act to make her point. To keep the legend of Mrs. Blackmore alive and to keep the people of Fairport out, she killed Farah Palmer at the first senior overnighter.

Only that wasn't Bianca's last act. Far from it. Because she killed again when Esther Lamb started looking into the murders. And then when Henry did.

"We're here." Caleb's voice jolts me from my thoughts.

I don't move. Instead, I sit and look out the passenger-side window at the hospital building.

Caleb places a gentle hand on my shoulder. "You don't have to come in if you don't want to."

I don't want to. I really don't. This is Caleb's friend, not mine. And after everything we went through that night in the ruins, I'm nervous. I have no idea what to say.

Still, I owe it to Caleb to be supportive. "I want to come." Besides, we can only stay a few minutes. Then we've got to get to school.

"I'd understand if you didn't. It's a lot. Too much."

I'm not sure which part is the hardest, honestly. If it's being back in this building so soon after being discharged. Compared with the others who were with me that night, my injuries were minimal. No concussion, but my fifth metatarsal on my foot was fractured, thanks to Mr. Nielsen. It was sheer adrenaline that kept me alive that night.

After Caleb caught me, I was no longer able to put any weight on it. Paramedics had to cart me into the ambulance on a stretcher. Now I have a cast and crutches; no volleyball for six to eight weeks. That means no preseason, and I'll miss most of the regular season too. It's not like I was going to college on a volleyball scholarship, but it still sucks.

Maybe the hardest part is knowing that my father was never even given a chance in a facility like this. With loved ones surrounding him. Instead, he died all alone.

Then again, maybe the hardest part is not knowing how to act in there. Because after everything that night in the ruins—I still don't trust this person.

Caleb's friend wasn't the only survivor. Bianca recuperated after her injuries too. The medics eventually arrived. It turned out Naomi was right. They couldn't get the ambulance through all of the fences and overgrown paths, so they had to make it to us on foot. The cops found Bianca in the crawl space, unconscious after that blow to the head with a femur bone. She made a full recovery.

I can't say the same for her husband. Caleb managed to subdue Mr. Nielsen until the first responders arrived. But by the time they reached the hospital, he'd succumbed to his injuries.

The detective in charge of the case says they were able to follow my tip about the knife that killed Nicolas Blackmore. They found it wedged deep between the boulders at the Founder's Slab. Bianca confessed to everything in interrogation, claiming her husband aided in all of the recent murders. Mr. Nielsen was the one who tried to kill Caleb and me in the weight room. It turns out he works as a biomedical equipment tech, so he has a free pass in and out of hospitals. That's how he planted Caleb's phone in his sweatshirt pocket. And since he periodically inspects the AED and other equipment in the school nurse's office, none of the staff would've batted an eye at his presence on campus the day of Diego's murder. He was the one who stalked us. He even scared Victoria that night in their pool, hoping she would beg us to quit our investigation.

But there's one thing Bianca Nielsen has refused to own up to: the murder of Esther Lamb.

It doesn't make sense for her to hold back on this one confession, not after coming clean on everything else. Not when she could easily put the blame on her deceased husband. The detective says it can't affect her sentencing, since—provided the jury is awake—she's going to end up in prison for the rest of her life.

Sometimes, I think her punishment is too easy. I know she lost her husband, but I wish I could take away more. I almost wish I would've ended Bianca's life down in that crawl space, the way she ended my father's.

But then I'd be closer to knowing what it's like to be her, to have blood on my hands. And I don't think I'd feel better at all. I'm glad the blow I landed with that bone only served to aid in my escape but didn't end her life—even if she deserved to die.

Instead of focusing on my father's killer, I've tried to shift my thoughts to Mom. It's been a lot for her. For both of us, but especially her. I think her grief is tied up in extreme guilt for believing the lies about Dad all these years. One night I walked past her room, and her cries trickled out. I thought I heard her whisper, "I'm sorry I never tried to come find you."

Grieving my father has been strained and awkward. It's not like when a close family member dies. Dad hasn't been around for the past decade; it's strange to mourn the loss of someone who wasn't actually there. We had to reacquaint ourselves with the man we used to know, the one we thought was gone. We had to resurrect him, only to watch him die all over again. Only then could we begin to mourn the loss of what would've been. What should've been. We now grieve for the husband and father we could've had but never will.

Arturo Rodriguez and Cecelia Durham have been by the house

to see Mom. At first, I didn't think she'd let them in. But she did, and they not only apologized but offered her a position in the company as well as some financial compensation for the past decade. I asked if she thinks they're trying to buy her silence, to keep anyone from asking questions about how much they really knew. But she shut my entire line of thinking down. She said she was glad to finally have Cecelia back in her life, and that it would be nice to work somewhat normal hours again.

I didn't push her on it. I think Mom's in the same place as me, unwilling to chain herself to hate or grudges. Because that's all they really do: hold us down. Make us prisoners.

Maybe it was Caleb who helped me see this, even before I ever found my father's killer. Sure, he has the ability to entrance me with those eyes from time to time. And when he threads his fingers through mine, I might as well be his captive; I'd follow him anywhere. But the instant I let go of my ridiculous age-old grudge against Caleb, I became free.

That's why I'm telling myself not to fixate on everything I hold against Caleb's *dear friend* as we head up the elevator, me on my crutches and Caleb at my side.

We knock, and Victoria's biological dad, Travis Whitlock, lets us in. I remember Mr. Whitlock from when my dad was still alive, before Mr. Whitlock and Bianca got divorced. Now I can't help wondering why they divorced. Was Mr. Whitlock simply one more person in the world who knew what that woman was capable of—or did she have him and everyone else fooled?

"Hey, guys," he says, his smile warm.

We find Victoria lying in bed, watching the television mounted on the opposite wall. Some sort of cooking show is playing. "Hi," she says weakly, trying to sit up.

"I've got it," Caleb says, crossing the room and grabbing the remote control.

"Thanks."

Mr. Whitlock picks up a laptop case and loops it over a shoulder. "I'll be down in the cafeteria answering some work emails. If she needs anything, hit the button." He shuts the door behind him, leaving us with Victoria in the cold room that smells of antiseptic.

Once Caleb adjusts the headrest, he pulls a couple of chairs closer to her bed. "How are you doing today?" he asks.

Victoria offers a tight-lipped smile. "No signs of infection. Meds are working."

When the paramedics arrived that night in the ruins, Victoria was immediately whisked away to surgery. It was touch and go for a while.

Caleb came to visit her as soon as he was allowed, but I've stayed away until now. I can't blame Victoria for her parents' crimes—only I'm not convinced she's entirely innocent. I wasn't sure what I'd find when I finally looked her in the eye.

Despite Victoria's apparent shock at finding her mother and stepdad underneath those hoods that night, some things simply haven't added up. Like the fact that she was in the ice cream parlor with the boys the day Caleb's phone went missing. I was so focused on Jameson, but it could've easily been Victoria who snatched it up and sent those texts.

Victoria was also supposed to leave the crawl space door open for us, except she didn't.

Then there was the fact that she claimed to have been chased by the killers when she fell on the pipe in the ruins. But why the hell would Mr. and Mrs. Nielsen chase their own kid? And isn't it a little convenient that hers was the only injury that night with no witnesses?

I guess I have another theory floating around in my head. One in which Mr. and Mrs. Nielsen believed that no one would ever suspect them if their own daughter was chased by the killer, especially not if she ended up injured. And the bonus in this plan? Should they ever be caught, her injury would garner sympathy. Just like it is now.

I'm not sure how exactly this scenario would've played out. Did her mother or stepfather stab her with that pipe, only it stuck in a little too far? I guess we'll never know.

The last little detail is the one that keeps needling at my mind. Victoria was sitting on the porch when her stepfather—who we believed had passed out—got up and came at me with a knife. Sure, she was severely injured and half out of it, but her eyes were open. She could've warned me.

Only she didn't.

I know, Victoria never personally attacked any of us. And there were countless opportunities. This fact doesn't squash my doubts. I keep thinking about how she called out Jameson's name in the ruins. She claims that in her panic, she only thought she was being chased and that she assumed Jameson was behind everything because of the idea that *I'd* planted in her head.

Now she folds her hands over her sheets, an expectant look on her face. "So? Did you go to school yesterday?"

"Yeah," Caleb says, and I nod.

"And?" She furls her hand in a *go on* gesture.

"And there were boring classes and"—he looks at me in confusion—"teachers?"

"Ugh." Victoria rolls her head back. "You guys are my only window to the outside world. If nothing happened, make something up."

"I got a bout of locker combination amnesia, thanks to my trauma?" Caleb offers. This elicits a laugh from her, which causes her to cringe in pain.

There was one interesting development yesterday, one I won't share with Victoria. It was my first day back at school since the ruins. I had every intention of booking it off campus for lunch with May the moment the bell rang. I wanted to avoid the stares and questions about that night. But then I saw Caleb, looking alone and lost at his locker. Only it wasn't because he'd forgotten the combination; it was because he didn't know where to go. All of his friends were gone. Maybe that's part of the reason I've kept all of my Victoria-related theories to myself. This girl who lies covered in bandages and white sheets is one of the last friends he has.

May and I brought Caleb along with us, and on our way to the parking lot, Naomi cut us off. I thought she might ask about Bianca and how the woman won't cop to murdering Esther. Instead, she asked if she could have lunch with us.

May being May, defender of the weak and mother bird to all flightless birdlings, welcomed her wholeheartedly and paid for her chicken bites. I guess Naomi just needed a friend or two.

Over lunch, I asked Naomi if she and her parents were going to fight to get justice for Esther. She thought about it for a moment, then said that every day she lives without her sister is an injustice; convicting Bianca Nielsen of Esther's death wouldn't help to take away her pain.

I didn't understand it, her willingness to accept things. Not wanting to fight. But I had to respect her wish to move on with her life. A trial would be a huge ordeal to put her already fragile family through.

One good thing has come out of all of this: Adelina finally has justice for her brother. Caleb and I visited her at Fairport Brew a few days ago. She thanked us for clearing her mother's name. For now, her identity is still a secret. But it's only a matter of time before the media hounds sniff her out. Maybe she'll sneak off in the night and find a new life. Or maybe, now that her family name has been cleared, she'll be able to hold her head high in Fairport.

"When is Jameson's thing?" Victoria asks quietly.

A pang shoots through my chest. The way it does every time I hear Jameson's name. Every time I think of him.

"Oh," Caleb says, reddening. "It was on Saturday."

Victoria nods. She knows how unwelcome her presence would've been. "How was it?"

He shrugs. "You know."

It was complete and utter hell. I almost left halfway through. That night in the ruins, Jameson saved me. Even though I accused him of being an accomplice to murder. I hate myself for it. I think a lot about the way I treated him that night. Did he deserve it? Probably. Do I regret it? Absolutely.

People sometimes say to live life with no regrets, but I'm not sure I agree. I want to keep looking ahead, to learn to forgive myself and others. But part of forgiving myself is accepting that I made a mistake. So I think it's okay to have regrets. We learn from them. We pick up and move ahead, becoming stronger and better versions of ourselves because of them.

Jameson's tribute was held in front of the entrance of the Fairport Village ruins, a move intended to reflect his valiance. To proclaim that we know this was all caused by one woman, not by curses or an evil as ancient and formidable as the boundless sea.

And yet, Starlight Developers, a.k.a. Surfside Cleaning, barely waited for the attendees to leave the grounds before they demolished the place.

The company—*Mom's* company now—plans to develop a brand-new resort. There's already a new sign posted in front of the property, beside all the old ones telling people to stay out. It shows 3D images of the plans. The resort looks amazing, a vision of bright colors and clean lines that stand in stark contrast with the formerly dark crumbling hellscape.

But the plan also has its opponents, the Fairport residents who say they should leave well enough alone. There's already a town meeting scheduled to discuss it. I'm not sure where I fall. I want to support Mom and her company. I want to believe the neighbors who talk about how much finding the killer has laid decades of fear to rest. But when I pass by the empty land, I still hear the whispers telling me to flee. Something about that place still thrums with a sense of doom.

"I wish I could've gone." Victoria sniffles, and it's not some false display of emotion.

"I know," Caleb says. "Jameson was—"

"Did someone say *hero*?" The deep voice makes my abdomen clench.

I glance back to spy Jameson's face through the cracked door. Try as I might to make strides with Jameson O'Sullivan, I find myself constantly backsliding. This guy makes it impossible. "Keep it down, bridge troll," I say as Caleb gets up to let Jameson's wheelchair through. "Are you trying to scare the hell out of a girl on her death bed?"

"Hey!" Victoria says before wincing again. "I'm not dying."

"Well, you're going to have to do a lot better than *not dying* to break out of this joint." Jameson rolls up right alongside my chair. "So proceed. Keep talking about me."

Caleb slumps back in his seat. "Actually, we were talking about someone else's hero tribute ceremony."

Jameson grins and crosses his arms. "Just look at you three. Sitting around, talking about how I stared death in the face. How I saved Eden's life."

I clench my molars and tap Caleb's arm. "I think Victoria needs her rest. We should go."

"Yes, we are leaving," Jameson says. "We're going to the Chicken House."

"No, we're not." I look at Caleb, who throws up a hand. "We have school."

"That's not fair," Victoria whines. "At least bring me some chicken."

"Is that part of your dying-girl diet?" I ask, standing up before she can attempt to leap off her hospital bed and strangle me.

The Chicken House isn't the only thing Victoria will miss in the wake of her parents' crimes. She won't be finishing out her high school experience in Fairport. Her dad lives down in Orange County, where hopefully no one will ever figure out who she is or what her parents did.

We say our goodbyes, and I find myself the last one in the room. Hand on the doorknob, I glance back at the bed, and Victoria's gaze meets mine for a moment.

"You know what, Eden?" she asks, her voice light despite her condition.

I stop in the doorway. "What?"

She narrows her eyes, and that familiar uncanny sensation snakes up my spine. It's like witnessing the dead walk the earth or a seemingly impossible curse materialize. "I'm glad we're friends now," she says, voice void of emotion. "We needed fresh blood in the group." She turns back to the television without awaiting a response and raises the volume.

———

We arrive at school right as the bell rings. By the time we get Jameson's wheelchair down from the back of the truck, help him into it, and I hobble my way through the parking lot, students are already tucked inside their classrooms.

Jameson rolls off down the hall, leaving me alone with Caleb.

I flick my head toward the lockers lining the wall. "I have it on good authority that someone at this school wants to kiss me right here, in front of the lockers."

He lifts a brow. "What could've possessed me to tell you about that?"

"You found me irresistible," I say with a devilish laugh. "And now every locker door only reminds me of my power."

"You can't be that powerful if you needed Jameson to save you."

"Oh yeah?" I hop back toward the lockers, one crutch at a time.

"What are you doing?" He crosses his arms, trying too hard to look unamused.

"Just running my mouth in front of the lockers. You might need to silence me somehow." I tilt my head, twisting my lips in a way that I hope is demure.

"We're late for fourth period." But he takes a step closer.

"Ooh, then I've got a better idea. I mean, since we're already not in class, we might as well *ditch* class, right?"

"Your logic never ceases to amaze me."

"See? I amaze you. That's power."

He stops a few inches away, his narrowed eyes glimmering down at me. I press my back into a locker door, but the handle stabs me, and my demure look turns to a disgruntled cringe. "Ow," I say, trying to rub at an impossible-to-reach spot. "That went off better in my imagination."

"Mine too, to be honest."

I swat him in the leg with a crutch, and he laughs. Before I see it coming, his hands reach out, wrapping my waist as he kisses me.

"Get to class, hoodlums," booms a voice from the heavens or down the hall. We startle, Caleb scrambling back as I catch my toppling crutches. Then I pretend to open a locker I have no combination to.

But Jameson's rumbling laugh spills through the hall, and I turn to glare. "You're not in class either, O'Sullivan," I quip.

"I'm TA for Snyder this period."

"Well, I'm TA for the little gremlin that lives in this locker." I yank on the handle again; it doesn't open.

Beside me, Caleb shakes his head softly.

"Whatever, Stafford," Jameson says with an eye roll. "Pretend you're not eternally grateful to me all you want." He smirks and rolls off down the hall.

I turn to Caleb. "Remember when we were in kindergarten and we put brown paint in Jameson's chair, and the teacher sent him home for having an accident?" I start to crack up all over again, but Caleb frowns.

"We ended up in the principal's office for that."

"Well, I think it's worth the risk to reenact it now. We should go to the art wing and find some paint."

"We should go to fourth period."

I sigh. "But mathematics wears on my near-death stress condition."

"Perfect. Because fourth period is U.S. History." He threads his fingers through mine and walks me to class. Then, because deep down, he will always be the boy I love to hate, he whispers, "Besides, you know better than to prank the town hero."

I whack him in the shin with a crutch, and together we hobble to fourth period.

EPILOGUE

NAOMI LAMB

ONE OF MY EARLIEST MEMORIES IS MY SISTER, ESTHER, tying my pale blond hair up into two ponytails. She was around four years old, so she didn't use a comb or really know what to secure them with. She found a pink hair tie for one side; on the other she used the filthy rubber band off a rolled-up newspaper.

When my mother tried to undo the pigtails that night before my bath, my hair was so knotted, she nearly resorted to cutting it all off. I screamed and hollered. Not because I was particularly attached to my hair at the tender age of two, but because my hair was the same as Esther's. And the only thing I wanted in life back then was to be like her.

Nothing much changed as we grew older. To me, she remained in this lofty place, high up there with the clouds. Maybe that's why, even now, it's impossible to accept that she's down in the dirt with the worms. I adored Esther. Her words meant more to me than anyone's. A kind word from her could lift me up to the sky, right there alongside her.

But a harsh word could bring me down harder than a sledgehammer.

Esther loved ghost stories, anything spooky. She'd written a scary short story for Fairport High's online literary journal, and it won her an award. So it made perfect sense that she'd get sucked into the legend of Fairport Village. It made sense that she'd scribble furiously in her diary about it and research the murders until it took over her life.

Only she never did any of that.

On Esther's last night, she was out at the wharf with her friends. I followed her, hoping she'd let me hang out with her. That she'd finally see that I fit in with them. They were only a year ahead of me after all, and everyone always told me I was so advanced.

I guess *advanced* didn't apply to social circumstances so much. If I'd had my own friends, I wouldn't have cared about Esther's.

I walked into the ice cream parlor where they were all seated, pretending like I just happened to be there too. Esther's friends said hi and waved me over, and I acted surprised.

But Esther's face went a frightening sort of calm.

I noticed that one of the girls at Esther's table wasn't part of her regular crowd. It was Lana King, one of the most popular girls in school. Esther had been so excited when Lana started following her on social media, and then when Lana asked Esther to sit with her and her friends at lunch.

Esther managed to brighten. She laughed and joked with the other girls while I licked my cotton candy–flavored ice cream cone.

I didn't like the way Lana was looking at me, like my clothes were dirty or I had something in my teeth. I didn't like the way she pulled Esther aside at the end of the night and whispered to her either. But the other girls, Esther's longtime friends, were so nice to me, I forgot all about it.

When everyone said their goodbyes, I was still riding the high. Being part of the older kids' hangout made me feel cooler, bolder. "Dare you to sneak into the Fairport Village ruins," I said, my fingers sticky from the ice cream.

She rolled her eyes. "Dare you back."

I didn't notice that the entire walk over to the ruins, I was the only person talking. That I'd blabbed on and on about her friends and the hilarious things they'd said. That I'd repeated every compliment they'd paid me—on my hair, on the way I'd meticulously applied my makeup in an attempt to look older, on how smart I was.

When we reached the rusted fence, she turned to me. Her hair was pulled back in a low bun, and some wavy pieces hung loose, flattering her face in such a way that I made a mental note to style my hair exactly the same way the next morning. Then she gestured toward the hole in the fence and said, "After you."

All of my newfound intrepidness threatened to crumple like the cottage porch beyond the fence. I couldn't let her see it, not when I was so close to being *in*. "Fine," I said, gripping the cold metal. "But the next dare is mine."

She gave a small head tilt of agreement, and heart thumping, I crawled through the hole.

When I stood up, facing her on the other side of the patterned fence, her pale blue eyes grew ever so slightly. She was impressed, and it only served to fuel me on my course.

She made it through and dusted off the dirt from her jeans. "So?" she asked, looking bored. "What do I have to do?"

I pointed to a cottage. The ocean-facing one that the Blackmores called the Beachside Bungalow.

"You want me to break into that place?" She was trying too hard to sound unimpressed.

"Nope," I said, already striding ahead of her toward it. On the side nearest us sat a boulder, and next to it a tree so overgrown that the branches threaded through the cracked window and twisted to perch on top of the roof. "I want you to climb up there."

Her mouth fell open. "You're joking."

I wasn't joking. This was the smartest idea I'd ever had. "I'm going to take your photo, and then you're going to take mine. We're going to be legends, Esther." Forget just having nice older friends. If Esther did this, she'd be the queen of the school.

And she'd have me to thank.

She took a deep breath, and I could tell her mind was spinning as she stared down the cottage. "The roof doesn't exactly look safe, Nay."

"We don't have to perform a ballet routine up there. Just stand long enough to take the photos."

She licked her lips and zipped up her sweatshirt. "Fine." Then she strode toward the boulder without another thought, clambering up awkwardly. My sister was many impressive things—student body VP, head of the art club, and straight-A student. But an athlete she was not. Once she made it onto the boulder, she reached for a high branch and, grunting, pulled her feet onto the offshoot in front of her. Then it was a matter of climbing a up a few more branches and inching herself out onto the roof.

"Be careful!" I called up, noting the slant of the roof.

I heard her mutter something under her breath, but it was lost beneath the waves. When she moved from the branch onto the weathered shingles, the branch bounced, upsetting her balance. She wobbled, and my heart stopped. But she recovered, finding a secure spot a few feet from the edge.

"Take the pic," she said, voice as shaky as her legs.

I pulled my phone out as she positioned herself with one hand on her hip, the other making a peace sign, and a closed-mouth smile. "Wait. Let's take it together," I said, already following the path she'd carved out.

When I made it to the edge of the branch, Esther bent to hold it still for me. Straightening with her back to the roof's edge, she pulled her phone free. "I still want one by myself after this. That was the deal, remember?"

"Yeah, sorry," I said.

"Whatever." She shook her head. "Ready?"

"Almost," I said, watching my feet with every small step. "If I switch places with you, can you get the ocean in the background?"

Esther let out an exhausted sigh. "God, Naomi, no one is going to care about your stupid photo. You have like four followers on Instagram."

"That's not true." It felt like she'd knocked the wind out of me.

"What you did tonight was really shitty," she said, suddenly sounding like Lana King. Not like her real friends and not like my sister. "You completely embarrassed me."

"How did I embarrass you?" I started to sway, my feet unsteady. "Your friends love me."

"They're just being nice to you, Nay. They're nice people."

"Not *all* of your friends seem that nice," I said softly. "Not Lana."

"Can we just get down already?" she said, attempting to skirt past me.

"What about the photo?" I asked, starting to feel sick and dizzy.

"I don't even want it anymore. Not if you're going to insert yourself into it, the way you insert yourself into every damned part of my life."

The hurt dug in, making my eyes sting. It was followed by a bout of dizziness that nearly took my feet out from under me. "I think I need to sit down."

"Stop being such a baby," she said, trying again to move past me. "If you were halfway normal—if you weren't some weirdo who orders cotton candy ice cream on a sugar cone like a grown-ass *baby*, maybe you wouldn't irritate the hell out of me."

"Esther, stop," I said, trying to lower myself without sliding down the sloped roof. The wind was picking up, making it more and more difficult to keep my balance.

"*Esther, stop,*" my sister mimicked as the Village ruins turned around me in swooping waves. "Go find some weirdo friends of your own. And leave mine alone."

"Esther, shut up!" I screamed, taking one large step toward her and reaching to place a hand over her mouth.

Only she flinched.

She wobbled, just like the first time. Stepped back, catching herself, all like the first time.

Except this time, the battered shingle beneath her foot gave way. It slid out from beneath her to plummet over the edge.

My sister screamed, arms flailing as she tried to right herself. Then she toppled off the roof, following the shingle down and landing with a world-shattering crash.

I called to her, thinking she might get away with a twisted ankle and a good amount of bruising. When she didn't answer, I thought it was because she was furious with me. I was already planning my apology, planning how to get her to the hospital. Even as I scrambled my way back down the tree and boulder route, I didn't think she'd fallen far enough to cause serious injuries.

But then I saw her body, and I fell to my knees. Panic grabbed hold of my throat, strangling me. Esther's neck must've hit the porch railing on her way down. It was bent at a ninety-degree angle, her head dangling down over the bottom porch step. The rest of her body was sprawled over the higher steps, covered in small cuts and many fast-forming bruises.

I tried to wake her up, knowing it was no use. I wanted to cradle her and tell her everything I'd been thinking on my way down. How sorry I was for ruining her night. How sorry I was for scaring her up there.

But deep down, I knew better than to get her blood on my clothes.

Instead, I took my sister's hands and dragged her body to some bushes, where I concealed it beneath the leaves. I needed time to think. It had been an accident, sort of. But accident or not, it had been my idea to go inside the Village ruins, to climb on top of a sketchy old cottage. I made her fall. My parents never would've forgiven me if they'd found out the role I'd played.

Already, the legend of Fairport Village began to seep into my veins, through my skin. I could hear the cries of the Founders, could feel the thrum of the land, the ancient evil that drove Mrs. Blackmore to madness and took Farah Palmer's life.

The land practically whispered the plan into my ears.

By the time I reached my house on foot, I knew what needed to be done. Using a stack of magazines and newspapers I dug up from a neighbor's recycling bin, I constructed the note from "Mrs. Blackmore": *I warned you never to set foot in here again.*

Next, I found an empty diary in Esther's things, a gift from our mother. Just like everything else I'd copied from my older sister, I'd practiced copying her handwriting from a young age. I had it down pat. I wrote the entries, which gave the authorities a reason for why Esther had been in the ruins that night. It also gave them a reason to bring their CSI unit to Sea Glass Shore instead of the place where Esther was actually killed: Beachside Bungalow.

Clothed in a dark hoodie, I crept back out of the house, swiped a sage leaf from my mother's garden, and snuck inside the Village property again. I cleaned up the blood droplets on the steps as best as I could. The ruins were too filled with trash and decay for them to find a few specks, so I bleached it and moved some trash on top of it. Then I uncovered Esther's body from the bushes. I whispered my apologies and goodbyes in the shadows of the ruins. Then I dragged my sister's body over to the fence. I didn't want my parents to have to search forever; it was the one thing I could spare them after everything I'd taken. After everything I would keep for myself.

There had been murders in the ruins before. The police would have to group them together, and they'd get nowhere. Because the murders weren't connected at all.

I left the diary for the cops to find, a few feet away from Esther's body, in the dirt. I dropped the sage leaf and a couple of beads nearby to validate the journal entry about the herbs and beads for the ritual. Then I tucked the note I'd crafted inside her sweatshirt pocket and snuck back home.

Thankfully, I never snapped that photo of Esther with my phone. The cops believed my story that she'd been upset with me after the ice cream parlor and that I'd walked home alone. Apparently, Lana corroborated my account, since she was the one who leaned over and whispered that Esther should ditch me in the first place. In the aftermath of my sister's death, Lana loved to publicly lament about being the last person to see her *dear friend* Esther Lamb alive.

Once the case went cold, the diary was returned to my parents.

And when the Fairport High seniors started digging things up again, I went to the overnighter to keep an eye on things. I made sure Henry and his camera didn't venture too close to Beachside Bungalow.

But then he was killed, and my panic started to set in all over again. I knew the police would be back, snooping around the property. I overheard Diego in the school hallway, talking about Mrs. Blackmore back from the dead. I followed Eden and her friends a few times, overheard conversations about searching the Village ruins for the knife that killed Nicolas Blackmore. I couldn't risk the cops finding Esther's DNA mixed with mine on the steps of that cottage. I needed a way to deter Eden and the others, to keep the authorities out of Fairport Village. They'd given up on my sister's murder, and I needed it to stay that way.

That's when I dug up Esther's diary again and showed it to Eden, so she could see how dangerous the curse really was. But she and the others refused to listen; I had no choice but to accompany them into the ruins. To keep them away from that cottage, no matter what it took.

In the end, my sister achieved that fame she so desperately craved. But only in death. It was as a result of my plan, but not because of some photo showing off her bravery to the students at Fairport High. She achieved infamy as the next victim of our town's dark legend.

A legend carved of sand and stone. A tale rooted in ruin. A lore built on lies.

Read on for a sneak peek of

THEY'RE WATCHING YOU,

another page-turning thriller
from Chelsea Ichaso!

EVERY SECRET SOCIETY HAS ITS PRIVILEGES...
AND ITS SACRIFICES

THEY'RE
WATCHING
YOU

CHELSEA ICHASO

AVAILABLE NOW

ONE

"YOU DO REALIZE YOU'RE GOING STRAIGHT TO DETENTION," I say to my lab partner Gavin Holt. He's wearing a white button-down shirt adorned with his signature bow tie—all the boys wear ties. It's a requirement, though Gavin is the only guy on campus who insists on the bow variety.

But this time he's gone off the rails and paired it with plaid pajama pants. Strictly against dress code. Torrey-Wells Academy, named after its two founders, has a bit of a double standard when it comes to attire. Guys have to wear slacks and a tie to classes, chapel, and to the dining hall; girls can wear pretty much whatever they want as long as it covers the necessary parts. For example, I'm wearing sweatpants and a ratty TWA sweatshirt—my daily uniform— and am in no danger of violating the code. Apparently, when the school opened up to girls back in the seventies, the board found altering the academy handbook too much of a bother.

Which is fine with me.

Gavin shrugs but scoots his stool closer to the lab table to hide his lower half. "I woke up late."

I roll my eyes.

"And then I had a small Pop-Tart smoke alarm emergency."

"Well, you look like you're ready to crouch by the Christmas tree and unwrap a package of Hot Wheels."

"You're one to talk, Sweatpants Girl."

Fair enough. I scan the list of ingredients again. "I guess this means I'm getting the water. Try not to blow anything up while I'm gone." I grab the beaker and head over to the sink. There's a sixty-six-point-six percent chance that Gavin will ignore my warning and blow something up while I'm gone, if we're basing this on stats from our last three assignments.

With a wave of my hand, the fancy steel faucet turns on. The Lowell Math and Science Building, constructed four years ago thanks to a rich donor named Lowell who made his money genetically modifying crops, is a state-of-the-art facility. No penny was spared, from the touch screens the teachers use in place of whiteboards to the observatory fit with a massive telescope. Handle-less water faucets were important too, I suppose. Water starts spewing out the sides of the beaker before I realize I've been gazing off into space. I shut it off with another wave and dump some of it, glancing over my shoulder at Gavin.

His lips are quirked, eyes squinting at the tray full of materials. He's definitely contemplating lighting something on fire. I watch as he adjusts his glasses, picks up the spatula, and begins prodding at the sodium metal without his gloves on. A sudden wave of frustration rolls through me. My best friend, Polly St. James, should be sitting here next to me, not Gavin.

If she hadn't left, I wouldn't be so stressed about my grade in this class. Whereas some teachers tend to show leniency toward the athletes, Dr. Yamashiro is extra strict. To keep the GPA required for my financial aid, I can't get anything less than an *A* on this experiment. Or on any assignment, for that matter. But with Gavin for a partner, I might have to settle for getting out of the building alive.

I return, setting the beaker onto the glass tabletop with a clank. Water droplets splatter the ingredients list as well as our findings sheet.

"You okay?" Gavin asks, leaning closer, his jade eyes narrowed behind his lenses. His scent is sweet with a hint of smoke, like he downed an energy drink on the way here or tried to ignite a Jolly Rancher.

"Fine. Put your safety goggles on."

He obeys, placing the goggles over his glasses, and I add a few drops of phenolphthalein indicator to the beaker. But he nudges me with an elbow, and I almost fumble the dropper. "Well, you don't look fine."

I take a deep breath and steady my hand. I'm not about to tell Gavin that life pretty much sucks now that my only friend has abandoned me. I'm not about to tell Gavin that I suspect something bad might've happened to Polly—that she didn't just up and run away like her parents and the police say.

I would never tell Gavin Holt that my eyes are stinging with tears because even the best-case scenario means my closest friend chose to leave me and never return my calls or texts again.

"I'm just tired and sore. Still recovering from hell week." Every year, at the start of lacrosse preseason, Coach makes us attend 5 a.m. practices before classes, and again at 5 p.m. after classes. It helps to get us in shape. It also makes every inch of my body feel like it's melting off.

"And maybe a little upset that Polly is…" Gavin pushes a strand of dust-brown hair off his forehead. "You know, gone."

"Maybe." But the truth is I started losing Polly months ago.

A few weeks into our Form III school year (Torrey-Wells Academy can't very well call us juniors and seniors like every other school in the United States), Polly was suddenly too busy for me. Even though we're roommates—we've been roommates since Form I—I didn't see her as much. Polly's straight *A*s always came with a healthy dose of cramming; this year, she never felt like studying. Then there was the staying out and sneaking back into the room after curfew, reeking of booze. It wasn't like her.

At least, it wasn't like the Polly who was friends with me. She'd vaguely mentioned her wild-child days, but people change. We were content to drink soda from the vending machines and spend Saturday nights in our pajamas.

Until she started getting buddy-buddy with Annabelle Westerly and joined chess club. This has to be the only school in the country where chess club is cool, and it's all thanks to Annabelle. Polly and

I used to joke about how Annabelle Westerly's endorsement could probably make pin the tail on the donkey the next school fad. But suddenly, Polly wasn't laughing much with me anymore.

She was laughing with Annabelle, who's trouble veiled in designer labels and a posher-than-thou lexicon.

Then two weeks ago, Polly wasn't laughing with anyone. She was gone.

I tried to tell Mr. and Mrs. St. James about Polly's new habits, so they'd do more to try and find her. But my claims only supported the police's conclusion. Polly had left a note, after all, telling her parents she'd taken a break from school to clear her head.

Authorities ruled her a runaway.

I'd seen so little of her this semester, I could hardly argue with them. I wasn't exactly an expert witness on Polly's habits or state of mind.

I put on my gloves and slap Gavin's hand as he reaches for a small green vial he must've stolen from the supply cabinet, because it has nothing to do with this experiment. Then I remove a tiny piece of sodium metal from the container with the spatula, drop it into the water, and thrust my arm to the side to keep Gavin back as the liquid sputters and reacts, leaving a pink trail through the beaker.

Across the room, Dr. Yamashiro eyes us, having learned from past experiences. Gavin pulls off the whole clueless thing so well that he hasn't been busted yet. Take, for example, whatever happened in his dorm this morning with a Pop-Tart.

But I'm on to him.

I think Gavin is actually a freaking genius.

He scribbles down our findings, just as Dr. Yamashiro starts to wrap up class. It's probably for the best, considering Gavin's fingers are spider-crawling across the table toward that green vial.

"Lord, help me," I whisper into the fumes.

"Maren, you know I'd clean up," Gavin says, "but if Dr. Y saw me..." He glances down at his PJs.

"You wore those stupid pants on purpose," I say, snatching the beaker off the table. Gavin grins, grabbing his books. He waits for Dr. Yamashiro to turn to the fancy screen that looks like a portal into another dimension, then shoves himself into a cluster of students headed for the door.

Gavin could probably come to class in no pants and still end up with a clean record. My cheeks heat suddenly at the thought, so I rush to the sink and stick my hands beneath the cool water.

Back in my dorm room, a cozy cube still plastered in Polly's vintage Hollywood photographs and my lone Lionel Messi poster, I throw myself onto the bottom bunk. My gaze drifts toward the photo collage—the one we made together last year—hanging on the wall between our desks, but I force myself to stare at the bedframe slats above me.

Polly's top bunk remains empty; the school hasn't forced a new roommate on me yet. It should be nice having the place to myself, except I loved living with Polly. We used to study together in here, comfy on our beanbag chairs, our dusty desks neglected. We'd lie in our beds, chatting for hours after lights-out, keeping our voices low to avoid shushing by the Form IV proctor.

Polly's parents came by and picked through her things. They took what they wanted but left the majority. Like they're convinced she'll regret her decision and return any second. I've been through everything dozens of times, hoping I'll find some clue concerning her whereabouts.

I shut my eyes and replay our last conversation. It didn't happen in this room—over the past few months, we never spoke more than a greeting to one another in here. I'd spotted her out at the Commons, across the large expanse of pristinely cut grass. I watched her for a few seconds, the way she walked with her head tucked into her shoulders. The sun bathed the campus in a warm glow, but she tugged the hood of her expensive new coat—most likely a gift from Annabelle—over her auburn curls.

When it came to money, Polly was like me. In fact, money was the way we'd met. During Form I orientation, we both attended the financial aid seminar with our parents. Torrey-Wells is ridic-ulously expensive, and my parents are not rich. They had to figure out how to send me here through a combination of payment plans and scholarships. There are only a handful of us scholarship kids at Torrey-Wells, and something about sticking together made sense. It felt safe. After a few minutes of listening to the droning financial aid advisor at our parents' sides, we stole through the side doors of Henning Hall, giggling as we explored our new campus, inventing histories for every statue, giving imaginary freshmen the tour. Bonding over lattes in the café.

During our first two years, while the other students were out gallivanting all over town on weekends, throwing around wads of cash, Polly and I were content to hang out in the dining hall and watch movie marathons in the common area of our dorm. At least, I was content. I guess Polly had her sights set on Annabelle and the rest of them.

That day on the grass, I called her name and waved her down. We were both headed to chemistry. But she turned and spotted me, and for a split second, I thought she might keep walking.

"Hey," I said, jogging to catch up. "Can I walk with you?"

She nodded, and up close I could see beige-colored patches where her attempt to conceal the dark purple bags beneath her eyes had failed.

"Where'd you sleep last night?" I asked, though it was obvious she hadn't slept at all.

She shrugged, pursing chapped lips. "In a friend's room."

"So, Annabelle's room."

Another shrug, but she wasn't running away from me. Her fingers fidgeted and her gaze floated away, searching the grounds. My chest pricked. She was probably worried about being seen with me.

"Are you okay? You look…stressed," I said.

"I've had a lot on my mind. Chess isn't going so well."

"Chess?" I asked, wondering how a club could be the cause of whatever I was witnessing in my normally lively and fresh-faced friend.

"It's not really working out. There's a lot more to it than I thought." She hitched her bag higher on her shoulder and massaged her temples with her fingertips. The hood fell back, and her tousled curls glimmered bronze in the spring sunlight. Then the words came out in a jumbled rush. "It's not just pieces and a board. It's...more. Too much, maybe." Her eyes widened as she finished, shining with something like terror.

At first, I was too stunned by her rambling to respond. Had the sleep deprivation really gotten to her? Was it drugs? Or was this something more? Finally, I reached out to touch her arm. "You don't have to play chess anymore, Polly. Is Annabelle pressuring you to stick with something you hate?"

She exhaled through her teeth, rustling her curls. "No, it's— forget I said anything." She reached up, removing my hand from her arm, and slowly, her fingers began to squeeze. "*Please*, forget it."

"Yeah, fine." She dropped my hand, and another pang shot through me.

"Polly!" a voice shouted from across the grass. I glanced over to find Annabelle Westerly, dressed in a slouchy sweater and tall leather boots.

"I've got to go," Polly said softly, looking at the ground.

"I miss you." I cringed at the way my voice cracked. "I miss our movie nights and our beanbag chats. I miss—"

"Let's meet tonight," she interrupted, spinning around to face me. We reached the end of the grass, and a large statue of Lord Torrey himself towered behind her on the cobblestone walkway. The cathedral bell tolled in the distance, reminding us to hurry along. "We can catch up."

"Okay," I said, the word dragging. "We don't have to meet. You could just come back to the room for a change—*your* room."

She shook her head and glanced over her shoulder. "I want to show you something. Meet me at the fountain." I knew which fountain she meant. *Our* fountain. The one with the white iron bench where we always had a quick coffee while waiting for our next morning class. "I'll see you in chem," she said, rushing over to Annabelle.

My heart buoyed in my chest. The meeting. It meant something. She was coming back to me. She'd seen the error of her ways.

After dinner, I sat on the bench by the fountain. Beneath the glow of the lamppost, I waited for an hour, checking my phone every ten seconds for a text from Polly that never came. I thought about texting her, asking if she was on her way, but it felt even more desperate than sitting alone in the cold night air.

When she never showed, I was furious. Hurt too, but mainly incensed that she'd gotten my hopes up. I made my way back to my dormitory, panic streaking through my chest that I would miss curfew and be locked out. Torrey-Wells is one of these sprawling New England establishments built on two thousand acres, complete with two orchards, four ponds, and fifteen student housing buildings; ancient, ivy-laced brick buildings stitched occasionally with newer models, like the Hamilton Fitness Center, to keep up with the times. I had to sprint to make it, and when I did, a cocktail of anger and adrenaline pumped through my veins, making sleep impossible.

As I lay there, the silent hours passed as I prayed for the beep of the room key. I hoped the door would click open and I would find Polly standing there, an apology ready on her lips.

Instead, in the early hours of the morning, I finally drifted off, and the top bunk remained empty. No creak of the door. No soft steps on carpet.

The next day, Polly missed all of her classes. When she didn't come to dinner, Annabelle Westerly started asking around, and eventually Headmistress Koehler reported her missing. The academy's state-of-the-art security cameras failed to pick up anything useful, so the police were brought in. Being her roommate, I was soon questioned. Her teachers were also questioned. Polly's parents were notified, and by the time their plane landed, the police had discovered Polly's note in the top drawer of her desk.

I voiced my concerns to the police. To her parents. Polly was supposed to meet me. Why would she run away?

But her parents took one look at the note, in Polly's own handwriting, and their faces fell. They pressed the cops to look for her, but even their pressing was half-hearted. Apparently, Polly had run away before. Back in middle school. Part of the reason they'd opted to try private school in the first place was to keep her on the straight and narrow. Yet here they were again, thousands upon thousands of dollars later, their daughter wandering somewhere out there in the wide-open world.

ACKNOWLEDGMENTS

We Were Warned is a book I wrote a few years back as a much different story in a completely different genre before deciding to shelve it. My brain refused to abandon it entirely, though. One day, I got the wild idea to rewrite it from scratch as a thriller. I have many people to thank for taking it from that spark of an idea to the book it is now.

To the brilliant Wendy McClure, thanks so much for your wisdom and enthusiasm on this project! From the get-go, I've felt so fortunate to be working with you on yet another story.

To my fabulous agent, Uwe Stender—for your belief in my writing and unwavering support along the way. I'm always grateful to have you in my corner.

A huge thanks to the team at Sourcebooks: Gabbi Calebrese, Thea Voutiritsas, Karen Masnica, Rebecca Atkinson, Delaney Heisterkamp, Monica Palenzuela, and Jenny Lopez. Thank you to Casey Moses for the fantastic cover!

Thanks to my dear friends and critique partners to whom this book is dedicated. To Julie Abe, who likes books about magical cupcakes and sparkly unicorns but puts up with my dark, twisted mind anyway; and to Laura Kadner, whose stories make me laugh and whose help always improves my books.

Thanks to the early readers who encouraged me to keep going with these characters and this eerie beach setting: Tara Tsai, Sarah Harrington, MK Pagano, Emily Kazmierski, Heidi Christopher, Julie Abe, and Laura Kadner.

To Brian Ulrich, thanks for letting me pick your brain about cameras and documentary-making.

Thanks to my parents, George and Rebecca Kienzle, for listening and cheerleading through all of the publishing highs and lows. To my Ichaso family, your support means the world.

To my husband, Matias—for always being my first reader and the person who talks me through every single new idea or plot struggle. I couldn't do this without you.

To my children—keep writing your stories. You have far more imagination than I ever did at your age. Thank you for thinking that my job is cool and for being the best people ever.

To the bloggers, Bookstagrammers, and Booktokers—thank you for supporting my books. Every post and photo means so much to me.

Finally, thank you, dear reader! You're the reason I get to keep writing, and I'm endlessly grateful that you picked up this book.

ABOUT THE AUTHOR

Chelsea Ichaso writes twisty thrillers for young adults, including *Dead Girls Can't Tell Secrets*, *They're Watching You*, and *The Summer She Went Missing*. She is also the author of the adult thriller *So I Lied*. A former high school English teacher, Chelsea currently resides in Southern California with her husband and children. She likes to think she plays guitar and would succeed on a survival television show, though neither is true. You can visit her online at chelseaichaso.com or on Instagram @chelseaichaso.

sourcebooks
fire

Home of the hottest trends in YA!

Visit us online and
sign up for our newsletter at
FIREreads.com

···

Follow
@sourcebooksfire
online